SHELTER

CHAZ BRENCHLEY

BLOODY BRITS PRESS
Ann Arbor and Alnmouth
2007

This one's for Harry and for Helen,
because they want everything, they said so,
and this is the best I can do.
Besides, they give me shelter …

FROST and fire, fire and frost: you could say that both were simply weather gone wild, temperature *in extremis*, thermal shock. Or you could say that they're both chaos in action, disorder under strict control; or that they're both manufacturers of pattern, one liquid and one still. As always, there's a lot that you can say and very little that you actually do. You always tell less than you know.

Except that chaos is control, control is pattern, it's all the same thing in the end. It's all the same story. Just depends on how you look at it. Or how you tell it. How I do.

In my mother's telling, all the country was wild as the weather once, and the sky was wilder; and all the wild country had its peoples, naiads and dryads and oreads and all, though there was nothing Greek about them. The Greenfolk, she calls them: creatures of wood and earth and water who surged and slept with the seasons, whose hearts were hard or hard to find, whose thoughts and needs and hungers were obscure.

At my mother's tellings, children and adults alike will sit enraptured, though some must surely carry nightmares home to bed like shards from a broken spell. All my life has been twisted round with dreaming; I've had it worst, I've had to live with her, but I can't be the only one whose sleep she has invaded.

In my mother's telling, all stories have ambiguous endings. Not so in mine. Only be patient, you'll see. I'll give you solid rain-washed gray to her green and growing, concrete to her questing tendrils.

1

In the valley where she made me live, there was wood and earth and water, little else. The lane we lived along still hadn't got used to its tarmac; every winter it tried to shrug the hard stuff off. Electricity and telephone came courtesy of the farmer up the hill who'd paid to have the cables run so far—literally by his courtesy when the snow came and the cables crashed, and there was only his generator to keep the dark at bay—but man, young man (boy in my mother's telling) shall not live by light alone, nor even by light and food and radio and mum.

Which is why, one reason why I drink so much.

You'll see.

Drinks (1)

The Agric is a sad drink, an old man's drink. But when you're fifteen, sixteen and living in the valley, it is at least an accessible drink. Rose who runs it isn't picky whom she serves; and when you're a little older it gets to be also an enduring drink, Rose doesn't watch the clock. Lock-ins a specialty, except that she never bothers to lock the door. Midnight, one o'clock, she might still have a customer come by. Everyone welcome, and the local bobby not barred: he grew up with Rose, as we all did.

So the Agric gets to be a habit, for those kids who don't break out and move on. For a breakaway boy come back, it was a natural site to hit, hard and fast. Not my first night home, nor yet my second, I owed my mother that much company; but my first night out, oh yes.

The Agric—properly the Agricultural Hotel—is one of those big square buildings that stand alone and draw the eye, gray stone calling to the passing trade. It's at the head of the valley where the road crosses the river and the river runs beside the old railway line, rails ripped out now and a trail laid where the track used to run, long and level and another attraction to us when we were kids, when we had only our pushbikes to get about on.

Back in the valley, I was back on the bike tonight. As soon as we could we'd graduated to scramblers, a couple that were ours and others we could borrow, enough to move the whole gang of us if we doubled up; and the old track was our highway then too, despite the law. That had never been a bother to us, either in theory or in person, in the person of Barry Carter; he had a big

3

police BMW, but he couldn't follow us if we took to the fells, and he seldom even bothered to chase. Some nights we'd set off home-made fireworks in his garden, and he'd chase us then; but we always had a start, we'd learned to make slow fuses that gave us time to creep away.

I'd never had a scrambler of my own, there wasn't the money; and no surprise that there'd been no lifts offered tonight. I'd phoned my closest mates and they'd all said *yes, of course, the Agric, fine, brilliant, see you there.* No one had said *I'll pick you up, Ro*, and I hadn't expected them to. Too much to ask; it was enough that they were coming.

So it had been out with Old Trusty, old rusty-and-squeak; pedal-power had brought me down the lane and along the road in the early dark, moon-shadows of the trees beneath my tires and no lights on my bike to disrupt them, only the occasional car's headlamps washing out the world for the few moments of its passing.

No lock for the bike either, but no worries. I'd dumped it where three muddy scramblers stood ticking gently against the cool, and walked through the ever-open door of the Agric.

It's no Tardis, this, not near so big on the inside as it is out. It must have been a real hotel at one time, earning its keep by keeping people overnight; God knows what they use all the upstairs rooms for now. All my knowledge of it is limited to one bar and the toilet; I've had an intimate relationship with both.

You walk into a lobby, where engraved glass in the doors directs you on; to the right the lounge, gentlemen-farmers and their genteel wives, any passing trade it can still pick up. In all my years of coming here, I've never been to the right.

To the left, the public bar. An open fire and a bare floor, hard settles and harder stools, hard faces and a hard welcome maybe to a stranger. I wouldn't know.

Tonight I turned left, pushed the door open, walked in—and stood there, stock-still as I had in my mother's doorway two nights earlier, the prodigal come home and finding it prodigiously hard to move further. Just the fact stopped me, that I was here. I was back

4

and I'd brought so much with me, I was so deeply changed, and surely something here should be different?

Nothing was. Or so at least it seemed, in that deceptive moment. Fire, floor, settles and stools and the faces of my friends below the dartboard, turned to face me as they had been so often before.

Of course it was not the same. I was changed, and they were changed towards me: smiles were tight, forced, shifty in their shift-lessness. They needed that moment too, and a little longer; I'd found my feet and the concept of movement, connected the two and taken a couple of paces over before any one of them stirred.

Then it was up and rush, big hugs the order of the night; or else it was sit quiet and wait it out. Depended who you were.

First up was Malcolm, tall and broad and already losing his hair and his waistline both. He grabbed me, banged his forehead against my shoulder as an expression of manly sympathy, squeezed me vigorously and handed me on to the next in line. Farmer's son, Malcolm. One of my oldest friends: heart of gold in a crock full of gilded shit. You really had to dig, to find the real thing.

Toby was a hugger also but the genuine article, and not at all awkward about it. Gentle soul, gently stubborn, stubbornly percip-ient. His parents worked the sheep for Malcolm's father; Toby worked the system. He'd left school at sixteen and done endless training-schemes since, six weeks here and three months there, "school you get paid to go to" and no threat, no danger of a perma-nent job at the end of it.

Arms around, warmth and comfort and his breath on my neck: Toby was the one who'd worried me most, when I thought about coming back. How close he'd get, how close he'd want to get. How much he'd see, of what I'd done and what had been done to me.

"Hey, Ro. Good to see you back, mate. Thanks for coming."

He didn't mean to the Agric. I nodded and gave him a smile, as thin and twisted as any of theirs; he tiptoed up to kiss the stubble on my cheek, and nothing awkward in that either, because he wouldn't at all see why there should be.

Then he peeled away, and there was Michael waiting. Michael my best mate, Michael my rogue angel, my companion in many

5

sins, my guiding light; and if anyone should have come to the cottage to collect me tonight it should have been him, and that he hadn't only underscored the monumental nature of the night, the depths of his difficulty and everyone else's.

No hugs, no need for hugging: we didn't need to announce anything, either to the world or to each other. Michael looped his arm up around my neck and pulled me down to share a short bench with him at the table's end. My pint was there already.

As were Dan and Lindsay, non-huggers the pair of them. Hands stretched over to shake mine one by one, weird formal gestures to substitute for words they couldn't find. I doubt we'd ever shaken hands before, but it seemed likely that we would again, from here until we'd run our course together and were separate or dead. After years, so many years a handshake marked an end, a limit, closure.

No girls. Girls were another thing, a later thing than us; they would have been inappropriate here. I didn't have a girl in the valley, and didn't want one.

Five of them, and me: that was the roster, all bar David, and we didn't take David into pubs.

I thought it was right too, fitting to the occasion, that all of them were there before me. Rare, but right tonight. I don't rate conspiracy theories, I didn't think they'd conspired. I thought that each of them was aware just how much they didn't want to be alone with me, they didn't want to be the one to meet and greet when they were so uncertain; and that they cared enough for each other not to let that happen to any of them. My mother would say that it was a bonding, perhaps a woodland spirit's whispering that drew them all and drew them early. I thought that it was just friendship, though I thought that probably only Toby would have articulated it even to himself.

Whatever, here they were. Here we all were, all with drinks and theirs all but drained already, mute evidence of just how early they'd been. They'd have been sipping, I thought, not gulping; and that little or nothing to do with the fact that three of them had charge of bikes tonight.

Malcolm was on his feet and gulping now, now that I was here:

6

draining what was left in his glass and gesturing with a finger around the table, accumulating nods. Dan went with him to the bar; even Malcolm's hands, even mine couldn't carry six pints at once.

Good manners should see me lifting my own glass and gulping also, draining it in one, not to be behind the others. I could feel their eyes on me, though, watching to see if I would; and there was too much symbolism there, they might read altogether too much into it.

I did lift the glass, but only to sip, to savor, to swill beer around my mouth and declare it acceptable with a nod. Another point in Rose's favor, she kept her ale well. It was her good work in that department had taught us all discrimination.

It also felt good to have something to do with my hands, against the silence of my friends.

I'd been prepared for this, as I was sure they had too. What, after all, could they say? Their lives were suddenly made small, too much a sideshow to be offered as the main attraction, the first thing we talked about tonight; and my recent life they knew all about already, or all that mattered, what the papers and my mother knew between them. They couldn't talk about that either, and they certainly couldn't ask me questions.

So. Awkward fidgetings, cigarettes being lit and offered round, eyes jerking all over while minds circled and circled, trapped in the orbit of a single unacknowledged fact, a black hole to conversation. Too big to skip or evade, too dangerous to skirt ...

I sipped beer and watched them, watched myself reflected in my glass, vastly distorted and that must be how I looked to them also: malformed, freakish, sucked by an alien gravity out of all known shape.

But they were still my friends, and for the moment all I had. When the boys came back from the bar, I lined my second pint beside my first and waited for them to settle, then gathered everyone with my eye. Not hard, they were all of them watching me, if sideways.

"One toast and then leave it, guys," I said. "Okay?"

Slow nods and slower smiles, glasses already being lifted. They liked that; if we could pick this thing up only to put it out of the way, that suited everyone.

"Okay, then. I'd drink to absent friends, except that you none of you knew him; so let's keep it simple. Home is the place where, when you have to go there, they have to take you in. I did, and you have; so here's to us, to all of us, and here's to coming home."

I lifted my glass solemnly, and drank, and so did they; and then I tipped my glass and did at last drain it in one long, long swallow, and banged it down on the table, and looked at Michael beside me and said, "How's David, then?"

A question I could legitimately ask, the absent friend indeed: not missing, but likely to be missing me.

It was predictably Malcolm who said, "David's fine. Going great guns at that center of his, it's really made a difference to him. He still comes up to the farm at weekends, too. Doesn't he, Toby?"

"Yeah, right. It's not us who are the big attraction, though, Malcolm mate, so don't you think it. It's his sheep he comes to see, his little lambs get bigger ..."

And then we were off, we were through the gate and away. When all else fails, there are always sheep: old jokes and new, true stories and slanders and dreams. There are even songs, though we weren't drunk enough for that yet.

We drank more; and still didn't sing but laughed a lot and were easy with each other, lamented the lack of a pool-table and threw darts instead, ate Rose out of her stocks of exotic crisps and made noise enough to let the old folks grumble. They must have been grumbling thirty years, as each successive generation of kids thrived here under Rose's regime; it would have seemed a shame to deny them the chance tonight.

At last—back at the table and back to talking, my tongue running wild with some fantasy that had left them all behind long since except for Michael but never mind that, they were used to me, they'd be glad to see I was not so very changed after all—I felt long cool fingers unexpectedly in my hair, and heard a voice I'd been expecting for two days now.

"Well, well. How's my *idiot savant*?"

"Feeling idiotic," I said, tilting back as she tugged, so that I could see her upside down and framed against the ceiling.

"Don't," she said instantly, instantly solemn. "You mustn't."

Which told me all that I really needed to know, answered my unvoiced question. My friends might not talk to me about anything that mattered, they might be avoiding her, but someone somewhere was spreading the glad tidings ...

Well, hell, of course they were. My mother was a storyteller, yes? And I was her favorite story. She might not have seen or spoken to Juliet directly, but ripples spread. A still, quiet valley like this, a stone of a story so heavy, such a splash: ripples would spread far and fast.

Besides, it had been in the papers. I had been in the papers. Someone was safe to have told her that, if she hadn't seen them herself.

It must have been something close to wishful thinking, some native or nurtured urge to tell my own story while it was virgin still, that had had me planning this little exchange differently in my head: how she'd find me by chance or whisper, in this pub or that pub or out somewhere on the cold hill's side or leaning on the rail of a bridge above dark water.

How she'd say to me, "So what did you come back for, Coffey, you sad creature? Meet smarter folk than you, did you?"

"One," I'd say. "I met one ..."

Howl

I have seen the best minds of my generation—
and I was not impressed.

I don't know why I expected anything different. Boys will be boys,
and girls similarly: I knew already—who better?—that being so
sharp you cut yourself daily is still no guarantee against behavior
that is tedious or vulgar or simply unsanitary.

Bleeding from every pore, I went up to Cambridge like a dew-
spangled rural fool, dragging a chain of achievements in my
wake—too many exams passed too well, and God help me, I still
thought that was good—and a burden of fancies at the chain's
further end. Or call it a rope, say I was roped to my own intellect
and add that you could find my expectations at the bitter end of
that rope.

Whatever, for a smart boy I was excessively dumb. Perhaps I'd
read *Gaudy Night* too often, perhaps I thought to find Sayers'
Oxford within my Cambridge, sixty years on: the charm and
intrigue of learning for its own sake, where Senior Fellows were so
enwrapped in their specialisms they'd all but sleepwalk through
the quotidian world; students who were pulled both ways, whose
pulses raced for the millennium but whose souls could still sing in
trochaic dimeters, whose minds blurred into a bridge between and
never lost cohesion.

What I found instead was a college so hungry for funds that half
its enrolment was from overseas, Greeks and Malaysians squeezed
three to a room and charged abundantly for the privilege; lecturers
so overburdened with work they had little enough time for their

11

tutees and none at all for their own research, so that all their applications for sabbaticals or Fulbrights were doomed *ab initio*; and students—

Well. Let me tell you about the students. Better yet, let me show you. Here is the bar, of a Thursday night in midwinter. It's a single room stretched out of all proportion, occupying the entirety of a bland rectangular building that hides its infelicity behind an appropriately poor mockery of a Georgian façade; the beer is as boring as the décor, fizzy and weak, its price its only appeal.

The foreign students are here in force, as ever, and colonizing as ever, making islands layered with smoke. Each new arrival—and they are constant—pulls up a chair or sits on a table's corner, lights a cigarette from the glowing butt they came in with, extends the territory with no thought for whomever they might be crowding in on. They have no concept of other people's space; their drifting smoke is herald to their drifting bodies, and their voices build a wall as emphatic as their backs.

Just as exclusive, just as loud, the rugby boys have claimed a corner by the bar. No latecomers to their circle: they came in as a team and they'll leave as a team, carrying their fallen in fraternity and triumph. *He ain't heavy, he's my brother*—but they won't sing that. Nothing so subtle or so well-considered. They're singing now, as a matter of fact, something long and dull and sexually unlikely; singing will lead on to drinking-games, and the losers—or possibly the winners, the rules are as obscure as their pleasures are mystifying—will stand on the table and drop their trousers, to the cheerful encouragement of their confreres and the deep disinterest of their wider audience, us, who have seen those vast buttocks before and will again next week and all the weeks that follow to the end of the season. Did they win their game today? Who can tell, who cares?

Oddly, rarely, there's a third disparate group with us tonight. These are the rich kids, slumming. Of a normal night they wouldn't be seen dead drinking with the hoi polloi, but occasionally they deign to spend an hour or two in our company, only to emphasize the difference between us. They won't have dined in hall, they'll have booked tables in three different restaurants—all under *noms*

12

de guerre—and eaten at whichever took their fancy when the time came, or else somewhere entirely other; these are not people whom a wise maître-d' turns away. But now here they are, playing among the poor people; if anyone cheers the rugger boys to greater volume or bolder deeds, it will be they. The girls smoke Dunhill or Cocktail Sobranie, the boys toy with a cigar; they drink the champagne that the college keeps especially for these occasions.

We sit in the middle of the room, Simon and I, because all the corners have been taken. Squeezed by empires on every side, we hunch and huddle together, forced into too close an intimacy by the pressures at our backs,

Simon is a nerd, as I am not; his soul is tainted with memories of anorak and acne, but I would choose him to sit with of all these groups that have no claim on me, because Simon at least has a brain. That and nothing other brought him here, as my own brought me. We were rivals indeed before we knew it, candidates for the same purse of money and prestige which he won and I did not. Not a normal scholarship, we both have those; this was something extra, an in-house benefit bequeathed by a dead alumnus. We've been told that Simon's victory was narrow, a vote of three to two; I'm uncertain how I feel about that information, but then I'm uncertain of my feelings about the entire business. Coming second is a new experience, and I'm not very sure how I like it.

Are we friends, Simon and I? It's hard to say. Not soulmates, certainly. But I can at least talk to him, which is a blessing in this company. And I can drink him under the table, which I confess I enjoy.

Ah, Christ. I should borrow my mother's voice; I can sound such a shit in my own.

Hell, I can be such a shit when I try. But then, can't we all?

Simon was a friend of mine, yes. As most friends are: an object of derision sometimes, in other company; fallible sometimes, a weak link, all too human. Except that even our closest friends— which he was not—are never totally human to us, we only ever see

13

other people as a complex of cliché and prejudice, elements in our own ongoing story. Narrative has necessarily to be subjective; the tales of our lives are told to ourselves and by ourselves but made from the myths and histories told to us by others, the templates that are all we have to work with.

Simon was a friend, and one of many. I was a sociable soul and seldom alone in that bright and hectic year, year and a few weeks that I had in college. Simon was more solitary—cliché again, you see: egghead, nerd, no social skills. Perhaps we can't even see ourselves as purely human as we tell our stories in the world, perhaps we have to fall back on formulae to make sense of our own part in the comedy. But Simon was a rock, and there were precious few of those. He was my touchstone, my dependable mate.

And then he was dead, and my grip was gone entirely.

Hartopp Scholar and also-ran, we used to meet for a drink once a week or so, always in the college bar because he was broke and I was broker still. Quite why he was so short of money I never knew; that's how good friends we were, we didn't talk personal stuff. With grant and loan and scholarship and Hartopp and no observable life to drain it all away, he should have been all right, even in costly Cambridge. He was a strong and passionate swimmer, but that comes cheap, especially at early-bird prices with student discounts on top; regular swims and occasional drinks don't add up to a costly social life. For all I knew he was supporting a gambling habit, or an invalid mother, or both; or maybe it was just native caution, maybe he had cash in the bank and couldn't or wouldn't spend it. As I say, we didn't ask that sort of question of each other.

I suppose we were asking questions of the universe, and we were friends because we could talk that talk and walk that walk together. No one in college was stupid, let's be plain about that, although they could and did act stupid and boorish and obscene; by any drudge measure, though, if you could count smarts in any way that was meaningful, I think the Hartopp jury had it right. Simon and I had better engines, we went further and faster on the same fuel. Or maybe we were better drivers, or bolder, or simply more gripped by the ride. What's sure, there was no one there to keep up with us when we cut loose.

Call it luck, call it coincidence, call it foresight or clever anticipation on the part of the college: whatever you call it, it was something rare and fortunate that had brought Simon and me separately to the same institution in the same year. We were both of us synthetists, seeing patterns that played drag-and-drop across disciplines, turned perspective and possibility on their heads.

Put it crudely, I read number as narrative, the whole of mathematics as a progress through traditional storytelling forms, though that was analogy only: I could not tell those stories, only describe them. Simon saw the same data in terms of landscape, peaks and valleys and ever-moving rivers. He couldn't map it for others, but he could walk that terrain in his head; and the two of us could go together, there was some uncommon ground between his vision and my own. "The binomial theorem is more beautiful than mountain passes," Simon said once, but I knew that already. Mountain passes are the crudest of mechanical switches, this way and that way unfiltered, on and off with the weather. They lack fluidity, discrimination, grace.

I suppose our tutors hoped that we could synthetize together, make one whole and comprehensible thing from what obscure pieces we could share. They showed us a model in our first week up, a 3D-imaging program that could turn text into landscape, a story into a mountain scramble. Old hat to Simon, who'd been computer-literate before he was reading Blyton; all new to me, whose knowledge of such things had been somewhat limited by dodgy electrics, a school in the rural outback and my mother's profound antipathy to the silicon chip. I asked if there were a program that could do the reverse, turn a map into a tale. They laughed, told us to think about it, gave us the tools and the time to play.

We had formal tutorials together, and hours where they left us alone with a computer, a whiteboard, whatever more we wanted; and of course we had those regular nights in the bar where we still sought ways to talk about numbers and managed not at all to talk about ourselves. If that's a definition of friendship, then yes, we were friends. Certainly we depended on each other, or at least I depended on him. His securities were not so easy for me to judge.

But then he fell out of landscape and into story, with no chance to tell his own ending; he depended on us for that, on me and others, family and friends and strangers, and we none of us did very well for him.

It was on a Sunday morning that the first policeman came. I was in bed, and not alone there. Too short for me that college bed was, and far too narrow for two, but there we were: cramped and tangled, sticky of skin and thick of head, or I was. It was Ginny who shook me till my eyes cracked open, who hissed, "Ro, wake up, there's someone knocking ..."

There was. Someone knocking and calling also, "Mr. Coffey? Are you there?" A male voice, a stranger. No one who knew me would call me in that way; no one who knew me would call me at all, of a Sunday morning.

I groaned, half a response and half a protest; unwound myself from Virginia and staggered dizzily through strewn clothes towards the door; barely remembered to hook down the bathrobe and fumble it on before I opened up.

A policeman: but I told you that already. A young policeman, then; a blinking policeman, a blushing policeman, not short but gazing up, a long way up at me. Fixing his eyes rigidly on my face, not to see or to be seen looking at what else was on view, my length of naked leg—it is a very short robe, deliberately so—and/or Ginny in the bed behind me, no doubt tousled and peering, unless she was hiding under the duvet or trying to.

I didn't turn back to check, I was blinking myself, gaping maybe; I must have seemed sluggish and bewildered. A friend, a fellow student, even a member of staff and it might have been funny, fit for a story later in the bar—"Man, you should've seen it, he didn't know where to focus; score one for the bathrobe and one for me"—but a policeman was something else entirely. Not funny at all.

"Mr. Rowan Coffey?"

"Unh, that's me, yes ..."

"I'm sorry to trouble you, sir," and troubled I surely was, he was being way too polite, "but could I ask you to get dressed and come through to the Dean's study? As soon as you can?"

The Dean meant trouble, or should do, she was the college disciplinarian; but his demeanor definitely suggested that whatever they wanted me for, it didn't mean trouble for me. Not directly, at any rate.

"Yeah, sure. Give me a minute ..."

"Of course, sir. I'll wait."

Don't bother, I know the way. The last thing I wanted was an escort through the college, sowing gossip at every step. But he sounded quite firm about that, so I just nodded and closed the door on him.

"Ro? What does he want?"

"I dunno, sweets. Not you, though. You go back to sleep."

She grunted the impossibility of that but stayed where she was, curled in the bed as I rooted out some cleanish gear—not last night's party-clothes, definitely not those—and took a minute extra to give my teeth a scrub and swallow a handful of paracetamol and a pint of water.

Then I walked out into the corridor, closed the door behind me and led the way: trying to make it obvious how I was checking my natural stride to help the constable keep up, not to let anyone think I was dragging my heels from nerves or reluctance. Probably I only managed to look rocky on my feet after too much wine and lust and other stuff last night, but that was fine too. True, too.

There was a new administration block close by the college gate, all glass and concrete, the gift of an American millionaire who apparently wanted to maintain the tradition of having no two buildings in harmony; the Dean, sensible woman, had clung to her old office in the old building. Small though that office was, she still managed to divide it into two utterly separate zones of control: feng shui, variety Western academic. Under the window was her desk, from where she dispensed justice to the recalcitrant or the repentant, who had to stand before her awful seated majesty; around the fireplace worn leather chairs offered chill-out, a place for counsel and concern.

Today the atmosphere was total chill, under a warm sugar-coating. She welcomed me in and offered me coffee, strong black and sweet, antidote both to the hangover I had already and the shock that was clearly to come; she introduced me to Detective Inspector Charleson, a man with a gray suit and a difficult stammer; she waved me to one comfort-chair and him to the other, pulling a hard one for herself into the gap between while the uniformed constable perched himself on the corner of her desk, notebook in hand.

"Mr. Coffey—"

"Rowan. Please? Just Rowan." No need to make this harder or more alien than it was already, by calling me a name I didn't own.

"Rowan, then. Good. I'm told you're a friend of Simon Tarrant?"

"Yes," positively, "yes, I am. Why, is he in trouble?"

"I'm afraid he's dead, Rowan."

Sharp eyes watching me, nailing me to the chair, to the moment: that much I saw, and that was all I saw until the moment passed.

I dropped my head, gazed down at my hands, saw how they trembled; touched them slowly fingertip to fingertip, two by two like a pensive clergyman, and would have defied anyone watching to tell just how hard I had to press them together to hold that tremble back; at last looked up again, and asked the question.

"Why?"

Don't you mean 'how'? he might have come right back at me, and didn't. He understood, I think, exactly what I meant; or wanted me to think so.

"Because someone killed him, Rowan."

I made some motion of my head, I think, that was trying to be both a gesture of thanks for his honesty and a rejection of it, both at once. I know my hands came free of each other then, because I buried my face in them, I remember the dig of nails into scalp; I know that I breathed out once, long and slow, as a dead man might, just releasing air no longer needed.

The Dean's touch, warm and certain on the back of my neck; good in a crisis, any crisis, was the Dean.

"Rowan, do you feel faint?"

I shook my head, against my palms.

"No? Sit up and drink, then, dear. No, I mean it. It'll do you good." And the coffee was there in her hand, already lifted from where I'd set it down on the carpet; and in its place a box of tissues ready, in case I'd been crying. Very good in a crisis, the Dean.

But no, I hadn't been crying. Hiding, perhaps; absorbing, preparing, certainly. When I looked at him again we were ready for each other, he and I.

This time, I asked the expected question. "How?"

"With a knife. And put him in the river, after; but he was dead already." Hiding nothing, sparing me nothing was Detective Inspector Charleson. I could be grateful to him for that, perhaps. Later. If I tried.

"Where ...?"

"He was spotted this morning, lodged against a pier along the Backs. He could have gone in anywhere upstream; I was rather hoping you might be able to suggest somewhere likely."

I frowned, blinked at him.

"By all reports you were his best friend in college, Rowan— effectively his only friend." Right. Nerd, geek, no social life. No social life but me ... "Is that true, would you say?"

I'd say Inspector Charleson meant by the Dean's report, I didn't think he'd talked to anyone else. I hadn't realized she kept such careful tabs. "It's a point of view," I said.

"An accurate one?"

"I don't know. Christ, what do you want, a disquisition on friendship?"

"No, I want a list of the people he spent time with. At the moment, yours is the only name I have. Can you give us any others?" A glimpse of steel, behind the gentleness: just a glimpse, to match my flare of temper.

"No," I said, capitulating quickly. "We didn't talk personal stuff. I never saw him around with anyone else."

"That's what I've heard, too. So. Did you two have anywhere special you used to go? Anywhere on the river, say?"

"No. We used to meet in the bar here, or at the pool sometimes. Nowhere else, socially. He wasn't a social animal."

19

"At the pool. You used to swim together?"

"Sometimes. He liked it, it was the other thing he did really well." A nerd, but a wet nerd.

"You didn't go swimming in the river?"

The silence hung between us, long enough to interest him strangely; he waited me out, though, until, "I thought you said he'd been stabbed?" *Are you laying traps for my tongue, Detective Inspector Charleson?*

"That's right, I did. He was. Did you swim together in the river, ever?"

"No, we never did. He wouldn't like, wouldn't have liked that." Clean chlorinated water and the strict march, up and down and count the lengths like a metronome, that was what Simon liked. I wasn't sure if he even responded to the sensual tug of water over so much of his skin, the way I did. Simon would never have gone skinny-dipping, without undue pressure applied.

"All right. Did you see him at all, yesterday?"

"No. We were together Friday afternoon, in one of the computer rooms. That was the last time ..."

"Did he mention any plans to you, how he'd be spending the weekend?"

"No," again. "I said, we didn't talk about personal things."

"Fair enough. Tell me about your weekend, then. What did you do yesterday?"

I ran through the story of the day in my head first and then aloud, counting it off on my fingers to be certain. "I was working in the college library all morning. I joined some friends for lunch in a café, and we spent the afternoon together. Just hanging out, you know? Looking at books, looking at clothes, not really shopping. We finished off in a pub, a couple of pints to get the evening started. Then I went back to my room, about six o'clock. I was going to a party later, meeting up with my girlfriend there. I had a shower, got dressed, killed a bit of time, not enough. I didn't want to be too early at the party. So I went out for a walk. It's what I do, I'm a country boy."

"Where did you go?"

"All over. Just round the streets, along the river a way"—I saw that touch his interest, as I'd known it would have to—"and then back into town, to the party."

"What time was that?"

"I don't know, I don't wear a watch. Nine o'clock, maybe? Around then."

"It rained," he said, "most of yesterday evening."

"That's right."

"But you still went walking?"

"Yeah. I got wet. In my pretty party clothes." I grinned, just a little; couldn't help it. "It made my girlfriend fuss, but I kind of like that."

"Uh-huh. So you turned up wet at the party. What then?"

"We stayed late, came back here, went to bed." Together, but he could work that out for himself, or his young subordinate could tell him. If the Dean hadn't done so already.

He nodded, and then took me through it all again, with details demanded: name of café, name of pub, names of friends. The house where the party was. All of that. And then, "I'm sorry," he said, "but I'd like to see the clothes you were wearing last night. We'll need to take them away, for tests. I'm sure you understand ..."

Oh, I understood all too well. *With a knife*, he'd said; and it's a nuisance, to be the only known friend of the victim. That thought made me blink, a little. Simon had been a friend, yes, and a co-worker for a year now; it was hard to tag him suddenly as anyone's victim, let alone my own. Harder to accept that all that was done now, finished, unresolved. Death resolves nothing, I was learning that in a hurry. Frayed ends, threads cut short—*with a knife*, and I had that uncomfortable-seeming hole in my evening, where I should have had an alibi. Of course the police would want to see my clothes.

I let the constable lead me back through college to my room, where Ginny was hanging a wet shirt above the radiator. Scarlet silk, it looked much darker now. Her own blouse was on a hanger already, just as wet, and the floor was clear; she was wearing one of my shirts and a pair of my jeans, sleeves and legs folded into ridiculous turn-ups. She looked about twelve years old, and frightened by the policeman at my back.

21

"I couldn't sleep," she said to me, ignoring him completely, "but I had to stay, so I thought I'd just do this. Everything else is in the washer, but I did these by hand …"

I nodded; she always did. It was my companion forcing that nervous explanation from her, to me this was routine. My laundry habits revolted her; and she'd bought that shirt herself, and the trousers that went with it. My funds didn't run to silk, or to designer labels.

I pulled her close and hugged her, and made faces at the constable above her head. No doubt he'd take the clothes regardless, and clever chemists would scour them for the least trace of blood—which wasn't there in any case, unless it was my own or Ginny's maybe: not Simon's, that's for sure, he'd never bled on my stuff—but still I was glad it wasn't me would be explaining this to Inspector Charleson.

Fire and Fleet and Candle-Light

Juliet didn't stay. She had one quick whisky with us, for old time's sake—"I taught you to drink, Rowan Coffey, never forget that. Heavens, I taught all you boys to drink. Among other things"—and went her way, leaving me wondering and the rest exchanging glances, speaking glances, none of them speaking to me.

After she'd left, I realized I hadn't asked her about David.

Hadn't needed to. Maybe. She'd assume I'd make assumptions from her coming here.

But still, I should have asked.

Maybe ...

In fact, we none of us stayed late that night. Could have done, no trouble; the clock wound itself steadily past eleven and no one moved, I might have been the only one who noticed; but even so, it was well before midnight when Malcolm started to make sensible going-home noises.

Nobody argued. It wasn't a night for real roistering. We emptied our glasses and pulled on jackets and coats, the good boys among us—Malcolm, Lindsay—tugged crash-hats down over their hair, we all said a noisy goodnight to Rose and walked out into the quiet, quieting dark.

Which quiet was soon broken by the racket of scrambler engines revving loud, throttling back to a rumble. Malcolm and Toby were sharing, Dan and Lindsay also; Michael was solo. Ordinarily, I'd have climbed on behind him as a matter of course. I had Old Trusty with me, but ordinarily I'd have left that without a second thought; Rose would have taken it in.

23

Not tonight. Michael glanced at me, I shook my head and went over to tap Malcolm's shoulder.

"Go by my mum's, will you? Tell her not to wait up for me ..."

He gave me a thumbs-up in response. It was a message he'd carried before; it meant *leave the door on the latch, just in case, but don't expect me home tonight.* When we were younger he'd taken it further, lied for me, said I was crashing at his place. We didn't need to do that any more. Subtexts were taken for granted now, Mum knew where I'd be if I didn't make it back, and that was not at Malcolm's.

I stood and watched them roll away, watched until their headlights were lost in the night, listened until the last sounds of their engines were faded and gone; then I heaved myself onto the push-bike and started to push.

I loved this road in the dead dark, in the stillness: one reason why I didn't carry riding-lights. All my life I'd walked it, run it, pedaled it and driven it, by sunshine and starshine and no shine at all; I knew every bend of it, every buckle in the tarmac. It knew me also, from the babe I'd been in my mother's sling through child-hood and boyhood to the thing I was now, toppling towards adult. Adultery we'd called it, of course, when we were younger.

It was the road and not the river that carried my memories, held them for me to return to. So many days and nights, so much to remember. And yet, and yet ... These days—these nights—I could find only one image, one overmastering recall when I traveled it alone. Light nor dark made any difference. Be I burdened or enchanted, weighed down or lifted up, it had only the one song to sing me.

And so it sang, and so I rode along it. Past the turning to the lane, the climb, my mother's house, and on: on to another turning, another lane.

And so up. Working hard now but trying to work silently, barely breathing and cursing every squeak and grumble from the tired metal of my tired bike, I rose up from the valley floor and breasted the first foothill of the high fells beyond. There was the tarn, glimmering darkly, ruffling starlight under the breeze; there was the dark square shape of the old boathouse, long since abandoned of any boat; there was another glimmer within its black shadow, a single candle burning in the window.

I could have cried out then, I could have cried her name; I could simply have cried for the relief of it, not to have to turn the bike and freewheel down the hill again, praying that she hadn't heard me come.

I did none of those. I coasted to her door, and leaned the bike against the clinker-built wooden wall; I lifted the latch on the door and went inside, treading softly still, and breathing barely; I fumbled my way up familiar creaking steps, letting the creaks announce me.

Her bedroom door was ajar. I slipped through, remembering to duck beneath the lintel—and again, one more time, one last time I was seized by the moment, and could only stand and look.

Until she moved, until she stretched one arm towards me from the bed; until she said, "Rowan. I'm glad you came. I was afraid it was too early, or too late ..."

"Never that," I said, and never mind the words, my voice was all boy, husky and tentative. "Never either one of those."

She sat up, and the duvet fell away from her; I saw her naked by candlelight and my throat was full, I couldn't talk at all.

She laughed awkwardly, and hugged the duvet against her. Bare shoulders and bare legs, and the rest hidden from me; I wanted to cry a protest, and could not.

"I feel such a tart," she said, on another broken chuckle. "But it was stupid to wait up, not knowing if you'd come ..."

I shook my head. *Not a tart, not stupid, you must have known I'd come, you did know, you lit the candle.* All of those, and more. And if I couldn't speak, at least I could move now, I had my legs again.

Across the floor I went, and that creaked too, as it always had. Down on my knees I went and laid my head in her lap, in clouds of duvet; and felt her fingers once more in my hair, gentle, soothing, protective.

Again I could have cried, and did not.

25

"Oh, Rowan. What shall we do with you?"

I turned my face up, and not only to have her touch it like a blind woman, finding out my features, measuring the changes.

"Where's David?" The question I should have asked before, that might have saved me the anxieties of the ride up: would she want me, would she have me, would she let me stay …?

"David's with my mother." The answer I'd expected, predicted, counted on. It was almost a certainty; she would never have left him alone earlier, though he slept like a log or a logy child, unreachable. And if he'd been anything other than safe—in hospital, say: that happened—she would never have come cruising the Agric, looking for me or otherwise.

"Thanks," I said.

"Arrogant boy. There could have been other reasons he should spend a night with her. She likes to have him, sometimes."

"Even so," and I sat back on my heels now and gently, gently began to work that duvet away.

"Even so," she agreed. "I thought it might be convenient." *I hoped*, her hands said, which she would not. Not yet. "You could take a shower," she suggested instead. "You smell of beer. And cigarettes, and sweat. Boy-smells. There's a new toothbrush in the bathroom, too."

"It'll still be new in the morning," I said, heaving myself up to sit beside her, to work the trainers off my feet. More smells for her to grumble at, which she did. But that was only ritual, we were past the days when she could order me to wash and watch me do it. Nor would she have done that night in any case, there was too much else in the air.

When I held her, when I kissed her she smelled and tasted entirely of herself, of woman, of Juliet.

And took me to her bed for comfort's sake, hers and mine together; and all night we sought that elusive thing, and at last I suppose we found it. I did cry, then, and fell asleep in her arms like an exhausted child, reaching for what my mother could no longer offer me, the shelter that I craved.

And woke to a stiff neck and the absence of her, long-time absence by the coolness in the sheet beside me. Stumbled up and through to the bathroom, naked as I was—no David to disturb, alarm, whatever—to use toilet and toothbrush, shower and towel; and so back into yesterday's clothes, Juliet not having played washerwoman à la sweet little Ginny, and downstairs to where sounds and smells were crying breakfast to my belly.

The stairs led to a little lobby by the front door; sympathetic conversion had left open the rest of the ground floor. Water-floor, we called it, where the boats used to be kept: ostensibly dry now, a really wet winter could still bring the tarn indoors, bubbling up between the floorboards to Juliet's distress and David's high glee.

She'd heard me moving about above, heard me coming down; she called out, "Mind your—"

Crack! Too late: driven by my stomach's sudden urgency, my stupid head had forgotten to duck through the doorway. I yelled, and went through rubbing my sore skull. Not for the first time, probably not for the twenty-first. Like being ridiculously beautiful, being ridiculously tall is not always an advantage.

Juliet glanced round from the cooker, giving me a good-morning grin that was noticeably short on tender sympathy.

"Idiot," she said. "Are you bleeding?"

I checked my fingers, grunted a negative and slumped into a chair at the table.

One big space, kitchen and living room together, like a New York loft in a lofty place: and like many lofts, it was the view that made it special. The doors that had once given access to the water were replaced by windows, almost the height and width of the room; despite the damp and the chill of the house in winter, despite the inevitable paddling in times of flood, it was easy to see why Juliet persisted here. The tarn lapped just a foot or so below the glass, and stretched for a hundred meters or so beyond. A fringe of trees encompassed it, shielded from the wind by the bowl it lay in; above and behind them, the high bare fells thrust upward, changing their aspect as the weather changed. Calm and calling under blue skies and warm sun, harsh and dramatic in a storm—I could spend all day just sitting here and watching their solidity shift as the light and shadows shifted. Could and had, and would again.

Not today, though. Juliet slid a mug of coffee under my nose, followed it with a plate of bacon and eggs and local sausage with toast on the side, and said, "Look alive, lad. It's late."

I'd gathered that already, by the sun's height and her contained energy. I was grateful that she'd let me sleep in, she clearly had things to be doing. It was Saturday, so no school; by the same token, though, a teacher's weekends tended to be crowded with all the stuff that a week of school prevented. I knew that, from four years' observation.

"Sit with me," I said. "Please?"

Juliet smiled, fetched her own coffee over and sat opposite me, her head slightly askance with a question I wasn't going to answer.

As I ate, I looked at her. Tall for a woman, still slender as a boy; dark unruly shoulder-length hair framed a face that counted every one of its thirty-four years, that showed all the various stresses of her difficult life. Of which I was one, though not normally the greatest.

When I was fifteen, she was thirty. I liked numbers, I liked symmetry; my friends liked pin-ups, silky unattainable beauty, girls. They mocked me, and not entirely from envy. I scowled at them, sneered at their solitary beds, said you didn't look at the mantelpiece when you were poking the fire.

Lied and lied again, to keep my image pure. *Simon-pure, but no, don't think about Simon.* In fact I'd thought her beautiful even then, even in the days of my ignorance; now—like the changeable fells at her back—her every mood delighted, fascinated, entranced me. Like the tarn, however deep I went, still she went deeper and drew me further in. Sorry, Ginny, sorry a dozen Ginnys—but why paddle in the shallows, when you can dive the lake?

"What are you going to do, Rowan?"

Heavy talk, for a breakfast table: but for her, I could be heavy. I could be a lead weight if she wanted that, drag her all the way down to the dark, mysterious heart of her …

"I don't know," I said slowly, truly. "They've offered me a year

28

out, if I want it; but I don't know what I want. I don't know if I want to go back at all."

"Don't be foolish, Ro. It's what you've worked for, all these years—of course you want to go back." And then, when I didn't reply, "Were you very close?"

"Me and Simon? No, not really. He was a mate, of sorts, but not a buddy. I think maybe it was different for him, he didn't run to buddies, but I can't take that on board, you know?" She nodded her understanding. "It's not that, it's the whole thing. He was killed, murdered, and they thought for a while that I'd done it. Or they acted like they did, I think they wanted to believe it. They wanted to prove it, keep things easy. They had me down the station half a day, asking the same questions over and over, trying to make me confess ..."

And I was shuddering again, just at the memory. Juliet reached across the table, squeezed my hands urgently, said, "Rowan, it's all right. You're here now, you're home, you're safe."

I nodded, smiled at her weakly. "I know. That's why I came. That's why I don't want to go back, it'll never be the same now. Even if they catch someone, and they haven't yet. I'm never going to feel safe. Or that my friends are ..."

"Well, give it time, boy. Give it a year, if that's what it takes. Time changes things."

"Time changes some things. I'm not sure about this. They offered me the Hartopp too, I forgot to say. It'd make things easier, but I really don't know if I want it ..." My hands closed over hers, *don't let time change you.* Or maybe *I won't let time change you, Juliet ...*

How much of that she read, I wasn't certain. She slipped her fingers free and said, "Eat up. I'll run you into town, you can come and see Mum and David. How's that?"

"Perfect." Just what I'd been angling for, the last root wriggling home. One thing for certain sure, time would not have changed David.

Time nor weather, time's best tool, could change some things, or not quickly. As we left, I looked back at the boathouse in daylight,

29

and saw faint letters still large on the boards of the wall. One of my friends it must have been, who'd sneaked up to spray that message: a putative friend perhaps, or a real one in a sulk or a frenzy. Juliet had been flushed and furious when we found it. She'd gone at it with some chemical stripper, that had taken the paint off the wood but half the color of the wood with it, leaving the message blanched deep.

Ro, Ro, Ro, your boat, the message read then, and still read now. I hid a smile, slipped my arm around her shoulders for the short walk to her car. I'd never told her this and never would, but actually I liked it.

FEAR FACTORS

i

They were six and eight, and they had always lived in the Castle.

Once there had been a mother, just the one, though only the Gnome remembered her. Now they were mothered by all the mothers there were on the Ride, though not all the mothers had children and some women who did were not mothers at all. That seemed not in the slightest strange, not to them, not to either of them. That was how the Ride worked, and why people came along for it.

They still only had the one father. His name was Andrew, and he drove the Castle and he drove their lives, which was the same thing; and when there was trouble he met it, but when it was trouble about them he drove away from it, and so they had joined the Ride. There was always trouble on the Ride, but it couldn't ever find them, because they were so small and the Ride was so big they could all of them hide inside it.

They were six and eight, they were boy and girl; their names were Antony and Emma (though people sometimes called them Icarus and the Gnome, from the time when he tried to fly and only fell into the stream he'd meant to soar across, and she standing on the bank could do nothing but laugh, though she was the elder and he needed hauling out) and they were stardust, they were golden under their mud as all children everywhere, or so they thought who knew nothing but the Ride.

Emma the Gnome who could remember their mother could also read their home. Antony/Icarus knew what it said, but Emma could actually read it. *CASTLE REMOVALS* it said, *No Job Too Small, No Journey Too Short*, and then a number after, which they liked to chant together like a mantra.

When they asked their father Andrew what it meant, he said it meant that their home was their castle, and they could move it around whenever and wherever they chose. Which they did, or they used to do. These days, they only went along with the Ride.

Once they'd found ten pence in the road outside a phone-box, and thought that was an omen; they'd dialed the number on the Castle's walls, calling all the digits out loud as they took it in turn to punch the buttons. A woman's voice had told them that they couldn't be connected.

They didn't know any other phone numbers. If the money was an omen, then, it must mean something else; Emma had kept it safe for a time, in case its moment came, but quite soon she'd grown bored with the knowledge of it, with the constant looking out for its maybe meaning. She'd given it to Antony, who put it in his pocket with his keys-to-nothing, but the next time she picked up his jeans for washing it wasn't there. He might have lost it, he might have given it away; he didn't say, she didn't ask. It was only money. What could that matter?

Emma who could read the words and the numbers on their moveable Castle could also read a situation, better than Antony who was—their father said—the little friend of all the world, and thought that all the world was his. *You listen to your sister*, their father used to tell him while she listened, *stick with her, she may be little but she's wise, you do as she tells you.*

And he did, more or less, give or take. Which was why this day they were crouching side by side and cramped beneath the Castle, below the oubliette. In summer they spent a lot of time down here, lying sprawled and easy in the shade and the dark oily smells of it—but this was not summer, and neither were they easy. They huddled against the high tire and held hands for warmth in cold fingers, peeped out at the gusty world and were almost, almost hiding.

No reason for that, of course. This was trouble, to be sure, but it couldn't be trouble for them. They were immune, too small and the Ride too big for anyone to find them out inside it. They were being silly, no doubt, and so their father would tell them later. But he wasn't right here, right now, and the cameras were; and so they squatted in the shadow behind the bulging rubber wall of the tire, and peered shyly where they might have basked and preened, and listened as no common child would and so above all—in their father's absence, and under the camera's eye—they were glad to be just exactly where they were, sheltered below the Castle, beneath the ultimate safety of the oubliette.

ii

"That's the boy, like that, yes. No. Don't smile. I know you're nervous, of course you're nervous, but don't smile for the camera, don't say cheese. I don't like cheese. Do I?"

"No ..."

"No, that's right. I don't. So don't give it me, don't talk it, don't even think about cheese. Think about making me happy. Think how scared you are, in case you fail. Think how scared you should be. Good. That's very good. Don't blink at the flash. I like my kids wide-eyed and hopeful. Hoping to please. That's the way. Now lose the knickers. Just push 'em down to your ankles. And look up at me. Puppy-dog hopeful, puppy-dog cringing. Good. You're good, you know that? Good at this. We'll see what else, in a bit. Kick the knickers off now. Lie back on your elbows. Yes. Born to be a catamite, and lucky that I found you, you'd have been quite wasted else. Let's see you with a hard-on now. No, don't tug the thing, just touch it, tease it. Tickle it. Do it with your head, not your hand. Don't let me down, boy, you absolutely do not want to let me down ..."

33

A town, a street, a house: house in its garden like a green skirt laid around.

Park and lock; walk to the gate, to the door. It's all so familiar. He came here often and often in his innocence, with his friend or to see his friend or to take his friend away, to see him home. And also in his guilt later, often and often and never sure how guilty he should be, or how confessional. Never sure how much was known, or talked about.

Now in his most guilt, sure of being talked about and talked about and quite unsure of his welcome here, he hangs back like a child; tags along reluctantly behind her, like a child; only hurries to catch up at the last for fear of the other thing, of having to walk into the house alone and unprotected, like the worst fears of a child.

Walks in sheltered but not enough so, with her but not holding her hand as he wants to, as he always has wanted to here and everywhere and never has dared to here; and then suddenly doesn't need so much shelter after all, as he never has indeed except right there inside his head, where perhaps all the shelter in the world could never truly be enough.

He stands in the hallway, beside and behind her; and noise comes from the living room, and noises come from the kitchen. Television one, washing-up the other. She calls out, "Mum?" and her mother appears, in the kitchen doorway, wiping her hands on a tea-towel.

And hangs it on an invisibility behind the door, and comes not to her but to him. Holds his hand in lieu of her, damp warm skin that won't be so for long, age will fight back against Fairy Liquid and not lose.

Says, "Rowan, my dear, how are you? Such a terrible thing, I was so sorry to hear of it. Come in, sit down, I'll bring you a cup of tea. Juliet, you do the kettle, will you …?"

And so she leads him by the hand, and so he feels sheltered; and she takes him into the living room and motions for quiet though he's said nothing yet; and for a minute they stand behind the sofa almost smiling at each other, almost biting down laughter, almost playing a game.

The boy on the sofa hasn't heard them or seen them, his eyes are fixed on the TV screen. And that would be the game if they were playing it, to see how long they could stand there unremarked, how long they could hold their giggles in.

Easy enough he'd have found it, for a time. If they'd been playing. There's material in the room there, unexpectedly, powerful enough to kill any tendency to laughter in him as his eyes find it; and then there's the television, and that sucks at him too with its stories.

What's in the room, what's stacked on the table and leaning against the wall? Leaflets, posters, placards. A roll of canvas in the corner that must be a banner furled, its poles propped up beside it.

Reservoir Rip-Off—Don't Drown The Dale!

He's seen the leaflets in his mother's cottage also, he's heard her tell the tale. He knows they're surveying already, drilling boreholes to test the geology, the rocks that lie below the blanket of earth and water, trees and grass and heather. His security-blanket, but never mind that. Is it suitable for more water, much more water?

They're testing, drilling, drawing plans. Cost, capacity, constituency: all their numbers are in millions. To oppose them there's his mother, there's Juliet. Apparently there's Juliet's mother. Others too, all up and down the valley and around—but all like this, all small. A cottage industry against a multinational and more, the water company and the council and the construction firms lined up waiting to bid. Jobs, income, water sports, tourism, so much to gain; and so little lost, a handful of people displaced and a valley inundated, woodland underwater. There are other valleys, other woods. Not even a village needing relocation, barely a voice raised in protest bar those with a personal interest to declare. All in all, a perfect project.

A shoo-in, he thinks, with a shudder.

It's not even news for the TV, or not today. This is the local bulletin the boy on the sofa is watching, rather than watching his back; and that's not talking reservoir, though it is showing pictures from the valley.

Actually it's the lane that comes over the tops from the neighbor-valley, it's the moorland where Malcolm's father keeps his sheep, where Toby's father tends them. Even from this unfamiliar perspective, one glance is enough to know it. If the camera would look down, it would see a cottage between the farm and the dark tree-shadows, where Rowan's mother lives and sometimes Rowan too.

But the camera is looking up, and seeing hordes. It's seeing trucks and caravans along the wide verges, both sides of the lane; it's seeing police cars; it's seeing people, many people at a distance. Some in uniform, the police; others in jeans and hooded anoraks or heavy coats against the wind.

Close to, it's also seeing people. Three of them, and the woman in the middle holds a microphone. To her left is a girl with raven hair blowing, with ravens' feathers and silver rings woven into it, with black clothes beneath; to her right is a man in a suit.

They're talking, turn and turn about. The girl's saying here we are and here we remain, we have to stop somewhere and we've chosen this; the man's saying no, not possible, not permitted.

As the man sways and steps aside, struggling to hold his brief-case against a sudden gust of wind, briefly the camera finds two pale, anxious faces, children crouched in the shadows below an old furniture van, CASTLE REMOVALS it says on the side.

And that, just then, is when Juliet's mother reaches out an untimely, liver-spotted hand and touches the boy on the sofa. She lays her hand on his shoulder and says, "David? Look who's here, look who's come to see you."

And he turns his head grudgingly, up and back, showing how his hair is receding already although he's only a boy, not twenty yet; and his face is broad and round and oddly flattened, his eyes small and wide-set to show how much trouble he has with the world, not seeing it as others do, not well understanding how it works.

But his eyes work well enough for this at least, that he sees and knows who stands behind the sofa. His mouth spreads into a wide wet grin and shapes the name of Rowan, though it comes out mostly as a spluttering bellow.

"THE WOODS ARE LOVELY," said the guiser, *"and I willingly could waste my time withal."*

By which he meant, of course, that having come so far, this was where he wanted to stay and make his home.

Now he was a strange fellow, the guiser, and he spoke strangely; and all the point of that was to confuse, to mislead, to have people stare over his shoulder while he picked their pockets or their apples or their noses perhaps. He had long, clever, dirty fingers and a long and a clever and a very dirty mind, which he hid behind any number of faces.

As he strolled through the woods, every tree and every creature among the trees saw him and smelled him and knew him for what he was, which was unwelcome.

He came to a clearing and gathered dead wood and leaves, and made himself a fire as the sun sank, and soon he saw a pair of bright green eyes watching him from the shadow of an old oak. He smiled, and threw another branch onto the fire so that sparks leaped upward and the warmth reached out like a greeting.

He heard a low rumbling purr, louder even than the snap and hiss of the fire and the roar of the flames in the wind. He waited, as patient as any trickster must be, until at last the eyes blinked, the shadows moved and a great black cat slipped into the clearing.

"Good evening, Master Cat," said the guiser.

"And a good evening to you, too, stranger," said the cat, stretching itself out in the heat. "Do you hunt here tonight?"

"I do, if you will be good enough to tell me where best to set my snares."

"It will be a pleasure," purred the cat, "a fair exchange for this wonderful fire. I must whisper into your ear, though, because my secrets are my secrets and not for the ears of the woods."

The cat crouched, and pounced playfully into the guiser's lap; and spent a minute rubbing itself like a kitten against the guiser's clothes, purring all the while. Then it set its paws on the guiser's shoulders and whispered into his ear, all the places where he might find good hunting that night and every night.

When it was done, the cat sprang away and vanished into the night. The guiser laughed, seeing how much black hair the cat had left behind it on his clothing.

He sat beside his fire until it had died to a glow; then he rose, and went on his way through the starlit wood.

When he was gone, the cat crept from where it had been watching, and sat by the last glow of the embers to wash itself. Its purr was louder than ever, for it felt very pleased with itself. The guiser would find no good hunting, it knew, this night or any night; for he reeked of cat now, and all the small creatures of the wood would smell him where he walked and stay hidden in their holes and burrows. He would go hungry, the cat was sure; and when he was hungry enough, he would leave the wood and not return.

The guiser went from place to place, as the cat had told him; and where he walked, his trail smelled of cat. Wherever he found a hole or a burrow, he left a twist of cat-hair at the entrance.

When he was finished, he picked himself a meal of fruit and berries from the trees, and lay down to sleep.

The cat had no good hunting that night, nor the night following, nor the night that followed that. At last its hunger drove it from the wood. It left lean and spitting, and swearing never to return.

Drinks (2)

I met the children in the field below my mother's cottage, just on the wood's edge, where they were causing muddy havoc to more than their clothes.

It had been no part of my game-plan. In winter, they say, the days get shorter; I was doing my best to make that literal, sleeping and sleeping and also spending a deal of my waking-time in my bed or else in Juliet's.

This day I was at home, and well hung over. I didn't stir till midday, when at last and reluctantly I carried my full bladder and my aching head from bedroom to bathroom. Slow relief, pissing and pissing, trying to estimate the volume of my piss; when I flushed it away, the toilet flushed brown. The water in the taps was the same, dark and murky. I decided to skip washing and went downstairs, rubbing my finger over my teeth in lieu of brushing and carrying a few precious paracetamol in my other hand.

"Any juice, Mum?""

"Sorry, no."

"Ah, bollocks. I need something to wash these down, and the water's off."

"Is it? You can run up to the farm in a minute, see what's what. Before you go, though," my mother took a glass to the fridge and filled it from a carton, "drink this. It'll do you more good than those poisons you're so addicted to."

"What is it?" I took the glass and gazed at its contents suspiciously. Off-white and swirling thickly, it had a textured look to it, more tweed than silk.

"Soya milk."

"Ugh," I said, and ugh it was, though it served to swill the pills down my neck. I took them deliberately, one by one, letting her see. Macrobiotics was her latest kick, the latest of many; I was constant, loyal to my chemical crutches.

As to so much else. To my mother, for one. Never mind the fads and fancies, the inconstancies, the fey philosophies: she was something else beneath all of that, she was my root, my strength, my survival. It wasn't only Juliet had drawn me home.

Not even mainly Juliet. Nor mainly my mother, either. It was the package, the whole: Mum and Juliet and my old mates and David and the valley too, every tree and rock, every whisper of water in moonlight. It and they between them had made me and claimed me long ago; one thing I was not, one thing I could never be was free.

That morning—no, that afternoon I sat at the kitchen table and suffered, and watched my mother against the dull light from the window, and felt immeasurably secure. An imposing figure, my mother, tall and solid and so unlike so much of what she said. It was hard to correlate even those two aspects of her, the very real earth-mother and the scatty, credulous would-be hippy child of nature; add in the storyteller also and there you are and there you have it, the classic riddle wrapped in a mystery inside an enigma, there you have Alice Coffey.

Me, I was comfortable with any aspect of her or all of them together, she was all the definition I'd ever had of a parent or any kind of family. Every mood, every setting was familiar: as that lunchtime, where I was grievously hung over and she was dispensing quackery with no sympathetic sweetener, much as she had done days without number over the last half-dozen years. We understood each other perfectly, my mother and I: as that lunchtime, where she stood in the bleak light of the window and said, "Ah. No need to go chasing Mr. Gardale, Rowan. I see what's muddying the waters."

"Kids?" I asked.

"Kids," she confirmed.

Living as we did, remote from the mains, we were necessarily well-informed about what kept our amenities working, and how they could be sabotaged. Ask me anything about a septic tank, I can tell you. Ask me anything about spring-fed water systems, how easy it is to foul the water …

There's this stream comes flowing gently through that bottom field; just where it meets the wood, just where there's a handy supply of fallen branches, is a perfect place to dam it. We don't get many kids round there, it's not really tourist territory, but when we do get 'em they all play civil engineer in the mud. And the stirred mud backs up the balked stream, and it's incredible how quickly it finds its way into our water-pipes.

"All right," I said, sighing. "I'll go and sort them out."

Of course I'd go. I was the one complaining, wasn't I? Mum wouldn't mind a little of the good earth in her water. Gotta drink a peck o' dirt before you die; she'd take it in one wholesome draught, and then pass her tankard back for a refill.

I went out the back way, past the chicken run and the potato patch, over the fence between the rhubarb and the compost heap and so across the field. Not running, not even walking fast, not to scare the kids: just an ambling giant, me, happening that way. Nothing vengeful.

As it happened, they didn't seem the kind to scare easy. When I arrived at their construction site their glances up and up were wary, to be sure, but not nervous. Neither guilty, as though they knew no reason to doubt themselves or me.

The boy, the smaller and younger of the two, looked more impressed than anything behind his caution. He'd been crouched over, knee-deep in the beaver-pool they'd made, slapping handfuls of mud onto the timbers of their dam; now he straightened and waded out, stood wet and barefoot beside his shoes and socks where he'd left them on the bank and said, "You're tall, you."

"I know I am," I said, grinning, all disarmed in a moment. I hadn't exactly meant to vent righteous fury against their innocent heads, but a monumental hangover can make me less than kind. There'd been a biting sharpness ready on my tongue, which three words had undone entirely.

"Will I be you-tall when I'm big?"

"I don't know that, I'm sorry. No one does. What's your name?"

"Antony. And she's called Emma. She's my sister."

"Is she?" Actually, it was easy to see that she was. She had the same big eyes in the same narrow and fine-drawn face, only that both her face and eyes were still distrustful, where his were beaming.

"She's eight. I'm six, but I'm going to be seven soon.

"Uh-huh. My name's Rowan, and I'm nineteen. Are you cold?"

"No," he said stoutly, though his legs were blue and all of him was shivering.

Okay. "Where do you live, Antony?" Talk to the boy, as the boy wanted to talk; let the sister scowl.

"In the Castle." The way he said it, I could hear that capital letter.

"Do you?" It didn't seem likely; a scruffier pair of urchins I'd never seen. "Which castle's that, then?"

"On the top of the hill." And he pointed, up over Brian Gardale's land.

"Uh-huh." This must be playtime; no castle up there, no castle for fifty miles around. Never mind. They didn't seem at all anxious, the way kids get on their own a long way from home or family; and one thing for sure, I wasn't about to take responsibility for them. Neither was it needful. We didn't harbor monsters in this peaceable valley. I just yearned for clean water, a pint of coffee and a bath. "Well, look, kids," I said, "I don't want to spoil your fun, but you mustn't dam this stream. See how muddy you've made it? That mud gets into our taps, up in the cottage there, and all our water runs dirty."

They just looked at me: understanding, accepting, I thought, just uncertain what to do about it. Needing a grown-up to show them. I sighed, and bent down to unlace my trainers.

"Tell you what," I said, "why don't we make a bridge, instead of a dam? A drawbridge for your castle, rather than a moat ..."

Ten minutes later I was as wet, as filthy and as giggly as they were. Emma had decided that I was safe, it seemed, or had at least granted me the benefit of all her doubts; she was in the water alongside her brother and me, hauling away with a will. The water

44

was bitterly cold, as ever, but the work helped. Hard work it was too, pulling tangled branches apart against the sucking adhesive qualities of the mud they'd used for mortar. At last we had their dam in pieces, though, and the pool drained away around us. After a minute the stream ran clear over our feet; I heaved the kids out onto the bank and stepped up myself, sparing one laughing glance towards the cottage, where I was sure my mother would be watching through the window. I could feel her eyes on me, watching and approving.

We laid a couple of the longest branches over the stream from bank to bank, to make a difficult bridge; I balanced back and forth a couple of times to test it, before I let them try.

"Good defense for your castle," I told them. "Any enemies come, you can just roll the bridge into the water, and watch them splash ..."

"Too late," Emma said solemnly. "They're there already."

"Are they?"

Antony nodded. "Come and see," he said, holding out his hand for mine. "We'll take you."

Take me they did, once we'd pulled dry socks onto wet, clammy feet and forced our footwear on over. Emma tied Antony's laces for him, not trusting me so very far after all; but she took my left hand as he reclaimed my right, and together they led me to the lane and so up the hill, past our cottage and the Gardales' farm and higher yet.

I'd figured it out by then, where they came from, I'm not stupid; but I hadn't quite figured it all. I hadn't got the castle connection. Not till we were right there among the convoy, skirting the police in their cars and the little group of journalists with their cameras and mikes, big padded jackets and expensive wheels, bird-bright and eager eyes that had Emma suddenly slipping round to the other side of me, holding her brother's free hand instead of mine and losing her smile, closing down completely. These were her enemies, clearly, and she was right, she had no drawbridge to raise against them. It was altogether too late for that.

Dead ahead, first vehicle in the convoy was the ancient furniture van I'd seen on telly, when I was playing hide-and-seek with David.

CASTLE REMOVALS, it said on the side, and now I did feel stupid as the kids pulled me to the back, to where a set of steps led up to a rough wooden postern-door set into the tailgate.

Antony ran ahead, clambering up the steps and pulling the door open.

"Dad? Dad, we made a dam, and then we made a bridge, and Rowan helped us, and can he come in now? He's got cold feet, he says ..."

True enough, I did have cold feet, more ways than one. But Emma tugged at me when I hesitated, and so I climbed the steps and peered hesitantly inside.

"Hullo? Um, I'm sorry, your kids have kidnapped me, sort of ..."

"Don't be sorry. I'm sure it wasn't your fault. Come and warm your feet, and welcome so ..."

The voice came from the back—or the front, I suppose, the cab end—and it was dim in there, I could barely see a shadow moving. Likely he saw the opposite, though it must have amounted to the same thing: a rectangle of light that was the doorway and myself a silhouette, a shadow, masked.

Gray and heavy though it was, that light I stood in was enough to show me at least the near end of the van—but no, let's call it the Castle, as the kids did. This was evidently the practical end, generations of lino on the floor and the walls lined with cupboards, a sink, a calor-gas cooker. A genuine tin bath hung on the tailgate, filling my heart with joy; I hadn't seen one of those in use since my own eccentric childhood. Must be ten years now since Mrs. Gardale bullied her husband into putting a proper bathroom into the cottage.

No space for a bathroom here. No toilet facilities at all that I could see, unless one of those tall cupboards hid a chemical loo. I walked in—was pushed and pulled in, rather, four small and insistent hands underlining their father's invitation—and blinked rapidly, helping my eyes to adjust to what light came in at my back or down from three grimy skylights evenly spaced along the roof.

Lino turned to carpet underfoot, again several layers deep for better insulation. There was a sofa and soft chairs, torn and oozing horsehair, and a low table between; beyond, a single bed was pushed up against the far wall, and a ladder beside it climbed to the roofspace above the cab. That space was closed off by a curtain, the only divider anywhere; presumably the kids slept behind it, in their own private place which they might not realize also provided some vestige of privacy to their father.

Their father looked like he could have used a little more privacy just now. Seeing him clearly and in close-up, I wanted simply to apologize and go. He looked like I felt, only more so, and I was fairly sure he'd been napping on the bed before Antony came banging in to announce me. His graying hair was wild, one of his eyes was clagged up and his voice when he hailed me had been slurry and thick.

He knew it, too, he knew it all. He pushed his hands through his hair, rubbed his eye clear and hawked deep in his throat; then he gave me a tentative smile. "Rowan, did Antony say?"

"That's right. Rowan Coffey, I live in the cottage down the lane ..."

"And my two wonders dragged you up here before either one of us was ready for the day, by the look of you and the feel of me. My name's Andrew, by the way. We don't go much for surnames, on the Ride. Gnome, we need medicine."

Gnome seemed to mean Emma; whatever medicine meant, she clearly didn't approve, by the way she tutted and threw her eyes upward. But she fetched two small glasses and a dark bottle from a cupboard, brought them over and plonked them down on the table.

"You're wet," her father said, sounding utterly unsurprised.

"We all are. We've been playing."

"Well, get changed, please. And help your brother. I can't be doing with flu just now." He watched her herd little Antony up the ladder and through the curtain, then went on, "Rowan, do you want some dry things? I've got nothing your length—and your parents named you well, by the way, though the rowan is traditionally female: at least you've the height and grace to carry it off—but if you don't mind showing a bit of ankle, I could find you something to wear."

47

"Don't worry about me," I said. "I've been wetter than this, and survived it."

"Actually, so've those two. Often. But I have to make gestures towards being a good parent. Well, never mind, then. This'll warm you, anyway."

He poured a glass, and passed it. I sniffed warily, and blinked.

"What is it?"

"Gammel Dansk. Danish pick-me-up. Best thing ever, for the morning after. Down in one, lad."

He showed me how, tipping his own glassful down his throat so fast it couldn't have touched the sides. I imitated him, and almost choked on the stuff; felt it burn all the way down to my belly, blinked once more and breathed with care.

He laughed. "There you go. Sit down, you'll need to. I'll make some coffee, in a minute."

He dropped into a chair, and propped his head on his hands; again I copied him, feeling suddenly uncertain on my feet.

"Homeopathic dosage," he grunted. "Hair of the dog that bit you. Properly ought to be the same as you were drinking last night, but this is sovereign."

For a moment, I thought I was listening to my mother, only that her remedies never worked. His was potent. Too much so, perhaps; it was Emma the Gnome—and that was not fair naming, she was neither short nor squat—who made the coffee in the end, when she and her brother had come scrambling back down the ladder in clean jeans and T-shirts. Her father didn't even need to ask; he just waved a hand vaguely towards the kitchen and she went, though he did watch her carefully as she lit the gas and put the kettle on.

"Essential life-skills," he said, against the question I hadn't asked. "I say it's good parenting. And she's always cautious. Takes good care of us all, don't you, pet?"

She spared him a glance, no more, before turning her attention back to what she was doing, spooning Nescafé into mugs and pouring milk for herself and Antony.

"No mother?" I asked.

"No. Not for a long time now. I don't know where she is, even. Which is mutual, I suppose. I don't think she's interested; she didn't want any of this," and the gesture he made included not only the Castle and the lifestyle implicit in it, but the kids also.

"That must be hard," I said.

"Not really. I've got what I wanted, at any rate. Likely that's true of her too, by now. Clever woman, and pretty with it: she'll have found herself another kind of life. Something that suits her better. I was a teacher when we met, very settled, very stable. She couldn't have known what would happen, I didn't know myself."

"Er, no, right—"

"Meaning you want to know what did happen, but you're too polite to ask? Don't be. No secrets in the Ride—or if there are, we don't flag them like that. Half the point of how I live now is to be able to talk about it. More than half."

Oh God, he was an evangelist. Wanting to share with a half-met stranger—my skin crawled in anticipation. But I owed him something: head and stomach both were feeling suddenly better, after the shock of whatever-it-was I'd poured down my neck. And Emma was just carrying steaming mugs towards us, with exaggerated care; between them, they had me nailed here. So, obligingly, "What did happen, then?"

"I had an epiphany. More specifically, I got a broken jaw. I was teaching at a comp down in Surrey, I had a disagreement with a kid from Year 10 and he threw a chair at me. I took it straight to the head and got him suspended for the rest of term, though I had to threaten to resign and go to the papers even to achieve that much. That night the boy's father came to my house and beat me to a pulp. My jaw was wired up for three months; I had to live on liquidized slop, anything I could suck up through a straw. I couldn't go back to teaching after that, and we couldn't stay where we were; I had a young family, Antony was barely three and they'd both seen it happen, I couldn't expose them to that kind of risk again. We put the house on the market and lived with my parents for a while, but that was no solution. Something had to give, and in the end it was me."

He took a drink and paused for a moment, a technique I was well used to from my mother. His children had settled at his feet; this was storytime and they were equally used to that and comfortable with it. He smiled down at them, touched Antony's head lightly with his fingers and went on.

"My wife wanted to go back to work, she'd always been the more ambitious of us. That was fine by me, but I had a lot of time to think during those months, and I didn't want what she'd had before, I didn't want an empty house all day and just the routines of shopping and cooking and looking after the kids. I felt as though I'd been offered a gift, a chance completely to rethink my life, and I was determined not to waste it.

"So I did a bit of traveling, leaving the kids with my parents and going off on my own. It was like being a student again, it was like being free. I went to Glastonbury, first time in fifteen years. I went to see Dylan at Milton Keynes. I went to the west coast of Scotland, with a tent. And everywhere I went I kept meeting people, seeing people, hearing about people who lived that way all year round. People who lived in a bus or an ambulance, people who carried poles and tarpaulins in a truck and built themselves a tepee wherever they chose to stop, people who saw foundations as chains, as I was starting to.

"I was envious. For a while it was no more than that, it was just 'I wish I could do that' and forget it; but then 'Why not?' started up, sat in my head unvoiced for a while, finally broke out and demanded attention. To be sure, I had children; but children can be travelers too, it's the best time, they love it. And they learn so much …

"I had a wife too, and that was the difficulty. She couldn't see what I meant at all, she couldn't see the attraction. All she saw was bills, schooling, certainty. Proper parenting, she called it; responsibility, she said.

"We had rows. Then we had silences. Then she was offered a job, a career move, central London. No way was I taking the kids into London; no way was she turning down the chance. So she went, and I stayed behind. We ferried the kids to and fro between us for a while, trying to keep things going. But I was getting restless, more and more, and she was less and less a part of our lives, less and less interested in our lives or in us.

"Then I saw the Castle, and bought it. Just like that. Spent a while doing it up, pretending it would just be a holiday home; but as soon as we drove off in it the first time we knew, didn't we, kids? There was nothing to go back for anyway, no other home, only my wife's flat or my parents' house, nothing of our own.

"That was three years ago, and I've never been happier." And he looked at me, an open invitation, and I ignored it; at last he had to ask, "What about you?"

"Me?"

"How did you end up here?"

"I was born here." Which was never likely to be enough, so I added, "I should probably have been born in a trailer, my mum's almost a soulmate of yours," in the way that extreme opposites are. "All the dropout freedom alternative-lifestyle stuff, she's got all of that in spades. It's just that she goes for roots on the side, digging in and digging deep. She found that cottage when she fell pregnant, and she hasn't moved since. All kinds of work she's done to keep it, but now she's a storyteller. It's what she's always done best, only she can get paid for it these days. She really ought to be itinerant, like you, I keep telling her it's the tradition, but she just smiles and stays put …"

"I'd like to meet her. But I asked about you, Rowan. Born here is one thing, still here is something else entirely. You look college-age to me, and this is term-time …?"

"Yes. I'm at Cambridge, sort of. They've given me a year out."

"Why's that?"

"Something happened."

"I'm sure. And of course I want to know what did, and of course I'm not too polite to ask, you know all that, and if I was my kids are not; but we'll save it, shall we? You'll be back, we're here for the duration. Come and see the Ride."

Third time pays for all; I asked the question he wanted. "What's that, the convoy?"

"The convoy, the people, the lifestyle—how shall we tell the dancer from the dance? We are the Ride and the Ride is us, and anyone else who comes along for the ride. Don't ask me who named it, I don't know. Before my time. The Ride is an entity, a hive-mentality: people come and people go, but the Ride goes on forever. A bit of a helter-skelter, but you can't say that, it has unfortunate connotations. Summer in the south, faestivating; winter somewhere wild. Winter here, this year."

"Somewhere wild. Right." They could have no idea; I thought I'd better pass the bad news on. "Wilder than you want, I reckon, up here. We measure the snow in feet in a good year, meters otherwise. Either way, it'll be over Antony's head; and you won't shift till the thaw. Farmers' tractors can get up and down this lane, scramblers can if you're careful, but nothing else. It's never plowed. What'll you do for food, for fuel? You'll freeze."

"Oh, we'll do. We've a couple of Land Rovers can cope with most conditions. And we don't have a lot of choice. There's nowhere in the valley bottom we'd be let stay, and if we went any higher we'd lose what shelter we get from the lane walls here, and we'd lose the spring water too. This is a compromise, but it's good enough. We'll cope, if we're left alone."

By now we were out in the lane, and looking back towards the journos and the cops.

"You won't be left alone, though. Will you?"

"Probably not. If we just stick tight, though, they may let us stay. If we're stubborn enough, if the snow comes soon enough. They always fuss at first, but we have to go somewhere, and we'll do no harm here. We're blocking no traffic, these verges are so wide ..."

"That's not the point. They're all Tories round here. County Tories, which is worse. Gypsies, hippies, travelers—whatever you are, they don't want you. You're an eyesore."

"We're an eyesore? Have they seen that factory down by the town, a few miles back?"

They could hardly have missed it. A site the size of an international stadium, buildings made of Meccano and scrap by the look of them, steel chimneys pumping shit into the air, smoke too heavy to fly ...

"Sorensen's," I said. "Makes MDF, plywood, hardboard, stuff like that. Hideous, isn't it? No one quite knows how that happened, though there are plenty of rumors. Usual backhander stuff. They can't all be true, but some of them must be, I reckon. Anyway, the place employs half the town now, so they're stuck with it. You're different, you're no use at all. And I don't suppose you've got the money to pay bribes."

"You are so right. And thanks for the encouragement, Rowan, that really boosts my confidence."

Pleasant company he might be, but actually I wasn't in the business of confidence-boosting. To be honest, I wouldn't be sorry to see them moved on, harmless or not. This was my valley, my lane even, and I liked it as my mother liked it, unchanging as it had been all my life. The Ride was an invader, however benign. I didn't particularly want dozens of new neighbors all winter long, I wanted to nest with Mum and Juliet and my few good friends and no one more. And the one invader had brought others on its tail, press and police and not at all benign, and those I most particularly did not want.

Not that I'd say any of that, of course. It was just a selfish impulse, too embarrassing to air even to my closest. Mum, Juliet— they'd be brutally ashamed of me, and I had no defense at all. Even David wouldn't understand why I didn't want to be nice to such nice friends.

So keep the beast in its box, Rowan boy: I turned my head from the watchers in the wings, and ran my eyes all along the length of the Ride.

Eyesore it was, for sure. Its component pieces were parked up on both sides of the lane, where the verges indeed were wide; they needed to be, to take this motley collection of vehicles, this scrap-yard-on-wheels. There were a couple of genuine caravans and a few mobile homes with number-plates from the seventies, even one American Winnebago; for the most part, though, what I was looking at was conversion jobs like the Castle. None other so big as that; I saw one ancient ambulance, a couple of box-vans, a number of Transits. Way up where the lane bent, there was something that looked suspiciously like a hearse, although it had been painted a gaudy pink.

Closer at hand, a fire was burning in a gap left in the line, cheerfully bright against the gray light of the day. People were gathered about it, sitting and talking, passing a plastic carton round from mug to mug. Andrew led me, his children towed me; we joined the group.

"This is Rowan," Andrew said, "from the cottage down the lane."

Smiles and grunts to greet me; someone hunkered over to give me room to sit, someone else passed me the carton. I had no mug, so I swilled straight from its open mouth: raw and cloudy cider, scrumpy fetched up from some festival, no doubt. I wasn't sure it was exactly what I needed just then, but what the hell. I didn't want to seem ungracious.

I was introduced all the way around the circle, even to the baby that a woman was feeding at her breast; only one name stuck, though. That was the girl I'd seen on David's TV: my age, give or take, with bird-bright eyes bird-watchful. Black feathers in her long black hair, dressed all in black; I didn't believe her name, when they told it me.

The talk went on, no concessions to the stranger in their midst, and it was all would they be allowed to stay or would they be moved on again, was this their winter quarters or was it not? Some thought yes and some thought no; it was the girl who was most certain, most aggressive. They would stay, she said, come what may.

After a while she pushed herself to her feet and stalked away, and even her movements were birdlike. Contained rage, I thought it was that drove her.

"Andrew?" I murmured, close and quiet. "Why's she called Scar? I can't see one ..."

"Can you not? It's not on her skin, it lies deeper. That's a story for another day, another place than this. You think she should be called Raven, yes?"

"Well, yes ..."

"Well, she was. Once. But that was cut away from her. Now she's called Scar, so don't forget it. We don't have a leader, this isn't a hierarchy, but she's what drives the Ride."

A Short Walk in a Kinda Hush

David slept till she waked him, always; but there had been a change there, a great change. Five days a week now she woke him early, and he went to work.

In the next valley over, there was a center purpose-built to cater for those with special needs. It had been a part of David's life for some years now, initially giving him thrilling days out of school that he could brag about to us less fortunate students; they'd taught him to ride and to body-surf down waterfalls, they'd taken him up mountains and down mines, they'd generally given him skills and confidence and experience of a wider world than our narrow lives could offer. After he'd left school, they'd given him regular day-care while Juliet was at work, to provide some relief to his mother; now—and better yet, better than anything—they'd given him a job.

Mornings he spent in the workshop with a dozen others, making simple craft pieces to be sold to visitors and through mail-order catalogues; afternoons he helped in various ways around the center, taking responsibility in small ways that stretched but didn't challenge him, and bringing home his very own pay-packet at the end of the week.

He was full of it, he was on a constant high, oh so very pleased with himself. Now I was home too and very much around, staying at the boathouse three or four nights a week; David's cup ran over with delight.

There were drawbacks, though, to all this joy. One I discovered fairly quickly, abominably early in an unwelcome morning. Juliet prodded me awake, with a gleefully wicked smile on her face; she closed my unsteady fingers around a mug of coffee and said, "Up, up you get. David's dressed already ..."

"Is he? What the hell for?"

"You're walking him to work. Remember?"

I gaped at her, aghast.

"Rowan, you promised him."

"Christ, did I? Was I drunk?"

"Of course you were drunk, when are you ever not? We'll talk about that, but not now. Come on, you have to do this. David's really looking forward to it ..."

No doubt he was. David and I had been taking walks together for years. We'd always been pals somehow, ever since infant school, despite the obvious and unbridgeable differences between us; there'd been bad times, inevitably, when his many troubles got the better or the worse of him or my precocity of me, but we'd always got over those and come back friends again. It had actually been one of those small crises that impelled us into our first solitary walk: we'd been about eight years old, he'd come round to play— to give his mother a break, I guess, but I couldn't see it at that stage—and his clumsy stubbornness had led to a favorite toy of mine being broken. I still remember the blind fury that engulfed me, the way my leg had swung back to kick him, the tremendous effort I'd made not to let that happen.

I'd not been able to talk. Trembling, I'd stalked to the door and opened it, gestured him out with my head. He'd shambled after me, abject and terrified but following regardless, all the way over the field and into the wood. I hadn't been leading him anywhere in particular, only away, I think, away from my few precious things before he did any more damage.

But something had moved in the trees ahead, rustling the undergrowth. I'd stiffened, frightened myself for a moment, all my mother's stories coming back to me. David had been still and quiet at my back, and we'd both watched in wonder as a great dog fox had crossed the path, pausing for a moment with one paw cocked in the air as it turned to gaze at us, unhurried, quite unconcerned.

It had been a moment of magic that made my anger meaningless, then and later; always something to cling to, to remember, a constant reminder that what we shared was stronger far than what divided us. After that a walk in the woods had become a regular treat; we'd never seen another fox, but we'd seen deer and rabbits and hawks, we'd found a badger's sett and made impossible plans to sneak out, meet up and spend all night watching the brocks. Later, as teenagers, we'd managed the sneaking out a fair few times, though never for badger-watching purposes; and in retrospect, I think that the sneaking was just too loud, too amateur to justify the never getting caught. I suspect that my mother and Juliet both knew absolutely what we were up to, and made their separate or mutual decisions to let it happen. For David's welfare and personal growth, I guess, more than for my own. Mum rarely worried about either one where I was concerned, but then she rarely needed to.

So we walked, often and often; so now David wanted to walk again. Fine by me, in theory. In practice we'd not had the chance yet, so he wanted it now. Rather than his usual solitary bike-ride, he wanted to step it out with me. Seven miles, at seven in the morning. And apparently, God help me, I'd said yes …

You don't break promises to children; we never, ever broke promises to David. I dragged myself out of bed, splashed about in lukewarm water in the bathroom, pulled on some clothes and went downstairs. Ducked through the doorway, self-preservation operating even in my numbed state—and why hadn't it been operating last night even in my drunken state, why hadn't I said no?—and found David just as Juliet had promised, ready in his overalls and donkey jacket, beaming with pleasure at the sight of me. His sister's smile was a match for his, though her pleasure was a deal more complex than his, and inspired by evil.

"Here," she said, swinging a carrier bag in my direction. "Thermos of coffee, and a bacon butty; David's had his breakfast. You can munch as you walk. You'd better get off now, we don't want David late for work."

No, indeed. He looked frantic at the very suggestion, hurrying towards the door and making great beckoning gestures. I sighed, threw Juliet a glance of pure hatred which earned me nothing more than a chuckle and a blown kiss, and followed.

◆◆◆

57

Childhood walks, teenage walks—not the same thing at all. Any walk with David was both at once. And I might technically be a teenager still, my birthday still months ahead, but recent events had made a full adult of me, or I felt so. That added another level; I was far now from the carefree lad of a year or two back who used to stroll and giggle with his slow but solid friend, feeling himself so kind, so generous, so very content with himself for being who he was and doing what he did.

I couldn't tell you now as I couldn't have told you then what I actually expected of that walk—except that it was never going to be a stroll: seven miles and David urgent to get there, this would be a serious pipe-opener, and God only knew how I'd get back after. Walk again, most likely; there weren't buses. But I wasn't looking that far ahead, through the pre-dawn murk. No further indeed than the next few yards, a glance at the steep fall of the lane and then a glance at the butty warm and soft in my hands, a great tearing bite and then look up again, not to fall over as I chewed …

I think I went walking that day with no expectations at all, with no thought in my head beyond a yearning not to be doing this, a sullen silent cry for that warm bed behind me. Certainly I wasn't expecting anything monumental from David; he didn't do monumental, except in that he had made monuments of his mother, of his sister, of me.

After a few minutes the first fierce pace he set dwindled, as I'd known that it must. Not that he was blown—David was an ox, he could push his own weight on forever—but inevitably distracted. It might have been the sight of some scuttling thing between the cracks of a dry-stone wall, it might have been a sudden thought strong enough to blanket his urgency beneath its own imperative; as it happened, it was a question, and it came straight at me like a hurled stone. David was very good at hurling stones, I'd seen him take a rabbit on the wing. He was pretty sharp with his questions too, and this one hurt.

"Rowan?"

"Yes, David?"

"Why did that man kill your friend?"

Not the first time he'd asked it, actually. David was a terrier, he

58

wouldn't let go; when he didn't understand a thing he'd come back to it and back to it, like a dog at a wound. This time I wasn't ready, though, it was too early and I was too little functioning to handle the question with the finesse that my friend required.

So I prevaricated, always a reliable stand-by in emergencies. "We don't know if it was a man, David. Might have been a woman. They haven't caught anyone yet, so we just don't know."

He frowned, and shook his head. In David's limited universe, women did nurturing things and only men were bad, and only sometimes. He didn't have my advantages; all the stories from which he learned the world came from the television.

"No, but why did he?"

There'd be no respite from this; he'd go on asking until I gave him some kind of a reply, however unsatisfactory. And give it a day or two, the problem would rise irresistibly in his head and he'd ask the question again, and so on until I or Juliet or someone found an answer that would suit, that would finally close the file for him.

"Until they catch someone we really can't know, I'm only guessing; but I'd guess that it was just for money, David. Simon had nothing in his pockets when they found him, so he'd probably been robbed. Robbed at knifepoint," a good TV-journalist local-news kind of phrase that David would recognize and latch onto, "and maybe he resisted, maybe he put up a struggle and the thief just stabbed him …"

Picture poor Simon the nerd, the geek trying to make a fight of it, against some thug with a knife and all the advantages. Impossible picture, not to be believed. But it might settle David for the moment, let him dwell on it, let him puzzle out the unlikelihoods and give me some peace while he did so.

"Did he have lots of money?"

"No." Well, maybe he did. I knew about grant, loan and Hartopp; there might have been more. Family money, perhaps. I didn't know. "But the thief wouldn't know that, David. Not till after."

That one took him a minute, before he nodded. Meantime we'd come down from the tarn and the open fellside into the dense physical shadow of the woods, a single step out of clarity and into mystery and myth. David might have harried the question at me further, but did not. Trees to be grateful for, I thought, and let his silence carry me also into the subtle messages of that place.

It was conifers made that sudden border, shooting up dark and straight and tall, the very definition of a tree line; lower down there were broadleafs also, old English oak and beech and thorn to stand against the Scots pines and firs and other strange invaders. No rowans, not in such mixed company. We had a preference for Apollonian groves and solitude; this was a babel, survival of the greediest, the kind of wood that explains the root of panic.

No chance did it have of panicking us, we knew it too well; half my lifetime since it had made me shudder by sun or moon or starlight. Dry or wet or snowy, I was as much at home here as in the cottage, and David the same. More easily spooked than me, more easily by a distance, little would spook him in this wood.

Even so, we walked softer under the trees' cover, and talked less. At other times we'd pretended that was only so as not to scare the wildlife, not to attract attention if we were out late or without license; but we'd never fooled ourselves, let alone each other. In ignorant childhood or discourteous youth, still we'd felt how these woods demanded our respect, and we'd given it willingly. Trees many times our age, massively ancient some of them, how could we not? And that was to discount all my mother's tales about other, older creatures who still lived here and walked the very paths we trod ourselves. I might try to discount them, might and did try, but David not. David was always a believer.

So we'd rarely been rumbustious, within the margins of the wood; we'd saved our wilder ramping for the high fells and open spaces. Now, today, we had no time to wander paths and glades, the clock kept us on the tarmac of the lane and striding; but still we listened to more than our own footfalls, didn't add our own voices to the mélange of birds and breeze and insects, other sounds, creak and crack of tree-talk all around us.

Until David caught a falling leaf, and looked at it as though it were a star, something unbelievable but true; and said, "Why won't I be able to stay with Mum any more, Rowan?

"I don't understand," I said, "you do stay with your mum. Every

60

weekend," though it was noticeable that a weekend nowadays meant Saturday and Sunday only, which meant just the one night away from the boathouse. Precious rest for Juliet, a precious time for me; I heard the watchfulness in my own voice, and hoped that David could not.

"Yes, but Juliet says maybe not any more, soon."

Ah. Put it like that, and perhaps I did understand. Change upset David, especially when it was sprung on him unannounced; it was always wise to prepare him in advance, well in advance for anything major. Juliet might be looking years ahead here, to the time when inevitably their mother couldn't cope with the difficult, stormy, overgrown child that David would always be. Physically he was too much for her already, I thought privately; his sheer bulk militated against his being left in the care of an elderly woman. I'd not said so, though, from sheer selfish chicken-heartedness, for fear of hearing Juliet agree with me. No more than David did I love change, and I especially didn't want to lose those long lie-in Sunday mornings, where the greatest luxury lay simply in knowing that we were alone in the boathouse. David slept till she waked him, always, but his snores were a serious inhibitor.

"I don't know about soon, David," I said carefully, not knowing either what Juliet might have said in reply to the same question; he was bound to have asked it, time and time again. He'd be looking to me for back-up, for reassurance, to hear the same comfort in another voice. Last thing I wanted was to frighten him. "But every boy leaves home sooner or later." *Some boys come back*, but I wasn't going to say that, and I very much hoped that he wouldn't either. "It's part of growing up, and you've been doing a lot of that recently. You've pretty much left home already, haven't you? It's not that your mum doesn't want to see you any more, of course she does; I expect Juliet just feels that she's earned a rest from looking after you, now that you've grown into such a great big bothersome brute of a boy ..."

It was always an anxious moment, being rude to David; sometimes he took insults literally. Other times he loved them, and they could serve as a handy distraction. I watched his face and saw him grin, and allowed myself to relax.

61

"Tell me about work," I said, keen to change the subject, not to have either one of us dwell on an idea that could shake us both. "What are you going to do today ...?"

We walked, he talked, spluttering with eagerness as his feet carried him forward into his happy day. We came to the valley bottom and crossed the river, rose up through the darkness of the trees and out into light again, though not into sunshine; clouds were building, threatening rain.

And so up and over, hard going to climb the fell; we stopped to share a restorative coffee, sweet and milky as he liked it and I did not. Juliet would have smiled over that, too. Luckily, I carry a hip-flask with me whenever I turn my eyes and my feet to the hills; I let David drink first, then added a splash and a dribble that made it more than bearable.

Down to the tree line again, and again that abrupt transition. Here, though, we were on Forestry Commission turf and the trees were managed, poplars in serried ranks ready for the Christmas trade. At a turn in the lane we came to a locked gate and vaulted it—well, I vaulted; David clambered over, graceless as ever—and walked a wide ride, soft with rotting bark underfoot.

The ride led us down to another gate, this one open, and a public road beyond. From here our way was signed for us, or more accurately for the benefit of visitors, *The Ryhope Center*, with distances that diminished at every turning: a mile, half a mile, four hundred yards ... David cried every number aloud, and huffed with exaggerated relief at the last. We climbed a track to a group of ranch-style buildings, long and low, with paddocks and parking-spaces round about.

I saw David to the entrance and waved him in, waved him goodbye, promised that Juliet and I would collect him in the car after work, no need for him to walk home alone; then I turned and trudged back to the road, remembering to look behind me for a last wave before I disappeared.

David had had his walk with me, and that was what mattered. That I was stranded now, with no kind sister to retrieve me, was quite unimportant in the scheme of his life, hers, my own. Nothing but wearisome. I sloshed the last of the cooling coffee into the cap of the thermos, added another slug of whisky and drained it; and sighed, and set off on the long way back.

I wasn't entirely without resources, though; I had my thumb, and I knew how to use it. There was never much traffic on these roads, but some at least: farmers, commuters taking a back route, late-bird tourists at this dead end of the season.

Hitching meant sticking to the highway, no cutting up through the trees. Here, though, that was no great loss. Though it was this valley that had the attractions and drew the holiday-makers, though ignorance is bliss and certainly they didn't know what they were missing—and equally certainly I was not about to tell them— still it was far more than the hill between that separated our woods from these. Here was nothing hidden and nothing old, no survivors. No atmosphere: no magic my mother would say, though I was reluctant to. Even David knew the difference, even if he couldn't articulate it.

So no pleasure here in the gray shadows of those stiff trees in the quiet between vehicles, only counting my own footsteps and straining after the sound of another car. No hint of a whisper below the hush, the murmur of stored centuries, concentric stories contained.

Cars came and went, tractors too, though not many of either. Not enough to grow resentful yet, though of course I was resentful anyway: what else should I be? Anyone going up this hill came necessarily down the other side, and I wanted no more than that. Five minutes' wear and tear on their upholstery, and so farewell. The tractor-drivers mostly made gestures of apology, *no space for you up here, mate* or *I'm pulling off, next field, see me go?* Not so the cars: Volvos and Saabs, loads of room inside, and their drivers hurried past without a glance, unless it was deliberately in the opposite direction. The rain didn't help, I guess, one of those sudden steady falls that soaks in minutes, giving them more genuine concern for their upholstery which seemed utterly to outweigh any pangs of conscience they might have felt as they swept by.

63

At last, though, high above the trees now and my legs and lungs both working hard, both crying for a halt, I heard the sound of an engine slowing even before I hung my thumb out. *Just changing gear, shifting down, the better to sneer as they pass*, I thought— but no. It wasn't a sneery-sounding engine. I glanced round, risking the humiliation of visible hope, and saw an old VW camper van with rusting black paintwork. It chugged to a halt beside me, the door flew open and a voice yelled, "Jump in, quick! She stalls, we'll never get her started on this hill, in this weather …"

In I jumped, bedraggled and dripping as I was; away we went.

"Thanks," I gasped. "I'm only going over to the next valley, but …"

"Us too. Think so, anyway. We're looking for the convoy …"

Yes. I might have guessed anyway, from the vehicle they drove; now that I pushed rain out of my eyes and looked at them, I really didn't need telling. I could have told them. Two young lads with their hair in dreadlocks, wearing faded black deliberately ripped and ragged—they couldn't have been looking for anything else, around here.

When I looked behind me, into the body of the van, I saw the stuff of life, to be sure, but not enough of it. Sleeping-bags and kitbags, tools and tarpaulins: all good to travel with, not so good as sole sustainers. The convoy I'd visited was a community, if not wholly at one; these boys, I was sure, were no laggard part of it.

I wondered why they'd come, what they wanted. Not to sign up for the duration, that was evident. In the back of the van I also saw scaffolding poles bolted together into crash-barriers or the like; bags of sand, bags of cement; a canvas hold-all with baseball-bat handles sticking out of it.

I had them take me all the way, in the end. No point my going back to an empty boathouse, when I could find clean clothes and company at my mother's.

When we reached the convoy, it had grown. Grown by ten or a dozen vehicles, I thought; the newcomers were mostly young, mostly male, prowling the lane and doing big staring acts up or down, one way or the other, to where more police, more journalists stood watching, photographing, murmuring into radios or recorders.

BAD BLOOD

i

The fire burned all day; it burned all night. Even with the barricades up now, the police in numbers and the bailiffs always watching, no one ever hindered their going to the woods for wood.

The fire was a beacon, a hearth and a parliament, where all had rights of audience and the house was always sitting.

Scar was there often, was there now: first among equals. Her body, her eyes, her words said so, though she herself would not.

He said, "You sent for them, to make a fight of it. Didn't you?"

She said, "We have to fight, if we want to stay."

He said, "No. We've never fought before, and we've always found a place. You have to be patient, that's all. We used to be good at that. We're the Ride, we're a community; they're no part of us. They're mercenaries, they're only here for the fighting. You'll destroy us all."

She said, "We have to fight, they'll grant us nothing else."

He said, "I have *children.*"

One was asleep at his feet, indeed, and the other in a woman's lap a quarter-turn to clockwise round the fire.

She said, "Your children are our strongest weapon, and our best defense."

He said, "No."

She said, "Yes, of course. Yours, and the others'.."

He said, "My children are not human shields."

She said, "They exist, they're here. They're part of your community. That's enough."

You mean they're just along for the Ride. But he didn't say so. His mind was filled with visions: his children as chips, as bargaining-counters, earning their place. Their wildness, their freedom only a mirage after all, only a part of the price that he paid, his ticket for the journey. *Every farthing of the cost*, he thought grimly, bitterly; and had forcefully to remind himself that this revelation, this insight was still a blessing to be counted, where the alternative was war and the battered bodies of his children. If it was the frailty of those bodies that kept them unharmed—that classic doublethink of authority, *we can hurt them so easily, we dare not hurt them at all*—perhaps he should be grateful. If their frailty kept him and all the Ride unharmed, perhaps they should all be grateful.

Perhaps. But he lifted his daughter to his shoulder, and stood; scooped his son up in his other arm and walked away from the fire and back to his home, his castle, where he knew that their protection lay in him.

Tonight he would not sleep, and did not try. With anxiety and cheap whisky combining to make a roiling misery in his gut, he sat in the Castle's cab and gazed out at limitless sky, unreachable stars. Felt the turning of the world beneath him and saw its effect as the rising hills occluded the constellations, glimmer by glimmer; he thought he was on a slo-mo roller coaster caught in an endless loop, tipping backwards and backwards, fated never to fall.

Thought that might be the whisky, roomspin under the stars where the whole planet made his spinning room; but the planet did spin, and with timelag enough on your eyes you could see it happen, he was watching it now. And there was room enough, surely, he could find a place on this spinning world for himself and his kids in their castle.

He'd thought it was here with the Ride, but that was a castle built on sand, and the sand was slipping. The Ride had changed. Not their fault, it was the unwelcoming world that had changed it; but Scar and her friends with their tank-trap obstacles to block the lane and make the world unwelcome, they had made the Ride no place for kids or him. He would have left by now, he thought, only that he could not drive through tank-traps.

Those had gone up this day, suddenly and without consultation. It had been a classic, a beautiful maneuver, and certainly pre-planned. With the dawnlight more vehicles had come, strangers to the Ride but not to Scar. They'd packed the verges all the way to where the press and police were parked; and then a little later yet two more, one from the north and one from the south, old camper-vans and nowhere for them to camp.

So they'd stopped in the lane there and blocked it north and south, just at the perimeters of the Ride. Even then, standing looking, he'd thought of a wagon circle, a defensive wall. Long and thin and vulnerable, this one, no circle; but nonetheless the thought came, and he believed it.

The police came too, and told the drivers they couldn't stop there, they couldn't obstruct the highway. They said there was no place to park, unless the police moved their own vehicles just a little further back. The police said they couldn't join the convoy in any case, there was an injunction to move it on and it was in breach already; they said the injunction didn't apply to them as they'd only just arrived, and they weren't joining anything, just visiting, and they'd be happy to clear the highway as soon as the police made room.

Which the police had done, eventually, reluctantly; and while they were backing their squad cars away, the back doors of both vans had swung open and the small army of that morning's newcomers—small, certainly, but an army for sure—had swung into action.

Pre-assembled barriers had been dragged out and laid across the lane; Scar had organized women—preferably with babies at their breasts—to sit on them, a second line of defense behind the young men with their baseball bats who faced down the unready police while the journos gleefully snapped and scribbled, while other young men mixed concrete …

Outnumbered and outgunned, the police had done nothing but observe and report; and so those steel-and-concrete roadblocks were fixed and firm and solid now. The lane was blocked, the lines were drawn, there was no way out but war.

This he thought, he assumed, was what Scar wanted. Not he, not many of them; but they'd back her now, they had to. She'd stolen their choices; and her men were everywhere, arguing her case. "It's direct action, taking possession, reclaiming the land ... It's yours, common ownership, you've a right ..."

And so there would be a war, or at least a battle; and he wanted to take his children away from it, and he thought probably he would. Only that meant taking them away from their safety, the Castle; it meant making them deliberately homeless, after so many years of teaching them the meaning of a home.

Tomorrow, perhaps, he'd prepare them for that; tonight he couldn't bear it.

So he sat and drank whisky, and watched the world turn or the sky spin away; and in the dead before the dawn, in the first gray that spoke of a coming sun out there, he saw shadows move behind the walls on both sides of the lane and knew that the battle had come already, come too soon, when neither he nor anyone was ready.

ii

They were six and eight, and they still did everything together, including sleeping: in the same small space, at least, if not exactly in the same bed.

It didn't seem small to them, who could pose face to face on all fours and arch their backs like angry cats and still touch nothing, not wall nor roof nor curtain nor each other, only the soft foam rubber and heaped fabrics under hands and knees and the warm still air of this private place.

They had another place that was private to them, more intensely private and much more safe; but this was theirs for every day and every night, and they had grown far beyond the love of it. They possessed it, or it them. It lay under their skin, deep-graven in their minds, their high chamber within the Castle's walls.

Under the blankets, curtains, off-cuts and samples that made their bedding, under the foam that was their mattress, under the steel flooring was the cab where their father drove and they traveled, where they saw the world go by; where, sometimes, their father would sit wakeful with his whisky all night long.

Above, set in the curve of the roof was a skylight, to give them light by day and the stars by night, if they too should be wakeful. On the walls were bags that held their clothes and toys and necessaries.

Late stayers, semi-nocturnal sometimes like their father, habitually they were late risers also and no dawn chorus. This pre-dawn, though, when their father thrust himself hugely through the curtain into their space, head and shoulders and half his body else, when he shook them awake with rough hands, it needed only a few hissed words to have them quick and clear-eyed and moving.

"Into the oubliette. Hurry!"

This is not a drill. Repeat, this is not a drill.

He didn't need to say it even the once; they knew. They did have drills, but never like this, in the dead dark dragged from dreaming and that tight catch in his throat that they could hear, that wasn't letting his voice out. It was fear, that they knew. They'd heard it before, had understood it even before they had the words to understand. Fear for them it was, that shut his voice down.

So: up, awake, they scrabbled in the dark for bags. Emma's to the left of the curtain, Antony's to the right. Scrabbled and grabbed and came out and down according to the drill, Emma first and Antony after; and before their feet hit carpet their father had flipped the carpet back, to lift the lid of the oubliette.

Emma first, in this as in everything, drilled to show no fear to her brother. Drilled to ask no questions either, no "why do we have to?" or "what about you?"

She slid feet first into what was darker than the dark above. Her feet found carpet that rang hollow, like a muffled bell, as it always did. She wriggled and rolled down to the end, where she could hunker with her bare feet on carpet and her back against carpet and her head pressing up against carpet; then she wrapped her arms around her pajama'd knees, and shivered a little.

Just a little, and only briefly. Antony came down with a bump and a booming thump to join her; their father whispered a blessing, and then the hatch closed and they were on their own and she wasn't allowed to be scared any more. Not until Antony was. It was okay then, they could be scared together.

The oubliette was of course their father's idea, and of their father's construction, and so they loved it; it was their final refuge, the place of ultimate safety, and so they loved it.

It was a dark, cramped, ill-smelling hole that they used only when terror lurked, or when terror came rampaging, and yet they loved it. Terror was separation, hell was losing their father; to escape that, this. This was separation, this was them in here and their father God knew where and doing what but not in here, not being with them. And yet they loved it.

Unlike most children, unlike any children else, they never ever played hide-and-seek. Hide-and-seek was not a game. Besides, they only knew one place to hide, and they hoped very greatly that no one would ever seek them there.

The oubliette was a box, a steel box the size of a four-drawer filing cabinet, which once it had been. Bolted to the underside of the Castle and painted black, hidden among spare wheels and fuel tanks and axles, it could pass any inspection bar a mechanic's, and their father was his own mechanic. For MOT it could be removed beforehand, replaced after.

The oubliette was lined with carpet for comfort below, at each end and above; the sides were simple steel still, drilled for air and rare, rare whispers of light. There was a hatch above; there was a hatch below. Both were hidden by carpet.

Emma had her end, and Antony his. Both had their Rescue Bags, with food and chocolate and water, a change of clothes and a favorite toy. Enough for a day and a night of hiding, and they should never need longer than that. Their father said so, he said he would always come.

And so in, with the fog of fear clammy in her mouth but not to be breathed yet, not before Antony. The place itself was not fearful, it was their place as much as the place above the cab was theirs: built

70

for them, kept for them, used never by anyone else. This was their secret, and they'd never shown it to a soul.

One day, she supposed, they would be too big to fit it. Their father had carpeted the roof after she'd banged and rubbed her head enough to make a sore spot, and she was already taller now. But one day they wouldn't need it any more. One day they'd park the Castle in a field by a house, and they'd live in the house and only play in the Castle and never have to hide any more. That was the promise, and they both believed it. Their father would lie to the police and the Social and the schools and all sorts, but he never lied to them when they could catch him and he never, never broke a promise that he'd made.

Besides, they needed it. They needed to believe it. Kid she was, determinedly, but that much she knew already. Everyone needed something to look for: a change, a miracle, a new life, a pot of gold.

One day, and one day—but this was today, and neither of them. They were here and they had to hide, and they still fitted into the oubliette.

Why they had to hide he hadn't said, she couldn't guess. No point asking Antony; he knew less than she did, about everything, always.

She listened at the air-holes either side, and caught nothing but the touch of breeze against her ear, breeze made oily by its rubbing at the Castle's sticky black belly. Their father kept it foul down there, to stop anyone looking too closely. She put her eye to the holes instead and saw nothing but the dark, caught nothing but the greasy touch of that same breeze that made her jerk back, her eye watering and stinging.

Overhead she could hear nothing either, now that their father's footsteps had departed. If she knew him—and she did, oh yes she did—he'd be back in the cab by now, sitting and watching, waiting for danger and hoping to draw it entirely to him, altogether away from his children.

Here inside the oubliette she could hear Antony, his little uncomfortable shufflings and his hard loud breaths. He wasn't crying, though, not yet; she knew the sounds of that, and the sounds he made to hide it. Threatened but safe, he could fight the tears back; safe but threatened, he couldn't hold them back forever.

When he cried, so might she.

She hated to be in the dark, but she knew that sometimes light could be worse.

When she did see light, it was worse.

Though the oubliette was hidden as well as their father could hide it, it was too big to hide completely; there were air-holes that looked out past the axles, past the wheels to the world beyond. She knew which they were, and those were the ones she looked out through. Though the cold harsh breeze stung her eye and made it water—not cry, not yet, but water—still she came back to them, time and again, trying to see what their father had seen and feared.

What she saw was not the dawn, not the sun's coming; these were flashes, sudden fingers of light stabbing through the darkness, glimpsed and gone. On both sides of the Castle she saw those, and thought *torches.* Thought *enemies,* thought the Castle and the Ride were under siege.

And then came the noises, and she knew. Under siege, and under attack.

They were the worst kind of noises, men shouting and women screaming, breaking glass. A lot of shouting, screaming, a lot of breaking glass; all of it too near, and some very close indeed. She felt the Castle itself shake and thunder; and now she was scared, yes, and Antony too. He wriggled into her arms, and they hugged each other, sobbing. They were safe, they knew, they were sure; but their father not, and so they were not safe at all.

The noises went on for ever. She didn't know about the lights, she wasn't looking any more; only clinging to Antony, only being there with him as she always was, the Gnome and Icarus together and missing their father.

The noises went on for ever, but they stopped at last. There were still voices, but no shouting now; still screaming, but that was babies, not women any more. She knew the difference, and babies did scream. Women sobbed still, and she could hear that too, because she and Antony weren't sobbing any longer. They were in the oubliette, and it was important to be quiet.

Antony sniffed in her ear, whispered into her ear: "I need to pee."

So did she. It was all right, they'd done this before, they knew how to do it safely.

She lifted up the carpet from the floor, and found the hatch. Worked the oily bolt back gently, silently; gripped the handle and lifted, let the hatch fall silently onto the folded carpet.

A square of gray, dim light beneath them; she could have put her head down and looked both ways, but didn't. Safer not to. Someone might look back.

Antony fumbled inside his pajamas, found his willy and poked it out, peed down through the hole. There wasn't very much, but she knew how urgent he'd felt it; she was just the same, burning, desperate.

When he'd finished, he squashed up at the far end to give her room. It was harder for her, because she was a girl; she had to take her trousers off and crouch over the hole. For a moment she thought maybe someone would have seen Antony's little jet of pee, an enemy might be wriggling under the Castle now, coming to find them out, she imagined a face appearing suddenly under the hole, just in time for her to pee all over it.

It wasn't funny at all.

But she listened, and heard no scrabbling, coming sounds. She peed, and heard the hiss of that against the grass below; nothing more, no shouts, no splutters.

She closed the hatch and bolted it, and laid the carpet down again before she put her trousers on. Then Antony came back, and they lay full length and held each other for comfort in the dark. She felt him fall asleep at last, and sighed, and did the same.

He woke her with his wriggling. She looked out and saw the gray of day, but nothing moving; she listened hard, and heard no sounds at all except the birds.

They opened their Rescue Bags and ate biscuits and chocolate, and drank water. This at least was routine, or at least routine for emergencies: holing up through the quiet of the day, eating hardtack and silence, waiting for their father to come.

He always did, he always would. They knew that, because they had to.

The silence outside didn't last, though theirs did. They heard noises, voices, a big engine come and slowly go. Voices and laughter, briefly voices and anger right there, by the Castle. She thought she ought to try to understand, it ought to be important; but there wasn't anything important in the oubliette, except herself and Antony, and waiting.

iii

Word came to him from a friend on the force, a whispered message in a crowded mall: *you should get out, you should leave. Now. Stand not upon the order of your going, but depart. Do not collect anything from your last address.*

So he did that, he did it all. This was familiar territory, being warned off out of the blue, sent off in the dark and into the dark. He could always find a friend, on any force.

He hitched his bag a little higher on his shoulder, and walked away from friend, mall, town. He'd catch a bus once they were running, but not from here; they might be watching for him at the station. He might hitch, he might just walk for a while. He would not look back. Or go back, or even call back to warn friend or force or anyone of what they were doing by driving him away.

He would not speak of what he'd left living in a box beneath the garden of his garden flat. Let them look, let them find it if they could; if not, let the smell of the thing find it out in a couple of weeks or a month. Or not. Let them chalk up one more disappeared kid, and let it go.

Magnificently unconcerned, he walked through the dawn; and let his feet find a direction for him, this first day away. He had an idea already where he'd go to overwinter, he'd been invited and it suddenly felt wise, but no hurry. Why be urgent? Even death didn't hurry, unless you forced the issue, and he never willingly did that.

iv

Woken by the noise and not his mother, he finds the front door open and her a little distance from it, standing in the field in her bare feet and dressing-gown with her hair wild and a cat in her arms for comfort.

"What is it?"

"It's cold, you fool. Put something on, for God's sake ..."

"No, that," with a long-armed gesture towards the distant noise, the faint flashes of torchlight in the gloom. "What's going on?"

"Rowan, I'm not having you dancing around naked. It's wicked out here, and I can do without a sick son on my hands. Come and get some clothes on, I'm going to."

He suffers her to lead him back into the cottage, with a firm hand on his bare shoulder; but, "Mum, what's *happening*?"

"At a guess, I'd say the police are trashing the convoy. Wouldn't you? Get *dressed* ..."

She pushes him into his room and he scrambles obediently, distractedly into yesterday's clothes; and comes out to find her ahead of him and back at the doorway, gazing up the hill. It's gusting with rain now, and she's holding a newspaper above her head as she hovers indecisively between weather and whether.

"Come back indoors," he says, recognizing the signs.

"I'm going up there."

"No." His turn to seize her arm, to hold her against her will, almost the first time he's done that; both perhaps are surprised by his strength, his certainty of purpose.

"Rowan, there are *children* up there! Babies, women—and you know what the police are like, what can happen. I have to go up."

"Mum, listen. What do you think you look like? You look like

75

one of them," and she did, in her gaudy patchwork dress and her undressed hair. No cat now, but still she looked like a witch. "Whatever's happening to them, you go up like that and it'll happen to you too."

I'm not having that, unsaid but very present between them.

"But—"

"You can't help now, in any case. Not in that," with a jerk of his head towards the sounds of battle. "What are you going to do, drive the coppers off? Biff them with a rolled-up copy of the *Gazette*?" It seems so from the way she's holding it, pointlessly, determinedly; he takes the paper from her as he talks, as he talks and talks, flooding her infirmity of purpose with his words, hoping to drown it early and realizing his hope, feeling resistance leave her. "We'll go up together, soon, when they've stopped. We can help then," cups of tea and shelter from the rain, arnica for bruises, but he'd have to be with her or she'd fill the house with victims and call down her witch's curses on the police, talk herself into trouble regardless.

"Yes. All right, Rowan …"

He closes the door firmly against any change of mind, against the noise; and steers her into the kitchen at the back for greater distance. Sits her down and tosses the paper onto the table, fills the kettle and sets it to heat. Sorts out tea for her and coffee for himself, and then stands reading yesterday's news inattentively while he waits for the water to boil.

A story snares his eye: the local office of the water company has been deluged with letters of protest, about the proposed new reservoir. Despite his pale dependent mother, despite his own anxieties, he grins; he knows all about that. The council and the DoE too, but it's the water company catching the brunt of it, being taken by the flood and—hopefully—swept away.

The grin fades slowly, he feels it go, as he reads on. The scheme seems only to have one supporter locally, willing to stand up and be publicly counted; that's Sir Julian Ricks, MP of this shire and the man who owns half the valley, the man in fact who owns this cottage and the farm up the lane and all the woodland and a great deal more. He's hugely, massively, influentially in favor of the reser-

76

voir. He talks of jobs and tourism, he talks of man-made beauty outmatching nature, holding a mirror to the hills and sky; when he speaks of wonderful benefits to the area, what he means—the paper's reporter manages to imply, without actually saying it directly—is wonderful benefit to himself, his many bank accounts and offshore trusts. If the scheme goes through, the compensation-bill will be tremendous, and he'll claim the lion's share of it. Set that against the paltry rents he can raise from hill-farmers and sitting tenants, the article suggests mutely, and no wonder he's so keen …

Even Sir Julian's daughter Patricia (16) is apparently opposed to her dad's pet project. A weekly boarder at the exclusive Beston Hill—girls only, and too private to be called a public school; a convenient distance from her father's grand house, in the constituency but no, not in the threatened valley—she's quoted as saying that the idea sucks, that what the country needs is not more reservoirs but fewer industries using less and far less water.

Rowan couldn't agree with her more. Fewer industries, and preferably fewer people too. There were some the world could well afford to lose; as, for example, her father …

"DARK AND DEEP," whispered the guiser, "dark and deep, just like me," which was just the way he liked his caves to be: a home and a hiding-place and more, the promise of secrets, hidden paths and treasures.

He'd found the cavemouth among boulders on the hillside, a little way above the margin of the wood. For a while he stood looking into the darkness of it, seeing nothing that moved; then he stooped to pick up a handful of pebbles. One by one he threw them inside, each one further and harder than the one before. He listened to the clatter of each as it struck rock; the last made no sound of its own, but a moment later he heard a soft grunt, and the sound of a heavy body shifting. He sniffed deeply, and smelled bear.

The guiser smiled, and went away.

The next day, when the bear came back from the wood with berry-juices staining her muzzle and her fur dripping wet from fishing in the stream, she found the guiser waiting for her.

"Mother Bear," he said, bowing low, "I have brought you a gift, if you will take it."

She squinnied suspiciously at him in the sunlight, but he laid a heap of fresh-killed meat before her, in the shadow of the rocks. She lowered her head and snuffed at it, scenting nothing but rich warm blood; and so she ate and ate, flesh and fur and bone, until nothing was left but a stain in the dry earth.

"And now, great mother, a boon, if you will grant it. Lead me where my eyes cannot see, take me to the heart of this hill, your home."

She trusted the guiser not at all, but it was a law of the wood that a gift unsought-for must be matched with a boon; and what harm? She was three times his size, and had six times his strength.

And so she swayed into the cave, and felt his hand grip the shaggy fur of her back for guide; and so she led him past the boughs of her bed and further, in and down.

The cave became a narrow tunnel in the rock, that branched and branched again; at every branching the bear stopped and sniffed the air, so that her nose might tell her which way was best to go.

At last, before a narrow cleft where the floor plunged steeply, she stopped.

"I have been no further than this," she said. "There are rank odors below, where I will lose the scent of the breeze above and not be able to find my way out again."

"No matter, mother," said the guiser cheerily. "I am here with you; I will remember the turnings. On!"

The bear grumbled, but the boon was owed. She squeezed herself through the cleft and he followed, never losing his grip on her fur.

Down and deep, far from touch of sun or wind; through vast stone halls and bitter pools they went, and ever he urged her on.

At last they came to where they could go no further, where waters too deep to wade lapped at their fret. It was the guiser who called a rest then. "Before we go back to the air, mother, let us sit a while in this darkness and think on how we have trodden a path where no other creatures from the world above have ever dared set foot."

The bear thought of her weary legs, the food that lay heavy in her belly and the long walk back to light, where she must trust the guiser. One thing she was sure of, though: he might remember which turns would take them back to the cleft, but he could not find the way from there without her nose for guidance. Too many twists and branches ...

So she curled up around her exhaustion, and slipped into dreaming; and as soon as she was asleep, the guiser took a candle from his pocket and struck a flint to light the wick. Quickly and silently he followed their trail back, the trail of wet prints on dusty *floor. Back to the cleft and further, even there the bear's dripping fur had left signs that were not dried yet. He made other marks to guide him, hacking chips and gouges from the walls; then he carried rocks and mud down to seal the cleft for a while, for a time, for long enough. Even if the blundering bear should find it when she woke, she would not know it without the touch of moving air, the scent of the world above.*

In another month, he thought, he would break the seal and open the cleft, go down to find the stink of bear-meat festering. He might yet be in time to save the pelt, to make a fur to sleep on.

Drinks (3)

"When they've stopped," I'd said, meaning the noises chiefly; but the noises didn't stop all morning, though they did change register, as they had to. You can break glass and you can shatter lives, but only once for each. Nor can anyone scream for ever.

They broke glass and yelled, they screamed and screamed, but only for half an hour by the clock. It felt a lot longer than that to me, as I sat watching my mother's face, seeing how every moment told. She would put it all in a story, I knew that; and hate herself for doing it, I knew that too, and so did she. Relentlessly honest, she knew it all already.

But the breaking stopped, when there was presumably nothing left that was whole that could be broken; and the screaming stopped also. We were too far away to hear sobbing or swearing, or anything that didn't happen at the extreme edge of effort.

Noise went on, though, traffic-noise, as though the bypass were suddenly running past our windows. Van-noise mostly, the police bringing up the Transits they must have come in, that they must have left some way down the valley not to warn the convoy of the raid. Van-noise coming and going, coming and going again; and then heavier stuff, lorry-noise.

And then I was impatient, curious, driven by my own needs as much as by my mother's; I told her to stay where she was, while I went to see.

I didn't need to go far. Not so far as the convoy, not by a distance. I walked out of the cottage and saw a breakdown truck with police markings, rolling slowly down the lane; hooked up to its towbar was one of the Ride's campers with all its lights punched out. Following the truck came a tractor pulling another trashed van: Malcolm's dad Mr. Gardale, I saw, kindly helping out. There was a cop in the van, working the wheel and the brakes; God knew what they'd done to the engine, that it wouldn't drive itself. Unless there's a law against driving with a smashed windscreen, smashed sidelights, kicked-in headlamps and buckled panels, a law that applies even to policemen ...

Nah. Nothing applies to policemen, that we know. Just too proud, most likely. Driving junk on the public highway would be humiliating; being towed in junk was fine, was tantamount to saying, "Look what I did, I junked this ..."

Barry wasn't like that, Barry Carter, our very own valley cop; but Barry Carter wasn't here. I knew that without looking for him. He'd be away on the far tops, keeping his distance, as much as he could manage. This was not Barry's kind of police work.

It suited Malcolm's dad, but Malcolm not; that again I knew without asking. I saw him coming down through the thirty-acre, and went up to meet him. I think we were both glad to have a field's-width between ourselves and the lane, the milling policemen and the detritus of battle.

Not that Malcolm would admit that. He was loyal to his dad and his opinions, as I to my mother and hers; he said, "Best thing, really. As they wouldn't listen. Had to happen, anyway. We couldn't possibly have had them here all winter. For their own good, we had to move them on ..."

For his own good, perhaps, his voice faltered and failed. We stood looking at a slow procession of disaster, rolling wreckage; and I said, "Was anybody hurt, do you know?"

"I don't suppose so. All that shrieking, just propaganda ..." Still his father's opinions he was voicing, but then at last a touch of himself, a glimpse of big Malcolm's big heart. "They took them away in Transits, not ambulances. Of course they weren't hurt. Van after van. I don't know if they were under arrest or what, but they couldn't be, not all of them. Not the kids. There must be somewhere else they're taking them ..."

What, a refugee center? Kind people scurrying with blankets and massive pots of tea? I thought not. I thought that wherever they were taken, it would be a temporary police station and nothing more. There wasn't a real one for fifty miles with room enough for the Ride, but any school or village hall would do. They'd improvise. The kids might get a little comfort, but the adults I thought would be all of them arrested, as many as possible charged with as much as the traffic would bear. The cops had to justify the raid.

And the vehicles would be impounded, trashed or otherwise; and there would be new injunctions issued by handy magistrates, and the Ride would be scattered and broken up and gone, nothing left even for the press to make a fuss about ...

"Yeah, right," I said, looking at the Castle where I could just see its roof against the skyline. Not such a stronghold after all—but they wouldn't shift that with a tow-truck. Neither with a tractor. They had any sense, they'd hotwire the beast and drive it down, if they couldn't find the keys.

We stood a minute longer, then, "I'd better get down and tell Mum what's happening, this whole deal is freaking her."

"Me, too."

"Right. Drinks tonight?"

"I think so, yes. Um, what are you doing today?"

"Dunno." Today, nor any day. Filling time was a problem, while my friends worked. I didn't have the money for drinking alone, I got too thirsty. And Juliet didn't like it.

"I'm stoning up the hill, there's a wall down ..."

"Might see you there, then. Depends on Mum."

"Sure ..."

My mother was not so robust as she liked to make out, that morning had really shaken her; but once I'd reported—*nobody hurt*, I said, improvising only a little on the known facts, *and nobody left now, they've all been taken away*—she nodded, and got her robe out for a little soothing embroidery.

My mother's Robe of Stories was a masterwork, her needle as sharp and quick and silver as her tongue. It was a smart idea, too: a robe of crimson decorated with dragons and mandalas and trees, each separate figure a story in vivid silk. All the punters had to do

85

was point and she would give them the tale they'd chosen, tailored for her audience, kids or professionals or pensioners.

"New story?" I asked, seeing her start in with green thread on a bare patch.

"Mm-hmm."

What story, I knew better than to ask. Even I didn't get previews. I hung around half an hour, to be sure she was settled; then I filched a couple of bottles of beer from the fridge and set off up the hill. Across the fields again, not to run into any lingering police.

Something there may be that does not love a wall, but not I. Not any of us. These walls defined our landscape, giving shape and meaning and history to all the rise of land from the woods to the high fells; we loved them, and we cared for them.

We didn't always do that very well. We'd learned the craft from an old hedger, redundant in his trade. He'd seen his beloved hedges rooted up by JCBs to make space for giant combines, had headed north and taken up dry-walling in his fifties. He was competent, but no master; we were boys, twelve and thirteen years old. Between us, we'd stacked up some singularly scruffy walls. Malcolm's father had been rude but tolerant, letting them stand on the understanding that when the inevitable happened, in storm or wind or snow, we went straight out to rebuild them.

No surprise, it was one of those early efforts that had come down this time. Scanning the slope, I saw tractor and trailer drawn up beside a wall, a figure moving desultorily in the tractor's wind-shadow. When I got closer I saw Malcolm doing what I'd expected, disassembling.

"This one's a right mess," he grunted when I joined him. "If Dad paid that old fraud a penny, he was robbed."

"No, he wasn't. What he paid for wasn't Robson's labor, it was our tuition. He laid out a few quid then, and got free walling for life."

"Bad walls, though."

"Bad walls then. Not now."

We'd learned, we'd acquired the basics from Robson and then taught ourselves by doing and doing again, until our walls didn't fall down any more. This one had been abraded by sheep and

86

weather, till there'd been a major collapse in the center; not all, but half its length perhaps had to be taken apart before we could start to build it up again.

We stacked rocks in neat piles until there was nothing loose or shoddy left in the wall; then I declared a beer-break. Just the one bottle, shared between us as we sat on the trailer's tailgate. The trailer too was full of stone; God alone knew why, but a new wall always needed more than the old gave up.

"Your mum all right, then?"

"No, but she'll get over it." She was doing that now, indeed: sewing herself a bridge, a lift, something to raise her up for the sake of perspective. "Even her weakness she'll make out to be a strength."

"I don't get that?"

"She'll make a story of it, Malcolm. She'll put it all, everything she feels into someone else's life, and listen to the clapping after. Let's get back to it, can we?"

Picking and placing stones, judging them by eye and touch, the weight and shape of them and something more: there's an inner side to walling, a confidence that every stone has its place and knows it. That's what we didn't understand when we were callow.

We worked side by side, not speaking; and then there was a figure coming down from the fell and that was Toby seen us from on high and come to help, and the wall grew more swiftly.

It was hardly worth stopping for the second beer, with three to share it, but we did; and Malcolm said, "Drinks tonight, Tobe?"

"Suits me. Where?"

"The Coach? For a change?"

"Fine. And a starwalk after, if you're into it …"

"Not me," Malcolm said, trying to sound regretful, failing badly. "Early start in the morning, you know?"

"Yeah, right. Ro?"

"For definite. Transport?"

"Trust me."

The wall grew more swiftly with three of us to work on it, but that was not swift; you can't hurry a good wall. As teenagers, as children we'd been content to throw up hasty boundaries and blur them even in the making; as teenagers, as adults now we knew the value of a strong and solid division, this on one side—our side—and that on the other.

Even so, Toby had proposed a starwalk tonight, and I'd said yes without hesitation, without needing to think. A starwalk did more than blur a boundary or two, it tore them like tissue and opened doors where none existed.

And I'd said yes and Malcolm had said no, equally quickly. One side, and the other; and Toby straddling both, I thought, or trying to.

It was mid-afternoon by the sun before we laid the final coping-stones and nodded, each to each. Rubbed stonedust off our palms and pulled faces at embedded grit, or I did (grown soft, soft-skinned in easy Cambridge: they didn't say so but I read it anyway, thin-skinned as ever), and we said "Later" and "Drinks" and "See ya," and went home.

Home to a visitor in my case, a stranger in the cottage where I'd left my mother at her needlework.

Found her at her needlework again, picking splinters from his skin.

And no, looking at his face while she held his palm in her hand and peered at it so carefully, he was not a stranger after all. Not quite, though I knew him no better than I knew his children.

"Andrew, hi. How are you?" Not just a politesse for once, it was a question with genuine intent behind it, a need to know; he acknowledged that by making no serious attempt to deflect it.

"Sore to the touch, a little, from trying to defend my home and family from baton-wielding policemen. I used a length of four-by-two, and the splinters are worse than the bruises. By and large I'm all right, though. So long as you can tell me that the Castle's still where I left it?"

"Yes, I've seen it. From a distance. Too big to tow away. I wouldn't bet on your being able to drive it, though. Even if you can get access."

"Oh, I'll get access; and I don't want to drive away. My friends are here, and my life too, with what remains of the Ride. Trashing us was counter-productive, though you can't expect local politicians to understand such a concept. We've nowhere else to go now, and no way to get there if we did. But I'll get access to the Castle, don't doubt that."

"How are the children?"

"Safe."

"I guess I meant, where ...?" I didn't like to say it aloud, but what I really meant was *have they been taken from you yet, has the Social got its claws into them*?

"Oh," he said, smiling thinly, "they're in the Castle. You ever hear of a castle that didn't have its hiding-places, dungeons, oubliettes? They're in the oubliette."

"Oubliettes are for the dead," my mother said, sharp as her needle's picking.

"Please don't tell the children that," said Andrew.

As soon as my mother was done with his skinned hands, we all three of us set off up the lane to find the children and to fetch them down. He'd called at the cottage first, he said, to ask permission to camp in the garden; it was a chill damp day, and he thought the kids were better left safe and dry and hidden until there were arrangements made, until he could lead them direct from one surety to another. Trudging the valley in search of shelter would distress them far more, he said, than another hour or two in the dark.

There were no police and no reporters left now, all packed and gone because there were no travelers, no vehicles bar the one. No story.

"They'll be back," Andrew said, gazing at ruts in verges and shattered windscreen-glass, all that remained of the Ride. Whether he meant travelers or press or police, he didn't say.

The Castle stood where it had stood before, and looked likely to go on standing a while yet. No glass in its windows, I'd expected that; no air in its tires either, though, they'd slashed the lot of them. *Too big to move, so let's make sure that no bugger else can move it ...*

I watched Andrew's face, and barely saw it flicker. He stooped to glance beneath the giant truck—stooped further than he ever must have needed to before, it stood a couple of feet lower than usual with its wheel-rims on the ground—and then hurried to the back.

When my mother moved to follow, he stopped her with a gesture. "Would you mind …?"

This is private, he was saying. His meeting with his children, she'd assume; their hiding-place, their oubliette, I thought.

"I don't understand how he could leave them," my mother said in a murmur. "How he can be so calm. They're children, *his* children, and this was a battlefield, and he just left them …"

"He left them hidden and safe," *or I hope so, I like those kids.* "Better than trying to get them out, probably, in the chaos; it wasn't even light, remember. They're surely better hiding up in their own home, rather than being dragged off by strangers, separated from their father, maybe taken away from him altogether …? And they're resourceful, tough, they'll be fine …"

"They're children," my mother repeated stubbornly, but without conviction: perhaps she was remembering my own childhood and her approach to it, how I was let ramble the valley at will, day or night, fed or hungry, with friends or alone. She always said the most responsible thing you can do for a child is to let them acquire their own sense of responsibility. I learned mine the hard way, by falling into things and getting hurt; Andrew's kids the same, I thought, and my mother of all people had no right to criticize, and I was rather surprised that she wanted to.

We heard muffled noises that became muffled voices, that became Andrew jumping down from the Castle with a child on either arm and his face oddly twisting: one emotion too many for his features to tell, I thought.

"Here they are," he said, playing the grown-up with something of a strain in his voice, "safe and sound. Just a bit cramped up, that's all. A five-star luxury oubliette is still an oubliette, isn't it, sweethearts?"

I moved past him, wanting to see; he said softly, "I wouldn't go in there just now, Rowan. I really wouldn't."

Neither did I. But he'd left the back open, for reasons of air as much as convenience; by the smell, by the sight of it—glistening purple liquid staining rugs and walls and furnishings and books, the odd glistening little turd sitting proudly—they'd emptied the chemical toilet over everything.

No sign of the oubliette, he'd closed that up despite distractions. No hint of purple on the kids' clothes, though, and no smell of chemicals or anything other when I stood close enough to sniff.

"They'll be fine," Andrew was saying over their utter silence. "Truly, they will. They just need a hot drink, and a cuddle ..."

"They need a sight more than that," my mother said flatly. "Something proper to eat, and a good comfy bed to sleep in tonight, and a story to chase the horrors away. That much, at least. And that much I can do. You won't camp in the orchard tonight, Andrew, you'll come indoors."

"Well, actually," he confessed, "I don't think we could have camped anywhere tonight. I don't think the tent would be usable."

I didn't think anything in the Castle would be usable; I thought its lease on life had been revoked, walls and wheels and contents too.

"Good," she said, meaning *that's settled, then.* "Come along down, and we'll see what we can sort out. Are those legs working, children, or do you want your father to carry you all the way?"

Well, yes. That was clearly what they wanted, by the way their faces rooted in his armpits. But it seemed a little much to ask, so I took Antony. Leave the wary Emma where she chose to be, at least for the moment.

Even little Antony was no lightweight; I was glad enough to drop him bouncingly on the sofa when we reached that far. Glad also to make a very obvious point of looking around—*sofa, chairs, two improvised beds, max*—and then up, *one bedroom, another bedroom, that's it.*

"If we tuck the kids up here tonight," I said, "in front of the fire with the cats, they'd like that, and you take my bed, Andrew—"

"Oh, no," he said instantly. "No, you can't give up your own bed for me. I'll share with these two ..."

"There's no need. No room either, but truly no need. I'll go over to my girlfriend's. I spend half my time there anyway, it's not exactly a hardship."

"Not for you, at least," my mother said dryly; but she gave me a brief nod of approval, and I gave her a very neutral stare. *You were waiting for me to offer; how much longer would you have waited?*

Terrible thing, when a boy's adolescent rebellions become convenient to his mother. That must be one true marker of adulthood.

The kids didn't want to eat, or sleep, or run around. Post-trauma, all they wanted to do was huggle with their father. So they sat on his knee on the sofa, while my mother sat on the floor beside the fire and told stories. Simple stories mostly, nothing challenging; she alternated familiar fairy-tales with others of her own devising. Her own improvising also, I thought; certainly there were some I hadn't heard before, and those were the ones that dealt lightly and cheerfully with children left alone, children bravely concealing themselves in dark places, hiding from wickedness and waiting for the good which was sure to come …

My mother has a magic tongue. After a while I had to slip away, not to be seduced as they were, not to loll idiotically and think of nothing.

Cooking would be late and haphazard tonight, I thought; too late for me, in any case. I made myself a couple of doorstop sandwiches and stood on the step in the gloaming, munching while the world turned towards the dark.

From here I could first hear and then see when traffic came up the lane. When it did come, my promised transport, it was double what I was waiting for, two scramblers racing.

Toby, and Michael: they came round the corner neck and neck, if lights or bikes have necks. Boys don't, when they're hunched and speeding.

Hurtled up the hill, screamed and skidded to a halt—two separate halts, thankfully, one on each verge and neither one quite making contact with the walls—and gazed over at me, breathless, demanding.

"Don't look at me," I said placidly. "I didn't see you start, did I? I don't know which one cheated."

"It was him," they said, mutually. I believed them both.

"There you are, then. Now, what am I supposed to do? Straddle the saddles, with a foot on each?"

"That's it," Michael said, turning his bike as he talked. "We've a bet on, how far you get."

"Honey, I wedge my foot under your balls, if I come off then so do you. With added impact. You'd drive like you carried dandelion clocks to your best girl."

But I perched myself behind him, clutched him loosely and away we went with Toby as outrider, the roar of two exhausts all the farewell I offered to the cottage that night. My mother would understand, the kids wouldn't notice, who cared what Andrew thought?

The Coach was a bad drink, a tragic drink, an offense to the eye and the belly. Didn't stop us going there, though, once in a while, if only as a touchstone, *don't grumble at the Agric ever again, look what it might have become ...*

Properly the Coach and Four, once it had been a classic Tudor stopover; it had repro etchings on the walls to prove it, steaming horses and scurrying stable-lads, post-horns and carriages and half-timbered gable-ends and all. But the highway had moved, as highways do, and taken the trade away. In my childhood the Coach had been a moldering mildewed mausoleum: still gabled, but the plaster gray and weathered between the timbers, where it hadn't fallen off altogether to show gray and weathered Tudor bricks behind.

Alas, I'd never been inside then. Too young, no father to take me and my mother not interested in pubs: I'll never know what kind of a drink it was then, or how they kept their beer. They closed it, when I was nine or ten. They let it rot until even its listed status couldn't save it, and then they knocked it down.

Then the highway came back. Amid the clamor for bypasses and greater speed, someone remembered this old neglected B-road, perfect for upgrading ...

Dual carriageway now, with ambitions for motorway status, what it needed above all was a caravanserai. Who could bear to waste that passing trade?

And so this ghost, this revenant. The Coach and Four went up again, a grim shadow of its former self: a long brick bastard of a building, with function suites and parking and no sense of either history or modernity, a dreadful post-modernist joke without the irony. Prince Charles would have loved it.

Among its many crimes, the Coach kept no real beer, only fizz in kegs. Undrinkable. Fortunately, bottled beers were in fashion and above all it wanted to be fashionable. When we went to the Coach we drank Holsten Pils because they'd heard of that, or American Budweiser because they didn't know the original was Czech. Need I say more?

Toby could have gone on up the hill to collect Malcolm, but we'd learned that it was better not; family tea was sacred in that house. Disrupting it made for trouble, taking Malcolm away—or trying to—made for chilly troubles that dragged on for days. He'd come under his own steam, atop his own oil-smoke, when his father decreed that he was free.

Meantime we roared through the valley like the hooligans we were, breaking many laws; and were scarcely more inhibited out of the shelter of the trees and hills, although once on the open road we were out of Barry Carter's shelter also. Someone else's patch, the dual carriageway: the police drove Range Rovers out there, and gave us no immunity.

The Coach was only a couple of miles down the road, though, and we made it unaccosted. One of these days the luck would run out, or run the other way; we'd be pulled over at high speed, reckless, helmetless and very likely drunk. We'd have our day in court, and our parents would weep over us. But never yet, and not today. That was all the philosophy we lived by, in hooligan mode.

Left the bikes and sauntered in, pushing fingers through wind-tangled hair; collected bottles from the bar; made a beeline for the pool table in its corner. Arrayed ourselves about it in a manner designed to look aggressive and hooliganesque to outsiders, heaped up a stack of coins just to emphasis possession, and that was us fixed. We'd be happy now till closing time, passing the sticks between us, playing doubles for variety when Malcolm turned up. The day's shocks were still salt on our tongues, *news news* and we wanted to tell it to each other and especially to Michael who hadn't been there, hadn't seen; but we didn't really want to talk at all, just to be together and doing something else. Pack instinct, rat-pack maybe, always happy to run.

Except that when Malcolm did turn up, he brought a girl with him. A stranger, Alison her name was: he'd met her at a Young Farmers' bop the previous month, apparently, and hadn't managed to mention it to any of us since. She was small, blonde, elfin-pretty; quiet but tough, I rated her, and very much a coup for Malcolm. She was maybe the real reason he'd suggested drinks tonight, and surely the reason why he didn't want to starwalk later. A better excuse than I'd expected: I'd thought he was growing dull on us, settling down into his father's life, closing doors. Heresy, I'd thought that was.

It wasn't heresy to bring a girl to a boys' night out, even without warning; it had been done before. It made for difficulties, though, as it always had. We didn't know how much space to give them, whether we should cluster round the pool table or cluster around her. She seemed more comfortable than we were, happy either way; we fell into a compromise pattern, two playing and one sitting out, sitting with her and Malcolm.

When we sat, we had to talk. Girl-style, she asked questions that boy-style couldn't evade. She wanted to talk about the day, more deeply than we'd have chosen; and when that was all talked out, she asked questions that were no easier to deal with. Malcolm had told her too much about us, I thought. Certainly too much about me.

"Tell me about your friend," she said, "the one who was killed?"

And so I talked about Simon when I really didn't want to, about how his death had driven me away, how I was trying to hide up in the securities of home; and if she noticed any irony in her stripping me bare that way, she gave no sign of it.

Malcolm sat beside her, holding her hand and saying almost nothing. Mute of malice or embarrassment, I wanted to think, cold hard bastard that I was, especially to my friends; but I couldn't do it. He was mute of wonder only, gobsmacked at this treasure that he'd found.

Starwalk With Me

We drank till we could drink no more, because they would not serve us. No Agric this, no old stone hotel hidden among the hills with older trees to mask it. The Coach could be seen from the busy road it served, comings and goings could be noted down and held against it. The police were regulars, watchfully in and out; the pub ran its own ID for under-21s, and carded anyone they doubted. Carded even us: staff turnover was high, so they never learned our faces, and serving a minor was a sackable offense. As was serving after hours; the pumps at the bar turned off automatically at eleven o'clock, and red lights glowed behind the optics.

We left with bottles in all our pockets, against a certain later thirst, and drove in convoy till we came to Juliet's turning. Malcolm headed straight on, with our horns blaring a goodnight, our lights flashing good luck; I wondered briefly whether he would be taking Alison virtuously home, or wickedly elsewhere. Impossible to ask, impossible to guess. His father I thought would not welcome a girlfriend sleeping over, but there were outbuildings aplenty to play around in. Or he might stop over at her place, of course, if her family were easier than his, though he would still likely face trouble in the morning.

Michael and Toby and I turned off and went up, up and up, out of the trees' shadows and into the moon's light. It was a gorgeous night for a starwalk, crisp and clear, all clouds blown away and the convenient wind died down now. There'd be a hard frost before dawn, which would only add to our pleasure.

The boys throttled back before we came to the boathouse, came in slow and quiet, training become instinct, not to disturb Juliet or David if they were sleeping.

Lights were on, though, and as it turned out both of them were up still. David was having one of his difficult days, didn't want to go to bed; Juliet's first relief at seeing me was instantly soured by the others' walking in at my heels, adding to her troubles.

David beamed at me, at the three of us. We were his excuse, a gift provided by a graceful God behind his sister's back and all unexpectedly.

Hastily, hoping to forestall a tantrum, I said, "Hi, guys. Don't worry, we're not stopping, or not yet. Just looked in to say my mum's got company tonight, Juliet, so I've been turfed out …"

"Surely," she said, meaning *message received, that's fine*. "You lads want to crash here too?"

"Uh, maybe," from Michael. "See what happens, what the time is, how we feel …"

"Not a problem. I'll leave the kit down here," she said, turning back to try once more to outface David, meaning *go away now. Wait not upon the hour of your going, but depart …*

"Where are you going, Ro?"

And that was David and had to be answered; so I said, "Nowhere special, mate. Just out. For a drink," showing him the bottles; David didn't like drink. "In the rain, by the look of it," lying prodigiously, but David didn't like rain either.

"Starwalk," Toby said brightly at my back, not picking up any of the vibrations; I could have slain him mightily. Before it became our word for what we meant to do tonight, it had been another word entirely, and I had made it for David and me, for what we did together some nights, slipping oh-so-secretly away to look for badgers.

His face changed heavily, from disappointment to stubborn hope. "I want to come," he said.

"No," from Juliet, flat and final, just ahead of my own refusal.

"Sorry, mate. Not tonight. You wouldn't like it."

"I want to come."

"David, you can't. Truly …"

"They're going to be out all night," Juliet said, recognizing the symptoms in us, "and you've got work in the morning. Bed, David. Now."

"Don't want to go to bed. I want to go with Ro."

Juliet threw me a glance that said again *get out.* I jerked my head at the others, and saw them back away; then, reluctantly playing bastard, I said, "No, David. Another night, but not now. You're not invited."

His face changed again, to liquid betrayal; I fled before the tears came, betrayed them both. Actually Juliet would handle him better without me now, but it still felt like a betrayal to leave her to it. And still I did that, comforting myself as best I could, poorly.

We left the bikes and walked up the hill, silent till the chill and the wind blew that soured mood away from us; then talking softly and starting to laugh again, only in whispers because there are only two things you can do under such a sky in such a night, you can whisper or you can shout, and we weren't for shouting yet.

Up we came, not to the height of the fell but to a false summit, high enough for us, for now: to a spot where a natural outcrop of rock and millennia of weathering played at standing-stones between them, leaving half a ring of boulders jutting over a ledge, the other half presumably still buried in the rise behind. This was our place of ritual, where we felt hieratic and looked-down-on, the presence of something greater than ourselves; this was where we always started a starwalk.

We sat on the boulder on the ledge's lip, where the earth beneath had been undercut by rain and wind so that our feet dangled over fifteen, twenty feet of air before the slope would catch us if we fell. If we did fall—or if the boulder fell, which it must do one day and likely with us upon it so that we would all go together, rock and boys—we would fall and roll with nothing to stop us, nothing to fetch up against until we hit the water of the tarn. A dirty slide, and a cold wash after.

I sat and looked at the boathouse, saw the lights go out and huffed a little in relief. That was that, and now the night lay before me and my friends were about me and there was nothing more that I needed, except what Toby held out on his finger now.

99

A fragment of rough paper, a tiny square with a tiny image stamped on it, too dark to see but something simple and foolish, something utterly hippy for sure: a smiley face, a wizard's hat, a grinning Cheshire Cat. I took the tab on my tongue, and licked Toby's fingertip for my share of what was always left behind.

And swallowed, and watched the others do the same, and then and only then cracked open the first bottle and passed it down the line. We had to husband our resources; there was no going back from here, and what we carried had to see us through.

No going back, only going up; but we were still in ritual here, and it was the rule that we stayed just here on our rock till all of us were flying, just a little. Part ritual, to be honest, and part risk: we were lads, after all. We liked to start the night on an edge; we'd heard so many stories of tripping kids who thought they could really fly, and where better to launch ourselves than here, where that long drop sang to us?

It wasn't actually so much of a risk. We didn't linger long enough to get truly high, and we were none of us stupid enough to do this alone, there were always others to hold us back. We just fancied the dare of it, *maybe this time*, and nobody was going to play chicken in front of his mates.

So we sat and waited, sipped at the bottle and watched the sky and watched the fall beneath; and soon enough I saw the stars flare and dance all formally within their constellations. I thought I could count and name each separate one of them. And started to do that, even, rapt in their glory; but my eye was seized and snared by the moon instead, rising above the valley, and so I lost my count.

The moon had more than one face that night, it was polyhedral, a gaming die ready to roll; I could reach up and touch it with my finger, scratch my initials, send it tumbling to decide my fate and everyone else's.

And I reached to do that, but it slid away across the oiled sky; and Toby said, "Well, I'm away. The rest of you?"

"Supremely," I said.

"There are whales in the water," Michael murmured, answer enough. "Look, look down …"

We did that, and yes, there were shapes that lurked and shifted in the dark below the glitter of the tarn's surface. We'd seen them before; I'd told my mother, and she of course had made a story of them. Not whales, but something kin.

I didn't like the story, nor the sight. The sky absorbed me, neutral and distant, playing games with abstract rules; wet or earthy, earthbound life was something other. Visionaries were sometimes right, and even hallucinations could tell truth. I wanted no more life in this valley than I could name or number.

"Time to go," I said, sliding safely off the rock, very far from wanting to fly down there tonight. "Is this a starwalk, or what?"

Some nights—cloudy nights, rainy or snowy nights—we'd go down rather than up, down into the wood and wonder at how the trees groped for us, how their roots twisted about our feet, how the moss shone to guide us where the wood wanted us to go. I didn't like that much either, always looking for fauns or dryads, others of my mother's greenfolk, less kindly than the books of my childhood would have them. Clear nights like this were what I yearned for, when I could lead my friends up to where tripping opened doors in the sky and let us out to dance among the stars.

Tonight I was exultant, dancing for real across the turf, my confident feet never missing a step. Up and up we went, yelling and blowing at the climb; and then down again, finding and following the old miners' track that was little more than a sheep-path now but still offered safe footing in the moonlight, for lads like us who'd walked or run or danced it often and often, the best part of twenty years.

The best part of two thousand years, men had dug these hills for lead and a little silver. Since Roman times, and through to living memory: there were men we'd met at the Agric whose fathers had worked their whole lives underground, who'd been apprenticed to the trade themselves before rising water and failing seams had driven them out at last.

The mines were given over to other uses now, to potholers and inward-bound adventurers. Guides from local centers would lead parties of schoolkids down for an afternoon, or office workers come for a weekend's bonding. We'd been down ourselves when we were children, and again since, unsanctioned and unguided; wandering by weak torchlight through a maze of passages and chambers, never wholly sure of where we were, scaring ourselves thrillingly stupid. Once we'd done it tripping, by candlelight, truly stupid. There'd been genuine terror in that, but genuine wonder also when the light sparked and ran like milk off dewy roofs to flow like water down the walls and round our skipping feet, when the dark rose up like mist in counterflow. Eternal diamond is eternal diamond, but perhaps needs to be set in softer metal to achieve its utmost value; clear crystal experience perhaps needs the pulse and grip of emotion in its frame, joy or terror but nothing less defined, to hold its shape as memory-till-death.

Tonight, no question of going underground. We had no lights, and no ambition. We stood at the gates to hell, of course, each of the clefts or twisted mouths that marked the openings to the ways below; we stood at the gates and howled like wolves and let our voices echo down and down till they were crushed by darkness, but they had to be our plenipotentiaries this trip. No stars below to walk with, always a chthonic disadvantage.

Down, and so up again: where the hills went, there went we. Where the stars shone, there we shone in echo or admiration. We danced to the music of the spheres, which is not the music of time though astronomers (but not musicians) will tell you that it is; we lay flat as children do, and felt the weight of the earth upon our backs and that we dangled above a sea of stars; we lay and listened to the grass grow, closed our eyes and felt it grow high about us. Felt it interweave us, knot and tangle and possess us utterly, draw us downward into loam and rock.

But that was chthonic, and not for tonight; and besides I liked it not, it frightened me. I sat up and looked up, found my body my own and the stars my own also, and my friends unharmed at my side. I sat and watched the moon progress all stately, though she seemed to be squeezing water from her pocks, all those cratered seas turned liquid and reflective.

I loved the moon for her pallidity, her lack of focus, her determined lack of will. She felt the attraction of the earth and so she would attend it, regardless of criticism or temptation, utterly unperturbed; she needed no life, no light, no wider orbit of her own. She had what she wanted, right there in her sight, and that was entirely enough. I admired her so much ...

I could be a lunatic, I could howl at the moon too, and did. I could listen to a fox bark back in four dimensions, and did. I could find a beetle crawling on a rock and be lost in its scurry, my nose pressed into a forest of ancient lichen, tasting millennial dust on my tongue ...

The sky was still dark between the stars, the boathouse still dark beside the shining tarn when we came back. Quiet now, tired now, all out of beer and brio, we slipped inside to make tea and makeshift beds. I saw Toby and Michael settled, and then set foot on the stairs; but the burr of Juliet's alarm above forestalled me. I went back to the kettle and made another mug of tea, but decided against taking it up to her. I was still tripping gently, not yet ready to climb into her vacated bed and chase after sleep, no way ready to talk about the night just gone or whatever else might be on her mind.

I left the mug where she couldn't miss it or its meaning, its many meanings. And went outside again, and walked a little way down the lane, to the wood's margin. There was a gate there; I perched myself upon it, and sat listening to the life at my back while I watched the slow, slow fading of the stars.

At last there was a star, a bright star moving a little wobblingly down the lane towards me. I still had acid enough in my eyes to see it as a coruscation, a catherine wheel spinning sparks; but it was only a bike-light in truth, and I knew that too.

David's bike, with David aboard. He came freewheeling cautiously, hands on brakes, slow enough to see me, to stop, to speak.

See me he did, no doubt of that. His eyes fixed on mine, twisting his head round as he passed, causing him to wobble further. He didn't stop, though, he didn't speak a word. I waved, but not even that was welcome. He jerked, and turned his heavy shoulder to me.

I sighed, and watched his red tail-light burn like a blaze through

103

the wood; and thought perhaps I'd leave this handy perch before there were more lights coming down the bill, twin stars, Juliet's car taking her also to her work. I might even walk in the wood a while, and never mind what I might find there. Anything, rather than face the same recrimination from her ...

I swung my legs across the gate and slid down the other side. Stood looking for a while, nothing more than that; it was dark in there. Dark of design, in a way that the mines were not. Even the deciduous trees even in winter wove shadows around their roots.

But they were deciduous, many of them, the roof was made of branches and gaps, and the sky was there to be seen between the branches; and the sky was still full of light to my starglimmered eyes. I could see enough to find my way, to follow a true path. That was ample. What more was there, that I might want to see? I had strangeness enough inside my head; I'd be glad enough of deep shadows all about me, to hide whatever might lurk in the wild woods.

So on, eventually, at last: on and in, and the trees closed in around me.

There were paths, new-made trails for tourists and more ancient greenways that predated people, by my mother's telling. If she'd talked of Bronze Age man laying down lines of travel so deep in the land that the woods remembered them still, that I might have believed. Her mythical creatures, though, tree-shepherds and elves and nameless beasts—those, not. I laughed at her, and talked of tractor-tracks.

And still jittered sometimes in daylight, alone among these trees: not scared, no, but wary. In this pre-dawn hush and darkness, where every touch of light or sound or breeze against my skin was a trigger to my overstretched, oversensitized nerves, I did more than jitter. I had run wild through this valley all my life, tasted and claimed every square meter of it, and suddenly I felt a stranger, alien, observed ...

When there were sounds stronger than the rustling of the breeze or the scuttle of small creatures across a leafmold floor, at first I wanted to bolt, lacking a door to bolt against them.

Something held me, though—something like the stupidity of running from a noise in woodland, perhaps, when one was allegedly an adult and the woodland was English and so not inhabited by monsters. I froze instead, the other extreme, and listened to the steady knocking that was surely not natural, and the murmur that underran it.

Elapsed time is hard to figure, when you're tripping. I stood in the constant flow of that not-too-distant knocking, and the come-and-go of the murmur that was too hesitant to be a babbling stream; and it didn't seem to me that I stood very long at all, before I forced my legs into moving. But the sky was more simply bright above the trees, hardly pricked with stars now, and there was light enough to take my last excuse away.

I left the path and picked my way through scrub and under-growth, towards the sounds.

My head still full of my mother's stories, even when I was sure that the murmuring was voices I was yet half-sure of meeting monstrous creatures in the wood there. My rational mind said not, but with the dregs of the drug still kicking in my bloodstream, rationality slipped its gears, slipped and slipped again.

I walked on, though, dragging my feet noisily for security's sake, to scare what demons were not scared by the coming dawn. I heard the voices fall quiet against my coming, and drew some comfort from that; and then I stepped through a grove of silver birch and into a clearing and found no demons at all, or none that I was expecting.

What I found, I found two young women dressed in mud and denim, hauling canvas over severed poles to make a rough bender. I huffed a slow breath of relief and looked again; met their hostile glares, and could put a name of sorts to one of them.

She was the girl called Scar, refugee from the Ride, her long raven hair tangled with more than feathers now; and her companion also I had seen around the convoy's fire, that time I'd spent with them on the lane.

They had a fire here too, a low smoky glowing smudge in a hearth of rocks; fire and shelter they had, but I couldn't see much else beyond their attitude. I wondered if the canvas were salvaged or stolen, but didn't care enough to ask.

Not that I would have had an answer I could rely on, if I had asked. They'd recognized me too; and as a local, I was enemy. That was clear from their faces, from their mute antagonism.

Nearly mute. When I went on saying nothing, it was Scar who spoke.

"I said," she said. "We're staying. We've got nowhere else to go."

Fine by me. I nodded, turned around and left them, headed back towards the boathouse, home.

TROUBLED TIMES

i

They were eight and six, and they knew nothing, necessarily; and yet they knew the facts of life, any number of different ways of knowing.

They knew those facts as nearly as their father could explain them, in the all-but-meaningless ways of adult explanation. They could have passed examinations—if either had had the skill with pen and pencil, or the patience to sit so long over a sheet of paper—and been word-perfect in them, and still not have related what they wrote or drew to anything they really knew as fact.

They knew other facts, inevitably, by observation: they knew how dogs got tangled up and why, how puppies followed later. They knew what hung pendulous beneath a stallion's belly, or a bull's. They knew also, or at least they admitted that the equivalent thing hung in their father's trousers, and a seed-thing of the same in Antony's. However like they might be, though, the difference was greater. They knew that their father was not animal, that he did not do those animal acts in fields and streets and stables.

What their father did, they knew by long observation. Their father met someone he liked, a woman, and brought her home to the Castle. Introduced her nicely. If she was approved of—and he'd ask, anxiously, when she'd gone, "Well? Do you approve?"—she'd be invited back. He and she might sit up half the night, talking and drinking while his children slept and listened and slept again. But still, sometime in the night, the door at the back would open for her and close behind her, and she wouldn't even be walked home for fear of leaving the kids alone.

Another night, if all went well between, they'd be invited as a family, tea at her house. And that time, there, after tea and games and a bath borrowed and shared, Antony and Emma would lie cuddled together in a strange room and a stranger bed while their father, they knew, would be doing just the same. In her bed, in the dark behind closed doors and nothing like what he'd described to them or what they'd seen. Their father was the prince of darkness, they were certain, as he was lord of light.

The noises, the cries and grunts that reached through to them— well, sometimes their father called out in his sleep, and sometimes they did. All women had bad dreams, they thought, and so slept loudly.

Last night it wasn't quite the same, but almost. The woman Alice hadn't come to the Castle to be approved, but they approved her nonetheless; she told wonderful stories, both by the firelight and later, when she settled them into the big bed that was her son's, she said, the nice tall boy they'd met by the stream who'd helped them build a bridge. Their father had come in after, had kissed them both and asked once more if they were all right now, not fretting about that long time hidden in the oubliette. He'd forgotten to ask if they approved of Alice, but it didn't matter. They'd been too sleepy to think about it then.

Later, her cries had woken them; but she'd be all right, they'd told each other, she'd have their father to comfort her against her hard dreaming. It had taken a while, but at last she'd fallen quiet to the murmuring of his voice, which they could hear too, which had lulled them all back into sleeping.

And this morning she'd been happy, and so had he; and she'd said they could stay as long as they needed to, until the Castle was all fixed up and they could be away again. As long as it takes, she'd said. And their father had smiled at that, at her; and so had they.

ii

"Hullo, is that the police house? … Good, excellent. Who am I speaking to? … Constable Carter. Well.

"… My name? We'll come to that. You'll know it, if you read the papers. The tabloids run my picture any time they can. Listen to them, they'll tell you I'm a monster.

"What I am for certain, is listed on the Sexual Offenders Register. I've done fifteen years inside, on and off for playing games with children. I haven't touched a kid for years, of course; but the police at my last place of residence fitted me up with some porn in a raid, just to be sure to get me on the register. 'Just so we can keep an eye on you,' they said.

"Well, I'm a reformed character now, perfectly law-abiding. Never mind how it happened, I'm required to keep the local police informed of my movements, so that's what I'm doing. I'm informing you officially, Constable Carter, that I've just arrived on your patch.

"No, I'm sorry, I can't give you an address, I don't have one. I'm— camping, I suppose you'd call it. Living rough, in the woods here. I couldn't even tell you how to find me, I don't think I could find myself just now. But I'm here. When I move on, I'll let you know.

"Oh, my name. Yes. I've used a lot of names. You'll find my convictions listed under Edward John Halliday, but these days, people only call me Root."

iii

Marten Peters had had a trying day, and that only the latest in a sequence of days that had tried him and tried him and found him wanting out.

Work had been hectic for weeks, and he'd thought he wanted a break, an unscheduled holiday, just something—anything—else to be doing. But a man should be careful what he wishes for, because here he was having exactly that, and hating it.

It had started with his daughter Louise having flu, or so they'd thought. But after three days and nights of it, he'd followed his wife into their daughter's bedroom and found her pressing an empty glass on Louise's stomach and peering, pressing and peering again.

"Marten, look. She's got a rash, and it doesn't fade when I do this, look …"

He'd looked, while she pressed; then they'd gazed at each other wildly, across their daughter's fevered heedlessness.

"I'll get the doctor out," he'd said. No comfortable nonsense, *it's probably nothing, measles maybe, what do we know?* They knew what the school had told them, and that was enough.

The doctor had come, and then the ambulance; and for days he'd gone to work and wasted his own time and his employer's, staring blindly at a computer screen and seeing only the beat of his daughter's sickness there, the one word *meningitis.* Days of moments, each worse than the last, and at any moment the phone might have rung to tell him that he had no daughter any more.

The crisis had passed and Louise had come home at last, or at least a thin pale wraith that had something of his bonny daughter's features to her, and answered to her name.

Then the conspiracy, his wife and his boss uniting: *Louise needs a change of scene and so do you, a quiet week away will do you both the world of good; take her to the cottage, why don't you?*

No reason he could think of, not to agree. So here they were, here they'd been for too long already; and now he had reasons aplenty, when it was far too late.

A holiday cottage in the middle of nowhere was a fine place to be in midsummer, when there were hills to climb and lakes to sail and countless other things for a robust and happy family to do. In midwinter, for Christmas, it was equally wonderful: they could build the open fire high and roast chestnuts, drink mulled wine and invent revolting substitutes for Louise; tease her and each other about presents forgotten or not bothered with at all; go to church on Christmas Eve and hope for snow, then spend the next days rollicking, playing with new toys and pulling faces at the weather. They didn't really need snow.

In November and unexpectedly, it was a different case. No one had gone in before them to warm the cottage and stock the fridge, to sweep the chimney or to make the beds; arriving in a dank evening, they'd found mildew in all the bedding and sodden plaster on Louise's sodden mattress, where a leak in the roof had brought the ceiling down.

Worse, they'd found that this far out of any season, the local pubs had stopped offering hot meals. There were no restaurants, of course no Burger Kings; in the end Marten had had to drive another thirty miles with Louise's whining heading towards hysteria before he discovered a chippie that was open. The food had been greasy and unappetizing; he couldn't really blame Louise for only picking at it.

That had been the first time she'd said she wished they'd stayed at home. She'd said it again when she saw the nest of coats he'd made for her on his own bed, the best he could manage in the way of sleeping arrangements. Privately he'd agreed with her, thinking of the cold and uncomfortable night he faced on the sofa cushions; but of course he couldn't say so, and so he'd snapped at her, and so she'd burst into tears …

She'd said it again since, several times. He couldn't blame her; the first two days of this supposed holiday they'd had to spend waiting for plasterers and roofers, taking the bedding to a launderette, generally making the cottage fit to live in.

And when finally they had been able to get away, of course they'd found that all the tourist attractions were closed up; while the weather and Louise's continued weakness between them ruled out any more active pursuits.

He'd been mad to agree to this, he thought, driving aimlessly while his daughter sniveled in the back of the car. A convalescent ten-year-old wanted friends and fuss and comfort, not stress and isolation; he wanted to be at work, to celebrate her recovery by proving that he was himself again. Maybe he should just turn the car and drive home, give Louise what she was crying for, write this whole adventure up as a bad idea mishandled …

◆◆◆

111

But he saw a sign, *The Ryhope Center: Pony-Trekking, Craft Shop, Pottery*; and he turned the car that way, hope holding out one last time over experience. At least they couldn't close ponies up for the season; Louise liked horses, she had a pony of her own, maybe if they were allowed to snoop around the stables she'd at least belay the whingeing for an hour …

Wonder of wonders, hope triumphant, or so it seemed. Louise hung over a paddock-rail talking to a chestnut cob while Marten found a member of the staff and spoke to her. A pleasant woman of swift understanding, she seemed: *meningitis, very sick, convalescent, adores horses* and she was gesturing a young man over, a man whose loose head and jerky motion spoke of his slow understanding.

His name was Gary, and he would be delighted if Louise would like to help him with his work, looking after the ponies. Mrs. Wright said it to him, and he said it to Marten and seemed to mean it, and then he said it again to Louise, and she didn't doubt him at all. His slack smile spoke to her edgy excitement; they were all but holding hands as they went off together towards the stables.

"No need to worry," Mrs. Wright said, watching them professionally out of sight nonetheless. "She'll be perfectly safe with Gary."

It hadn't occurred to Marten to worry at all, he was too relieved.

Relief is instant gratification, though, it never lasts. Louise spent a couple of hours getting smelly in the stables, and only came away when he shouted for her at the gate, after he'd asked for her and then called her and got no response at all.

"What?" she said sulkily.

"It's lunchtime." It was past lunchtime, long past his; he'd been running all day on no breakfast, and he ached for food.

"I'm not hungry."

"You've got to eat, Louise. Dr. Hallett said so, remember?" She'd had a wee prepubescent crush on a junior houseman at the hospital; but not enough to override the call of horseflesh, seemingly. She shrugged, no more than that.

"Louise, come on. They do lunches here, if we're not too late, if

I haven't given you too much leeway already; you're certainly not getting any more."

"Can I come back, after?"

"We'll see," he said, classic evasion but meaning definitely *no*. Meaning, *no, you're exhausted, look at you: all eyes and bones and matted hair, you look like a refugee. I'm taking you home straight after and you'll rest, you'll go to bed if I have to take all your clothes away to make you. I'll have to take some of them in any case, everything you're wearing, that's another trip to the bloody launderette, and I'll have to do that while you're sleeping because you'll have hysterics if you can't wear those jeans, I know you will, they're blessed with horse-dung now ...*

Classic parent raises classic child: she read all that in his face, or enough of it to go mulish and stupid. He had almost to drag her across the gravel forecourt, her feet kicking a savage wake for that too-brief contentment.

The way to the cafeteria lay through the craft shop, simple wooden shelving stacked high with basic bowls and plates and mugs, earthenware under rough dull earthy glazes, blues and browns and muddy greens. There was wooden giftware also, toast-racks and coasters, bright-painted toys; and hand-sewn toys, fat and happy hippopotami.

But the pottery was closest, those were the shelves they had to pass between. And between the shelves also was a big heavy body hunkered down, green overalls and dark cheap-cropped hair beginning to thin, prematurely Marten thought though he couldn't see the face below the hair; and warm spicy sensuous smells were in the air, soup and coffee and good hot food, and he could see the cafeteria doorway in the opposite wall.

And he tugged Louise by the arm as he squeezed through the narrow gap between crouching body and high-stacked shelf; and she tugged back unexpectedly and he wasn't having that and so he yanked her, hard.

And she came staggering, flying almost and then flying almost in truth as she tripped and fell headlong over the man in the aisle.

Marten still had hold of one arm, he could half-save her from crashing to the ground; but her other arm flailed helplessly, and of

113

course caught a stack of bowls and sent them crashing, nothing to save them in the least.

And the figure she'd fallen over rose roaring to his feet, his own arms wheeling now, doing more damage, pulling down more piles of pots. Louise scrambled to her feet and saw his pale moonish face, saw and heard his incoherent rage, and screamed, and backed away.

Backed straight into a shelving-unit and sent the whole thing tipping, tumbling, slipping, smashing, bull in a china-shop, chaos and disaster.

The man—young man, boy almost, despite the hair—bellowed one more time, and drew his hand back hugely, and slapped her.

Marten grabbed his shoulder, too late; but turned him nonetheless, and in one heartfelt moment he took all his weeks of work and missed work, the days of worry and the past days of sheer bloody frustration, he put it all into one moment, one movement as he drove his fist into the young man's face.

iv

It's David's room upstairs that has the view of tarn and fells and overbearing sky; Juliet's looks back to the lane and down to the wood.

That's where Rowan's sitting this afternoon, watching the tree-tops with the binoculars that were her first material gift to him, way back when she was his teacher and not meant to give him gifts of any sort. A gesture of thanks, she'd said then, working up an unnecessary defense in case he was loose-tongued at school, a bragging boy: for his taking David on so many walks, giving him such a good time, she'd said.

Ordinarily Rowan keeps them for stargazing, with or without chemical assistance; today he has a different use for them, trying to spot where in the wood the girls from the Ride are camping. Even in winter, though, when half the trees are bare, there's too much cover to see down to the floor of the wood. He lowers the glasses in frustration and sits for a while only thinking about that camp and

114

what it may mean, what may result from it; then he spots a figure, a man walking down the lane, and it's nothing more than curiosity that has him lifting the binoculars to his eyes again.

A quick shift of focus, and the man leaps into view. He's a stranger, but Rowan knew that already, simply from the way he walked. A shock of shoulder-length hair that should have been pure white and isn't, is ivory-yellow instead, or nicotine-yellow perhaps; a lined and stubbled face, fiftyish or thereabouts. Dirty denims, jacket and jeans. No other clues, who he is or what he's doing here. He doesn't look like a tourist or a backpacker, any kind of walker. He looks like a city man from a bad city, utterly out of place; but he doesn't walk like a man displaced, he has a lounging confidence in his gait that says he will make his own kind of home, wherever he may find himself.

As he passes out of view, Rowan lowers the glasses again and wonders.

And is still wondering, still watching the road when he hears a car come up from the valley. Sees it a few seconds later, a Volvo estate taking the climb slowly, it seems, he thinks. Very slowly, and slowing still—and turning now, coming to the boathouse, coming to a halt.

He doesn't recognize the car, neither the driver. She's middle-aged, dressed smart-but-practical, exudes confidence and competence with every step as she walks around the bonnet of her car. She opens the nearside door and reaches in to help her passenger out.

Him Rowan recognizes, but briefly doesn't understand. It's David, home from work when he shouldn't be, coming back in a car when he left on a bike.

More than that, it's David in a mess: bent and shuffling and sorry, his face when he lifts it bruised and bloody and patched with plasters, his eyes red with weeping.

Whatever this is, Rowan thinks, it's trouble. And whatever trouble that trouble is, it's his trouble to sort it out …

115

"BUT I HAVE PROMISES TO KEEP," said the water-spirit, whom the guiser loved.

He had heard her first, as he sat on a rock in the dark musing on his secret kingdom and what he had done, what he must yet do to keep it his. A high pure voice he'd heard, singing of stars in water: enchanted, he had looked down and seen the stars reflected in a tarn below his feet. Stars and something more he had seen; a brighter light, no moon but a shining thing, a vivid green jewel in the night.

He had slipped silently down the hillside, a shadow among shadows, and found her floating among the reeds at the pool's edge. She was as lovely to his eyes as her voice was lovely, a liquid beauty whose hair tangled with the reeds, whose body glistened as darkly silver as the water that bore it up; and between her breasts she held a treasure, that glowing jewel, and he thought that was lovely too. He wanted them both to be his own, and determined to make them so.

For that one night, though, he had only sat and listened, sat and watched. When the sun rose, she'd slipped away from its light that even her jewel could not rival; she'd dived deep, and the black waters of the tarn had closed above her.

The following evening he'd come back, his hands full of flowers. The sun's last glimmer on the water had left him breathless; as soon as it was gone he'd scattered his blooms across the tarn and called her gently. "Lady, come forth ..."

A moment of stillness, of utter silence; and then the water had lapped at his feet and her head had risen, within the circle of his gift. One flower had caught in her hair; she'd reached long fingers up to touch it, laughing.

"Who calls me, who?"

"I," he'd said.

"And who are you?"

"A worshipper."

Again, she'd laughed. "And what good is that to me?"

"I can bring you flowers, lady. And more, if you will take it."

"I do not need your flowers." But her hand had moved again, to touch the one she wore so accidentally, to gather more from where they bobbed about her.

"No more you do," he'd said, betraying himself utterly. "One as lucent as you needs no adornment; you grace my gifts, not they you. But be not so cruel as to begrudge them that chance of grace, nor me the chance to bring them."

"Sweet-tongue, I will not. But a gift must be answered with a boon, that is the law. What can I give in return, who have nothing that lies within my gift?"

"If you would, lady, you could sing to me ..."

And so she did, that night and others; and so he courted her with all the pretty things that he could find, asking nothing of her but her love and never mentioning her jewel. Neither did she mention it to him, until one night when she found him sighing and sorrowful beside the water, his hands empty.

"What is it that troubles you," she asked, "my love?"

"Lady, you know that I am a thief and a trickster," the guiser said through his tears.

"You have told me this; but I have never known it make you sad."

"It is my nature; how can I grieve for that? But there is one to whom I owe a debt, and she has laid a burden on me. I must find a certain precious thing, a green stone of great beauty, and steal it for her; but I have searched all day for this thing and have not found it, and so I have had no time to gather flowers for you, and so I am distressed."

"I do not need your flowers," she replied. Her voice gasped, and he did not believe her; but he thought it was more than the lie that made her gasp so. "Tell me of this stone."

"It shines in starlight, and it is hidden from me; and so I must suffer for it."

"Suffer how, my love?"

"It is decreed, that if I do not find the stone and steal it, I must pay my debt in blood and pain. There is no help for me now; I had only this one day and night to bring it to her."

"I have the stone," the water-spirit whispered. "But I have promises to keep ..."

"What promises are those?"

"It was given me for safe-keeping, and I must break my oath to give it up; but I will do that for you, my love, because I love you."

"No," he said. "You may not. Your honor is worth more to me than my pain, or even my life."

"But not to me. I must lose one, or else the other; and I choose to lose my honor."

And so she did. She fetched the jewel from its hidden darkness, and gave it to him. He cried again for love of her, and kissed her; and swore to bring her fine gifts, wonderful gifts to mend her broken promise, and meant every word that he swore; and left her at last, at her urging, before the sun should mar the stone.

And left her with the stolen stone shining at his throat, and it seemed to him that all the stars were singing, and only she was not.

Crowded House

"He hit a kid, Juliet. A customer. Look at it how you like, you can't get away from that."

She couldn't, no—but oh God, she was trying. She was lining the story up every which way, to make David the victim and not the villain of the piece.

The kid's dad, I thought, had gone a fair way to helping her out there. The kid certainly hadn't been hurt by what was reported as no more than a slap—though a slap from David, I knew too well, could be a terrifying thing in itself, full of sound and fury, however little it might signify in the end—while David had most certainly and visibly been hurt by her father's response. He couldn't have done better for Juliet, couldn't have helped her out more.

And of course I had my own contribution, my own responsibility to lay before her when she resolutely refused to lay it out herself. "It's my fault, originally," I said. "If I hadn't come blasting in here last night with the boys, he wouldn't have got so upset at being left out, and he wouldn't have gone off to work in such a sulk this morning."

"It wasn't you who mentioned a starwalk," she said wearily.

"Maybe not, but I could've told them to wait outside, I should've known …"

"How could you?"

"I've known them a long time, Jules. David and Toby both. And I'm supposed to be good at predicting likely outcomes, that's what mathematical models are all about."

"Oh, right. Rowan the prophet, I forgot." She pushed a hand through her tangled hair, then shook it wildly. "It doesn't matter, anyway. We can all try to blame ourselves or each other, it doesn't change the facts. The only important question is whether the center will take him back now."

"She said they would." I'd talked to the woman who'd brought David back, and Juliet had had a long conversation with her on the phone since.

"On probation, she said. After a cooling-off period. But there's no guarantee he won't do the same thing again, now that he's done it once. His moods are unpredictable, they know that as well as we do. They're never going to trust him again, they can't afford to; and he'll be aware of that, he's very sensitive to atmosphere."

And he tended to react badly, where people reacted badly to him. This was old ground; school had been a hard road for David and for those of us who loved him, having to watch him and watch over him, having to step in again and again when he came up against those who loved him not.

We'd thought all roads would be easier since, his and ours, because of the center. If we were to lose that comfort now …

Well. We looked at each other, mutely reading minds; she said, "You'll keep an eye on him while he's suspended, won't you? While I'm at work? It'll only be a few days, hopefully …"

"Of course. As long as it takes. Won't be the first time I've looked after David."

"No." She settled beside me, sighing, at last allowing her head to fall against my shoulder. "No, and it won't be the last. But that's what I'm afraid of, Ro—that sooner rather than later there's going to be no more school and no more center, nothing more available for him, no respite. It has to happen eventually, I've always known that. Living where we do, where I've chosen to, options were always going to be limited; in the end they'll just run out. And then we'll have him home, and that'll be that. He can't go back to Mum, not for more than a night at a time, she can't manage him any more. God knows, I love the boy—but I don't know if I can love him full-time. I've always been scared to find out …"

"You don't have to," I said softly, stroking her arm. "There's two of us, at least. Job-share."

"Really? I've always been scared to find out about that, too. It

122

was fine when you were kids, I didn't mind dumping you on each other; but this is different. We're talking a lifetime here, Rowan. David's lifetime, most likely. You, uh, you do know about that, don't you ...?"

"What, that he's not going to beat Methuselah? Yeah, I know. I asked some people, medics I used to hang out with ..." Cases differ, they'd said, there were always exceptions and I wasn't to look on what they said as gospel, or even a prognosis; but as an average, they'd said, he'd be lucky to see fifty. Forewarned is forearmed, I'd said, and thanked them kindly.

"Did you?"

"I wanted to know," I said. "To be ready."

"Right."

"So don't sweat it, okay? He's got friends, and more friends than me; you don't have a monopoly on loving David. We neither of us do. But whatever happens—everyone else goes south, goes west, wherever—there's always the two of us. For as long as it takes, as long as he needs us. Trust me," I said. "Okay?"

"Okay," she said. And then, "You know what?"

"What?"

"I love you, Rowan Coffey ..."

Generous soul that I am, I gave her every opportunity to prove that, to demonstrate, to measure it by her body's length by mine; and then, in the damp and heavy silence after, I said, "I'm going to need some time off, mind."

"Mmm?"

"For good behavior. If I do David-sitting all day. You've got to let me run off afterwards, if I need to."

"Rowan," and she hauled herself up on to an elbow to see me more clearly in the darkness, a count of her confusion, "when did I ever not? When you're here you're here, and welcome so; when you're not, it's because you choose to be somewhere else that night. God, boy, I've never been possessive, that's the last thing, you know that ..."

I did know it, and still knew myself possessed: having to make my own rules as she would not make them for me, and my own excuses for them. "It's not a case of possession," I said, lying softly where I lay under the soft fall of her hair. "Things'll be different, that's all. If I'm here with David all day, if I'm here when you get in. At the moment I come and go, sure; but when I come I come for you, for the two of you. And I stay, I don't bugger off to do something else instead. You may have to let me do that, is all I'm saying. And you'll have to make it easy for me, because I'm going to find it hard ..."

"Ro, love, it's not me you're tied to. I'd hate it, if you ever thought that. The door's open to you, always, whether you're coming in or going out. We need to watch David for a while, that's all; nothing else is changing. You can love me and leave me, go home to your mother every night, go off with your mates and do mad things all night, whatever you want. I won't even ask questions. Just be back in the morning, before I have to go to school, that's all I'm asking."

"I will be," I promised, and drew her back down beside me, against me, and the duvet up to cover us both. She was wrong, she was very wrong, I was very much tied to her; but I needed her not to believe it, because that was so much what she needed.

Root and Scar

Having my license to roam, I didn't mean to use it. The next day Juliet cried off school, phoned herself in absent, to be sure that David understood what had happened and was now happening, and that he would settle under this new regime.

Me, I borrowed his pushbike and crossed the valley floor, to explain it all to my mother. Or to pretend, at least, that I was only there to explain—"I won't be around much for a week or so, I'll be all day at Juliet's with David, so I may as well stay over ..." In reality, I suppose I was looking for a lot more than the casual nod of acceptance such news could expect. She was a wise woman, my mother: I trusted her to see more clearly than Juliet could and hence more deeply, to understand just how big a commitment I was making here. A dose of that wisdom was what I needed more than anything, to help me find a path that I could follow.

It's a quantum universe, alas; there are realities and realities, and those that we build in our heads in transit, however credible, are not necessarily those that we step into at journey's end.

I leaned the bike against the cottage wall, ducked through the doorway and found myself walking into a scene of domestic bliss. Happy families, except that the family on show was not my own.

Two children, playing beggar-my-neighbor in front of a roaring fire; their father sprawled relaxed and contented on the sofa, a book in his hands, a cat in his lap and his eyes on his kids at their game. Emma and Antony, their father Andrew: and Andrew was wearing my old bathrobe and nothing else. It covered him more decently than it did me, but little more. He had the grace to check it, briefly, to pull it straight where the cat had made it gape before he glanced back up at me.

"Rowan. Your mother's in the bath," he said, and left me to draw what conclusions I might from the information.

Not hard. My mother is a wise woman but she has some foolish habits, and a particular passion for strays. That was how our cats had come to us, and stayed; other guests had come and gone, and not all the men had slept in my bed while I shared my mother's.

I nodded, gave the kids a cheerful wave and went through to the kitchen; came back shortly with a couple of steaming coffees, black.

"There's only soya-milk and honey," I said, "if you go for additives."

"This is fine, thanks. Sit down?"

He swung his legs off the sofa invitingly; I shook my head.

"I'm going to talk to my mother."

Two dozen words and the games we'd played with them, claim and counter-claim. Possession is nine points of the law, and we were both trying to establish our stakes here. Pointlessly, perhaps—my mother is herself and hers alone, she will be owned by no one— but the space about her is precious, and we both wanted a lion's share of it.

One reason, the main reason I went to interrupt her bath was to preempt his doing the same thing. It's a privilege that lovers assume; I wanted to make it plain to him that in this house at least, it was a privilege granted also to the son-and-heir. A privilege forced on me often these last years, when I really hadn't wanted it: aggressively unbodyconscious, my mother had taken no account of teenage sensibilities, assuming that early training would triumph over hormonal imbalance and/or adolescent angst. Which it did— but only just, sometimes.

Now that license was useful to me. I might have waited, but chose not to; chose instead to walk into the bathroom, where my mother lay in a bath of cloudy, cooling water. No question of the door being bolted against me, it wasn't even closed.

Head cushioned on a folded flannel, eyes closed and face dreamy,

126

face framed by tendrils of damp hair: this was a familiar vision, familiar from a hundred such visits to the bathroom, even if it had generally been her stentorian and utterly undreamy bellow that had bawled me in.

Cool, cool woman, my mother, though warmly pink just then in the misty light. She couldn't have heard either my arrival or my voice, she didn't open her eyes, she should have been expecting Andrew if anyone; but she knew the fruit of her loins by his tread or his breathing, she would have said his aura. All she actually said was, "Rowan. Sit down."

There was a chair, kept precisely for such social occasions. I dislodged the other cat from her contentment, sat down, sipped coffee, waited; after a moment the eyes opened and fixed me with a thoughtful stare.

"Well? How's it going, long lad?"

"Not so well just now," I said.

"Tell me."

So I told her about David and his sudden disgrace, how my life and Juliet's would necessarily be changed by it; and what I got in return was not the sympathy I did not want, but neither was it the unqualified support, the good sense I'd come seeking. My mother's mind is not unfathomable to me—how could it be, after so many years so intimate?—but even I find her sometimes unpredictable. Took me a minute to latch on, this time.

"David's always been a difficulty," she said, and I thought she was only being hard and practical. "And with Juliet it was always 'love me, love my brother.' You must have been expecting trouble."

"Yes, but not yet. Not now ..." *When I need it least*, I was saying, *when what I need is stability, fixed stars and certainty* ...

"Actually," she said, "it's quite convenient if you have a reason to stay over at the boathouse for a week or two. Andrew will be here a while, with his children, and there really isn't the room to squeeze you in. They need your bed, they're too young to camp, and you're too overstretched."

Physically or mentally, she might have meant that; either was true. Both were. But I was only slowly, slowly catching up here.

127

"Besides," she went on, "it'll do you good, to have someone else to focus on for a while. A year out is all very well, Rowan, but it shouldn't be a year wasted. Other people's troubles are a blessing, they're a source of growth. You concentrate on David, look after Juliet, you'll be the richer for it."

Leave me alone a while, she meant, which meant, *leave me with Andrew*. It wasn't my needs that she was focused on. She closed her eyes again, her hand dribbled water into the channel between her breasts, and I began at last to recognize the symptoms. Little blame to me, for being so slow: I hadn't seen this often. There had been men in plenty, but few who were in any way significant. This one, though—she thought this one might be a fixture. "A week or two", she'd said; in my mother's loose chronology, that meant a period of time immeasurable as yet, but almost surely longer than a fortnight. Limitless, perhaps, in the future she sought behind her shuttered lids.

A fixture till she breaks him, was my own sour thought, *or else he breaks away*—but that could take months, perhaps years to accomplish.

I took the kids out for a walk—"for an hour," I said, meaning *two*, meaning *time enough for a long slow shag on the hearthrug, if you fancy one, lady and gent*. It was very much in the air, I thought; they wouldn't even need to undress.

The rain had stopped around dawn, but even so I told the kids to wear hats or hoods; it was too cold to come home with a wet head, I said.

"But it's not raining."

"Correct."

They looked at me askance, recognized some level of teasing here, and fell quiet where other kids I knew would have badgered and pestered for an explanation. I found myself liking Antony and Emma more and more.

I led them down over the back field, across the bridge we'd built that was still sturdily surviving, and so to the edge of the wood.

In fact, the only reason I'd brought them this way was not to take them the other, up the hill and so past the Castle with its

128

inherent memories for them, fear and loss. As we approached the trees, though, they started to hang back and whisper, their eyes watched the ground and their feet crawled to a halt, and it seemed that I'd brought them to a place of fear after all. And of loss too, loss of that insouciance that I loved in them.

Well, that was a thing to be dealt with. I said, "What's the matter, Gnome?"

"We're not going in there, are we?" In a mutter, scowling fiercely at her wellies.

"That's the idea. Why, don't you want to?"

Two hard-shaken heads, and, "We don't like it."

"Why not?"

Because it was dark, apparently, and prickly and spiky; also there were things that made noises and moved, and they were fairly sure they'd seen monsters a long way in, one sunset. Real monsters, not made up. Like the ones my mother told stories about, *real monsters* ...

Turned out they'd only been in once themselves, daring each other monumentally and lurking just in the shadow of the canopy just for a minute or two, just long enough for honor to be satisfied.

I grinned, crouched down to their level on the wet grass and said, "Listen. I know it looks scary, but it isn't, truly it isn't. It's brilliant in there. There are foxes and badgers, and all sorts of birds; it's them you hear shuffling about in the leaves, just birds and moles and stuff like that. There aren't any monsters. My mum tells great stories, but they're only stories, they're not real. She makes them up," *and she shouldn't be telling the scary ones to kids who're going to believe her ...*

They didn't believe me, or not completely. But I was determined, I wouldn't let them stay frightened of one of my favorite places; I talked and talked, and in the end they gave way, beaten into submission more by the relentless flow of words than by any force of argument. They held my hands and skittered nervously on either side of me, and together we all three went into the wood.

Before long they were holding each other's hands and ranging ahead of me, chasing shadows and birds as I'd been certain they would. No credit to me, that was the wood's true magic; but I took credit for it nonetheless, and strolled along through the sullen drip-drip of long-fallen rain finally finding its way to earth feeling well contented with myself.

I made them swear great oaths of secrecy and took them to a favorite, very private hiding-place of mine. An old poacher had shown it to me when I was their age, seven or eight. "We was the real Home Guard," he'd told me. "None of that Dad's Army crap you see on the telly. We had to play along with them, that was our cover, Church Parade and exercise with broomsticks; but when they-all dismissed, we come out here. Five of us, there was, and we only knew one man else, our commander. We was saboteurs, see. If Jerry did invade, Dad's Army wasn't going to stop him, and neither were we, but we'd make his life bloody uncomfortable. Blow up his trucks and his trains, assassinate his officers—like the French resistance, see? This was our base. We had six months' rations here, explosives, guns, you name it. Safer than houses, no dog's going to sniff this out. One time I was caught by the game-keeper going in, and I had to kill him, it was that hush-hush. We buried him in the woods here, they never found his body …"

Was that true? I didn't know, but I believed it. Or maybe he didn't even say that, maybe he only hinted at dark deeds to impress a kid, and I was so impressed I romanced it into a confession. I've told the story to myself so often, I can't distinguish my own words from the original; we could be talking false memory syndrome here. It happens. But what is certain is that I never brought my friends here, I never told a soul except myself until I brought those kids along and gave them an edited version. When I was a kid I was too scared to talk, I thought Ethan would come and kill me too for spreading his secret when I'd sworn such heavy vows to keep it quiet; when I was early teens, when Ethan had died and I held it quite alone I thought I'd make a love-nest of it, I'd have a private shagging-spot to bring my girls to (blindfold, I thought happily, so they couldn't find it later, bring another boy: shagspots aren't for sharing). The heart of the wood, I thought it was, my heartwood.

But then of course there was Juliet, and with her came the boat-house and I didn't need any love-nest else. With her, I needed no girl else.

There's a clearing, a glade overhung by an old oak. Nothing tremen-dous in itself, there are many such and this is no gnarled monster fit to hide a king. That's one of the things about the valley, you can't see the trees for the wood, nor is there any need to. Individ-ually, they're none of them particularly special. It's the congregation that matters.

Somewhere in that glade—it might be among the oak's visible and writhing roots, it might be in a hollow rotted stump or under a rockable rock, I am absolutely not drawing you a map here—there's a hidden hatch that hides a greater secret. Below the hatch is a concrete tunnel, dark and damp; the torch I carried only made it seem darker, but the kids were brave now, crawling at my back and never raising a murmur.

The tunnel slopes steeply down for a distance, and then debouches into a broad chamber, space enough for five men and a heap of stores. Space and to spare for a couple of wooden crates and candles in bottles, the way I'd left it furnished. I used to come here for solitude, to escape mother and friends and all my life, to hide up in a cold dank tomb and think gloomy thoughts and like as not declaim some verse aloud; now I lit the candles and sat the kids on the crates, produced cokes and chocolate from my pockets and told them how privileged they were.

Antony gawped. "Have you really never ever?"

"I really have. Never ever. You're the absolute first. This is my big secret, it's where I come to hide."

Emma gazed around, gazed levelly at me where I sat on my jacket on the iridescent floor and nodded, said, "This is your oubli-ette."

"Nothing dead here, pet lamb," though there easily could have been. No need for Ethan to bury his gamekeeper in the wood. If he did, if it wasn't just a story. You could bury a regiment under that hard-packed floor; or not bury it at all, just stack it in the corners to molder and rot. This far below the leafmold and the beechmast,

131

no dog would sniff it out. I had Ethan's word on that, and Ethan knew dogs.

Emma frowned, Antony stared. "Your oubliette, she said. Not dead, nothing's dead. A hole to hide in, that's what that is. We've got one too."

To my surprise, Emma didn't try to shush him. "We'll show you," she said. "You won't fit, you're too big, but we can show you. It's under the Castle."

"The Castle's all locked up, though."

She beamed. "We can get in. We can always get in. We know where the key's hidden. It's a secret, mind."

"Of course it is. You know a lot of secrets, don't you? And now you know one more. I know yours, and you know mine. Sharing's fine, but you mustn't share this place with anyone else. Secrets spoil, if they spread too far."

Mutual explosions of outrage, from my two guests; of course they wouldn't, they'd never told anyone about their oubliette until they told me, they knew all about secrets and private places and how special they were ...

I mollified them with stories safer than my mother's, and teased them into entertaining me with their own stories of life on the road with their father; and at last we went home, cheerfully impressed with ourselves, to find equally satisfied parents waiting, mine and theirs. Andrew took one look at their hands and clothes and chased them noisily up to the bathroom, asking if we had a nail-brush; I kissed Mum's cheek and left, heading for home, my other home, my lover's.

Car missing, no one there: Juliet must have taken David into town. For a treat, most likely, tea and cakes, his favorite. And the cinema after, maybe. Probably not a visit to their mother; she'd not want her to worry.

With time to kill and plenty on my mind, too much to sit still and wait for them, I went out into the blustery wind and down the hill, just walking. Had no goal in mind until I reached the trees and the gate in the wall, where I'd sat and seen David pedal past me in his dangerous, disastrous huff. Trying not to think of that, not liking where those thoughts would inevitably lead, I thought of something else instead; and vaulted the gate and followed the paths until I came to where I'd found Scar and her friend making camp.

I didn't really need the paths, I could have followed my nose instead, the smell of woodsmoke on the wind like a herald to the sound of voices that came after. When I reached the clearing, I found it crowded; there were three competent-looking teepees where there had been one rough bender, and there were half a dozen people sitting huddled around the fire where I'd only been looking for two.

Of the newcomers, three I thought were probably survivors from the Ride, stubborn as Scar, as determined to stay. The fourth was the man I'd seen walking down the lane. I had no logical reason to classify him otherwise, I certainly hadn't seen all the complement of the convoy; even so, something about him made me doubt. Leaders like Scar and followers like Andrew may be opposites in many ways, in every way that counts, but they still have a common hunger for company, a mutual need to share. This man gazed at me with raptor's eyes, a loner undisguised.

Scar gazed at me with neutral eyes, neutral brushing lightly up against hostile.

"Something we can do for you?" she asked.

Well, you could go away. I don't like you here, too close, you could bring the press and the police back on top of us again. You make these interesting times in the valley, and that's not what I want. Not what I came home for ...

I smiled, shook my head, said, "Well, let me sit and visit a while. No more than that. No one's home, and I don't feel like being alone."

That much, she understood. Of course she did, it was aimed directly at her. She grunted and shifted a little closer to her neighbor on the one side, making space for me on the other.

How much can you read into the dynamics of a small circle? I'm not sure, and hindsight is deceptive; but the newcomer, the isolationist was Scar's neighbor on the one side, the one she closed the gap on. Which only emphasized how much of a gap there had been before, how much there still was on his other side, between him and the next in line. Maybe that was what I'd read before, to make me label him a newcomer: that they were giving him space where they took none for themselves. Maybe. I thought he reveled in his splendid isolation, though, I thought he looked for it. Might have come seeking it, even. He was surely seeking something; his body was at rest, cross-legged and easy on the ground, but his eyes moved and moved, restless at the molecular level and restless at every level else.

They followed the talk around the fire, those eyes, and they followed every motion, slow or sudden. They touched on me lightly, and came back to touch again; a dozen times, a hundred times. I wasn't counting, but I thought perhaps he was. I thought I was being measured, analysed and judged.

Judged safe, I thought, perhaps. Ineffectual, perhaps. Boy at a loose end, attracted by what was unusual, no more.

Fine by me. I sat and listened, hardly said a word except when a spatter of rain made the fire hiss. A girl leaned forward to add some more wood to the flames, and I said, "You're all right at the moment, but what are you going to do when the snow comes? You can't stay here then …"

"We're staying." That from Scar, flat and final. "We've lived rough through the winter before this."

"Not up here, you haven't. Trust me, it's wild. And what's the point, anyway, what are you trying to prove?"

"We don't have to prove a thing. That's not what we're about, not now. The Ride was making a point, sure, showing that there was another way to live within the world; but your cozy little world hit back, it didn't like us, so it destroyed the Ride. So now it's our turn. We're back in the world, and we don't like it, we're going to change it. You don't want to see this whole fucking valley flooded, do you?"

"No," I said. "No, I don't."

"So we're going to stop it. And not with petitions and protest letters, that's a waste of time. Direct action, it's the only way. They're drilling samples already, to test the geology; so we'll stop them drilling. And that's just the start …"

Oh, she was fierce, was Scar, with her feathered hair whipping in the wind and her eyes bright as a blade, her voice as sharp. She looked mythic in that wood that day, more than human; and myths are potent, powerful, I knew that from my mother.

The man at her side sat still, but his eyes absorbed us all.

The girl who had fed the fire said, "We need more wood," and scrambled to her feet; I was up a moment later, saying, "I'll help."

I didn't look back at the circle, but I didn't need to; I could feel the smirk. Well, let them think I was just a gawky lad with no graces, seizing any chance to be alone with a pretty girl. It did me no harm, and might be useful.

Her name was Lisette, she told me, and she was a college dropout, a year on the Ride and passionate about it, still shaken by its ending. Determinedly not going home to Mum, or not yet: she'd invested too much faith in Scar, and too much of herself in what she stood for. She didn't like this, any of it, the camping in the woods or the confrontations to come; but she was still a believer, she felt obliged to make a stand.

I picked that up as much from her body as her words, as we gleaned fallen branches from the scrub; and didn't challenge any of it, only asked, "Who's that guy then? The old one, the quiet one who just sits there and watches you all?"

"Ugh." Her face twisted; she didn't like him either. "He's a friend of Scar's, I suppose. He turns up every now and then, stays a week or two, never says much. He's called Root, he's got this tattoo all down his back like a giant tree-root. There's a scar underneath it, thick as your finger, God knows how he got that; but the tattoo doesn't hide the scar, it sort of celebrates it, you know? I think he's creepy," she added, sounding briefly younger even than she had to be.

I carried my share of wood back to the fire, dumped it and said goodbye. I think Scar at least was glad to see me go; she didn't share Root's view that I was harmless. Whatever else I was, I was still a spy from the world she'd declared war on.

I walked back up to the boathouse, and found it empty yet, still no car outside. Watched the wind ruffle the waters of the tarn, and thought a while; then went inside to leave a note for Juliet, to say that I'd be late home tonight.

Back on David's bike then, and down the valley to Michael's house. He was just home from work; I nuzzled his neck, whispered sweet nothings in his ear, oozed affection in front of his parents until he shoved me off, choking with laughter and saying yes, saying go on, then, take the bloody scrambler, Christ …

I borrowed his helmet too, for safety's sake; left the pushbike to his tender care and roared away.

Drinks (4)

Every game boy drinks Fentle's. And with good reason. The Fentle Arms is the last pub alive that still brews its own beer; turn up on the right day and you can smell the heady mix of yeast and barley wafting down the lane towards you, breathe too deeply and you can be over the limit before you've walked in the door, almost.

Even geriatric boys drink Fentle's. And with good reason. It's a fine beer on its own account, but the scenery is fantastic; and I don't just mean outside the door. Turn up on the right day and you can smell the heady mix of expensive perfumes and rampant hormones wafting down the lane towards you, breathe too deeply and you can have a nasty dose of priapism to deal with before you've walked in the door. Almost …

The Fentle Arms is a great drink on a Friday if you're a lusty lad or a lewd pensioner, or any grade of male in between. It stands all solitary on a height, a beacon to the valleys round about, and a beacon also to the girls of Beston Hill. The school lies half a mile below, shrouded in trees, only its rooftops and its playing fields visible from the pub. Conversely, the pub is effectively hidden from the school; but the lane that leads up can be watched quite easily from the windows. One girl—or an amenable boy—to keep *cave*, and there's no danger. A warning whistle will send illicit drinkers scuttling out of the back door and onto the safety of the wide fells before suspicious staff have found a place to park.

The landlord's perfectly amenable. He does good business on a Friday.

◆◆◆

I rode the scrambler noisily up the last slope, and revved the engine a couple of times before I killed it. Then I took the helmet off and worked my hand through my hair, unzipped my leather jacket and walked inside.

I was too early for the main rush, after tea. That's when the good girls, the prefects and post-16s collect their passes and are let loose for the night. They're not, of course, supposed to come to the pub, but many of them do. They meet boyfriends there by arrangement or else pick up boys by chance, though "chance" is hardly the word where both parties know just what they're there for. It's a teenage mating-mart, the Fentle of a Friday, and the introduction fee is a rum and coke and perhaps a cigarette. That's all it takes.

I'd never used it, of course, never needed to; by the time I was old enough to satisfy those girls, I had someone older who satisfied me entirely. But some of my friends had been regulars, and I'd come often enough to observe.

I knew I was early, but that was all right. There was another part to this low comedy of bad manners, and I'd watched that too before now.

After classes but before tea on a Friday, there's a general exodus of younger girls, the weekly boarders going home. They're not walking, of course, but you'd think they were, by the way they troop out of the gates. It's a school tradition that parents or other pickers-up don't come all the way; they wait on the road below, till their girls come to them. It saves traffic congestion, I suppose, on the steep and narrow lane; the girls talk about it as though it were as hallowed and ancient a rule as the angle that they wear their hats.

Whatever, it's a practice that some of them exploit, when they dare to. Year 11s, usually—fifth-formers in their own strange tongue. It's another custom of the school that departing girls are not supervised on that brief walk down, they're trusted; so the kids and the good girls turn left at the gate, while the bad girls turn right and hustle up to the pub to toast their freedom. The organized ones make sure their lifts come late, to save them having to hurry that first drink of the weekend.

◆◆◆

So I walked in, leathers and crash-hat and six foot four; and I heard an "Oooh," I swear I did, a gasp and a suck of breath.

I didn't look round, of course. Wouldn't want them to see me grinning; shame to blush 'em into silence, when they were having such fun. I went to the bar and got a pint, lounged over to a corner, all but put my boots up on the table. Then and only then did I check out the collected custom.

Old men on the settle, this evening as every evening, where they had been since lunch and before lunch too: sitting with their mouths open, breathing hard and drooling occasionally, relying on their age for their excuse. Younger men at the bar, taking a few pints aboard before going home to their wives and kids and dinners, refreshing eyes and throat and belly and libido all at once. Adolescent boys in clumps, in awkward places, uncertain of everything except that they couldn't keep away, couldn't possibly leave, not possibly, not now ...

And in the window-bay the cause of all this male angst and pleasure, a little group of girls. Allowed to leave school clothes behind, a cherished senior privilege, they were lamb dressed as mutton: sixteen trying to look twenty-one and failing, falling short. Four of them, all of them trying not to look at me and failing ...

Now I could grin, I could look them over and grin again, not to seem disappointed; and then I could look away, sip my beer, give the boys over yonder a sympathetic look that was almost an apology for stealing all their thunder, sit and wait ...

Sit and wait and listen, I could do that too, and did. Kids don't know how far a hissed whisper travels, further far than soft and natural voices.

"... gorgeous! Those legs ..."

"Spaghetti-sticks under the Levis, betcha. Skinny, knock-kneed ..."

"Leave it out, Trix. He's perfect."

"He is not."

"What's wrong with him, then?"

"Well, if he was perfect, he'd be over here buying drinks all round, wouldn't he?"

"Do me a favor. Why should he? Nothing in it for him."

"That's all you know."

"What? Oh, right. I suppose you're going to take him home and screw him senseless, are you?"

"Dad's away. But he should buy me a drink, first. I don't give out for nothing."

"Maybe you should tell him that. Is he meant to read your mind?"

"My body language, sweetheart …"

But she did it, to the gasps and hisses of her friends; she stood up and swayed her way over. Only out of the corner of my eye was I watching, and applauding; my head was turned studiously towards the brasses on the wall, and didn't turn until her shadow fell across my table.

Then I looked up at her, and smiled. Something more intimate than the grin I'd flashed before, something I used to practice for hours in front of Juliet's mirror, a woman's bedroom the only place it really should be seen.

"Hullo," I said.

"Hi." Her friends had accents of cut and polished diamond; hers was diamond in the rough, deliberately disguised, a posh voice scuffed in the street and stained in the gutter. As her clothes were, expensively scruffy; and her hair, chopped urchin-style by some genius so that each individual strand fell precisely, decoratively awry.

"Can I help?" I asked neutrally, very adult.

"Well, you could buy me a drink …" Not so much confidence in her now, and the half-glance back towards her friends said that there lay the real help I could give her, not to damage her credibility by refusing.

"Be a pleasure," I said, rising smoothly and extensively to my feet beside her, letting her see every inch of my unfolding. "Sit down. What'll it be?"

"Uh, rum and coke …"

Of course. I nodded, went to the bar and watched in the mirror behind it while she exchanged signals with her mates. *See? Told you* … and *Help! What do I do now …?*

Her rum and coke, and a whisky for me: I clinked glasses with her, and asked her name.

"Trix …"

"Hullo, Trix. I'm Rowan. You want to ask your friends over to join us?" for all the world as if I didn't care.

"Not particularly, no," showing how much she did care, how much it mattered; but then, she was dreadfully young.

"Suits me," I said, with another of those melting smiles; and then, meanly, "This your GCSE year, is it?"

"That's right," defiantly, trying to outface me while her cheeks flushed in despite of her will. "What about you, is this your cradle-snatching year? Or did you only come here to stare, like those poor sods?" One quick gesture of her head took in the whole clientèle.

This time, my grin was completely genuine. I might be playing a game, but she was serious; this was her style, her way of facing down a world she didn't trust. Even when she tried to pull—in front of her mates, pride on the line—she couldn't help snarling. Her idea of a charm offensive, this was, missing only the charm …

Except that actually I did find it charming, she delighted me.

"Three, four years ago I came to stare," I said, I lied. "When you really were in your cradle. Not now. And you're no kid, Trix, you know what you're doing. You came to me, remember?"

"That's right, I did, didn't I? What can I have been thinking of?"

"A free drink and a ride on my bike, perhaps?"

"That's not fair," she said, scowling, though I was willing to bet that those were pretty much the horizons of her hopes. "And don't *laugh* at me …"

"I'm not laughing," I assured her softly. She lifted her eyes from where her nails were picking at a beermat; big dark eyes that neither sulky defiance nor heavy mascara could spoil, they blinked up at me and I caught my breath, couldn't help it, had to swallow sharply. Internal organs performed cartwheels and butterflies to order, and no, I most definitely was not laughing now. "Listen, how's about this for a game-plan? We finish these drinks, we go for a bounce-about on the bike, I'll give you lessons if you don't mind getting muddy; then we'll just take it from there. Unless your mother's watching the clock for you …?"

"I live with my dad," she said shortly, "and he won't be home till tomorrow. My lift's at the bottom of the hill, we'd better tell him or he'll go up to school and make a fuss."

"Who's your lift? Not a boyfriend, is he?"

"He's the gardener," she said.

Her lift the gardener was no faithful family retainer, to wring his hands over the wild behavior of the young and adored mistress; he looked as sullen as she did, and glad to be shot of the responsibility of her. He gave me a quick once-over, took my promise to see her safe home as casually as I had made it, and drove off in the family Four-Trak. I concluded that this was not the first time his charge had dumped him in similar circumstances; so long as the crash-hat protected her skull rather than mine, he'd think his duty done.

So long as I didn't bring her home in a body-bag. There was some danger of that, the way she threw Michael's scrambler around the open dell I took her to. Nursery slopes, but she was no nurseling; she tried routes—mostly straight up or straight down—that would have made me hesitate, and when they failed, stall or fall, she turned back and tried the same route from some other angle.

"You done this before?" I asked, helping her haul the bike up after a particularly long and muddy slither.

"No," she said, panting, blazing, "but I'm bloody well doing it again …"

When at last she let me take her home, home turned out to be a high Georgian house set in its own parkland, sheep grazing the acres of lawn and horses chewing hay in the stable block at the back, where we left the bike.

"Dad hunts," she said with a dismissive jerk of her head, lest I think her a Pony Club kind of girl. "I don't," added needlessly and then expanded, "I think it's sick. I go out with the sabs sometimes, it makes him wild. There's a groom looks after the horses, he's got his own flat over the stables there; but don't worry, he doesn't come into the house. No one does," as she opened the back door to let us in.

142

"Except your dad, presumably?"

"Yeah, but he's in London. I said, he won't be back till tomorrow."

She was filthy, and I was none too clean myself; there was a scullery just inside the door—the mud-room, she called it—where we left helmet, footwear and wet socks, and padded on barefoot. A solitary supper had been set out for her in the kitchen, by the housekeeper she said who came in daily; she took my hand and tugged me on, through a grand hallway and up a magnificent staircase, down a corridor to her own big room.

She dumped her jacket on the bed, glanced through an open doorway into an en-suite bathroom and then a little uncertainly at me. I gave her no help, I was enjoying myself too much.

"Uh, I need a shower …"

"Okay, fine."

She chewed her lip briefly, while her fingers touched the buttons of her denim shirt, the buttons of her jeans; then she jerked her head away and walked stiffly through into the bathroom, pushing the door to behind her but not even closing it properly, definitely not bolting it against me.

Sounds of rushing water, a slow trickle of steam around the door: I wandered the room, touching her teenage things, stroking the quality of the curtains, killing time.

Eventually, the shower cut off. I listened to the sounds of hasty toweling, and wondered quite how she would come back to me, how she'd cope; and was answered when the door swung open and she stood there, damp and naked and a little tremble in her voice as she said, "Rowan? Please …?"

Now was the time to be kind; she might have brought other boys back at other times, but I thought probably none had got this far. I said, "Okay, sweets, if that's what you want—but let's not rush it, eh? I could use a shower too, I was waiting for you to offer …"

She watched me while I peeled my own clothes off, there in the bedroom; she stepped back to let me pass and watched me while I soaped and showered, while I used her towel to dry myself, all very slow and leisurely, letting her learn my body with her eyes. Then I came to her through the billowing steam, kissed her gently and ran

143

my hands feather-light across her skin, drawing forth shudders. I took her hands and guided them, letting her learn my body with her fingers now while her eyes were full of mine; and so at last I led her to the bed, taking a handful of condoms from my discarded jacket en route, and taught her some of the many things that bodies can learn of each other.

One girl's supper won't feed two starving teens. We scoured the freezer, and ate prawns and shepherd's pie, ice-cream and more ice-cream. She wore her dressing-gown, I wore her father's bathrobe, knee-length on me, soft and hooded and luxurious. When we were finished eating, she fiddled with a silk tassel on the belt of the gown and said, "Rowan …"

"What?"

"Can we, um, you know, do it again?"

"We surely can, sweets. Is there a double bed in the house anywhere? Yours is a bit cramping …"

Big grin, deliberate wickedness; she stood up, took my hand again, said, "Come with me."

Back up the stairs we went, and into her father's room. His suite of rooms: he had a bedroom and a bathroom and what must have been a dressing-room at one time, what was now his office. I stole a quick look inside, while Trix was peeling the coverlet back off his wide tester bed. Computer, fax, couple of phones; shelves of books, folders, couple of filing cabinets. Very nice.

"Rowan…?"

"Yeah, I'm coming. Let's just have the lamp on, shall we? Light enough to look at you, you're beautiful, but we don't need the chandelier. We do need these, though," producing the condoms again from the pocket of her father's robe. "You want to put it on me this time? Nice and easy now, it's a skill every girl should learn … It's okay, giggles never hurt a guy except in his pride, and I'm not that proud. You cry out if I hurt you, though, that's not what it's all about …"

✦✦✦

144

I was careful as I could be, and when she did cry it wasn't because I'd hurt her. I nestled her against me, and kissed the tears into choking little giggles; then I spread her out across the bed again and worked my slow way down her body, letting my tongue do the talking. From her shoulders to her filling breasts, lingering over the nipples till I had her gasping; and so on down, firm belly and sparse wiry hair and what was warm and wet beneath.

Made her come, which made her cry again. I stroked and soothed her, murmured quiet nonsense, held her close; and at last, at long last she fell asleep.

"Rowan?"

"Mmm?"

"What are you *doing*?"

"Waiting for you to wake up, sweets."

"I thought you'd gone ... What *is* that?"

"Just a game."

"My father doesn't have games on his computer."

"He does now. I downloaded it, off the net."

"He'll kill you. No, he won't, he'll kill *me* ..."

"No, he won't. I'll wipe it. Look—there it is, gone. He'll never know it was there. Trust me."

"Well, but—Turn it all off and come back to bed now? Please?"

"Sorry, sweets, can't do that. I've got to go. I only waited to say goodbye."

"Oh. Ohh ... Will I, will I see you again?"

"I expect so. No, don't sulk at me. I promise, all right? You're gorgeous. Give me a kiss, and give me your phone number. Here's a pen, write it on my hand so I don't lose it. Will I get your dad, if I ring this?"

"No, it's my own phone, in my room. There's voice-mail, if I'm not up there. I don't want you to go ..."

"I know you don't, but I have to. Shouldn't have stayed this long. I'll just get my clothes and vanish, don't you come down. Whoops—condoms! Better not leave those. And you'd better make his bed pretty, and sleep in your own, okay? Night-night, lover ..."

◆◆◆

"Rowan ...?"

"Nah, it's the nasty bogeyman out of the bitter black woods, that my mum's always telling you about. Shift over, Jules. I'm a big boy, me."

"Big boy who's been out late. Very late. What have you been doing?"

"Shagging a cute and eager sixteen-year-old on her father's bed, of course. What else would I be doing?"

"God, you're full of it tonight, aren't you? Got anything left for me?"

"Just my strong but tender arms, sweetheart. I'm all out of lovin' spoonfuls."

"Good enough for me. Is that comfy?"

"That's perfect. So are you. Night-night, lover ..."

WILD WOODS

They were eight and six, and they knew there were monsters in the woods.

They'd seen one. His name was Root. They knew him.

They'd been playing fairies in the trees, and they'd been so pleased with themselves, so brave. They'd come so far from the cottage, they couldn't even see the field from where they were, only the path that led that way; and there were so many paths in the wood, they might forget which was the right one. Or they could pretend to forget, they could play that they were lost. Emma had said that, she'd said, "Let's play one of Alice's stories, where the little children are all alone in the great dark forest, and ..."

"No," Antony had said quickly. "Let's play fairies. Our fairies, not Alice's ..."

He liked Alice's stories, but only in Alice's house, by the fire or tucked up safe in bed; he didn't like to think about them here, where they might come true. He thought they'd been brave enough, just to come this far on their own. Rowan had said the woods were safe and he did believe him, he trusted Rowan; but he didn't trust Alice's stories. Not in a magic place, where anything might be listening.

Emma hadn't argued. They'd started their game, she'd been the Queen of the Fairies and he'd been her servant, like he always was, and he'd been picking berries and pretty things for her bower when he'd smelled smoke and seen a shape through the bushes, a shadow, a figure coming towards him.

147

He hadn't screamed, though he'd wanted to. There hadn't been any air in his throat, for screaming with. He'd stiffened and stared, and seen that the figure was only a man, and for a second he'd felt released.

Then he'd seen who it was, the man.

He'd backed away from Root, and found Emma suddenly at his side, her hand gripping his.

"Hullo," Root had said, smiling. They'd always hated his smile.

"Hullo, Root ..."

"What are you two doing here?"

"We're staying with Alice, and Dad ..."

"The Castle's broken, we've got to wait till it's fixed ..."

He'd walked forward, and they'd walked backwards; and suddenly one of them had turned and tugged the other and they were off running hard.

And of course it was the wrong path, and they'd got lost, and it had been ages before they found their way home to the cottage; and when their dad asked them what the trouble was, why they were so dirty and why they'd been crying, they only told him about being lost and scared among the trees, they didn't say a word about Root. There wasn't any point, they knew that. He didn't listen, when they tried to tell him about monsters. Grown-ups never did.

Later, in the bath, Emma said that maybe they could tell Alice. She might take them seriously; she wouldn't laugh, at least.

"Or Rowan," Antony said. "We could tell Rowan. We showed him the oubliette," and there seemed to be a connection, at least to Antony, between the one thing and the other.

"Yes, okay. Let's do that. Let's tell Rowan."

ii

Well, well. So there were fairies at the bottom of his garden. Fairies that knew him, and knew enough to be scared of him. He liked that.

He'd always fancied fairy-cake. And a little of what he fancied, just a bite or two, say, two little nibbles, that always did him so much good ...

iii

Saturday morning: David watches cartoons.

Rowan watches David watch cartoons. Sometimes Rowan isn't sure quite where he stands with David. Even after a lifetime—two lifetimes, his own and David's, neither one of them can remember the other not being there—he's still occasionally uncertain quite what David is to him, or he to David. Especially he to David, especially at the moment. He's one of the triumvirate, he knows that. There's David's mother, there's Juliet and there's him; but who is Rowan, what is he? Friend, brother, guardian? All three, perhaps, another triumvirate, three in one. It's a question he can't answer, he can't see that far into David's difficult mind. Sometimes—now—it's a question that seems to matter.

Juliet bustles about, between David's guffaws and Rowan's silence. He can't ask her; she wouldn't understand why it was a question, and he couldn't explain.

"I've got to do some shopping," she says. "Anyone coming for the ride?"

"Yeah!" David says, and here at least his thought-processes are obvious, he thinks he'll get a repeat of yesterday, treats in town.

"Not me," Rowan says, glancing out of the window, at the rain. "Think I'll stay home today, do some thinking."

David's disappointed, but not enough, not to change his mind. Juliet just nods.

"Okay, you do that. Get that great brain working. Anything I can bring back for you, anything you need?"

"No, I'm fine, thanks."

"Are you? You're very quiet this morning."

"I'm fine," he says again. Wins himself a quick, amused kiss on the cheek, and gives her a smile in return, then sits and watches as she urges David into his coat and out of the door. It's a day for watching, he thinks; once they're gone, he turns his eyes away from the television and back to the window, back to the falling rain.

At length he hears an engine, but that's not Juliet's car returning, neither any other car. It's a bike, and not a scrambler: something heavy. He waits, to be sure it's stopping and not just passing by; then he goes to the door and opens up, gripping tight against the suck of the wind.

Big bike, police bike, blue and white with a big blue light; and astride it, dismounting now is Barry Carter looking like an alien in his waterproofs and helmet.

"Rowan. Come in, can I?"

"Yeah, sure, Barry. Just don't drip on the Aubusson, she wouldn't like it."

For a second he hesitates, before he sees Rowan's grin.

"All right, I'll buy it. What's an Aubusson?"

"Posh carpet. You come and drip on our bare boards, as much as you please. Juliet's not here, anyway."

"No, I saw that her car was gone. But the lights were on, so I was hoping you were driving it, and she'd be here."

"Not me; a bike's my limit, I don't do cars. Why do you want Juliet, what's she done?"

"Just a word of advice, if I can trust you to pass it on?"

"Barry, man. If she needs it, she'll hear it. Trust me."

"Fine. May not need it anyway, but just in case. There's a known pedophile camping out somewhere in the valley. Dunno where, I haven't actually found him yet; but he phoned to say he was coming, cocky shit. He's a bad 'un, served time for abuse, abduction, murder, the works. Playing games, he said, but then I looked him up. He says he's clean now, but they never are. You can't clean shit. They should be locked up for life, his kind. Or just put down. I'd do it."

"You're not worried about David, are you?"

"Nah," and he grins suddenly, they both do. "David can look after himself. That boy's a bloody ox. Broke your arm once, didn't he?"

"Sure did."

"But Juliet's got friends with kids, they come to visit sometimes, right? I've seen 'em. I'm warning everyone, don't let kids wander. Boys or girls, he's not fussy, according to his record. I'll move him on sharpish, one way or another, soon as I track him down; but in the meantime, tell Juliet to be careful, right?"

"I will," Rowan says. "Thanks, Barry. Have you told my mother yet? She's got kids in the cottage at the moment, looks like they'll be staying a while."

"Yeah? I was saving that side of the valley till tomorrow, but if there's kids there—Well, you couldn't live with yourself, could you? If anything happened ..."

"Right."

"Cheers, Rowan. See you around."

"Surely. Give Mum my love, tell her I'm homesick already."

"Will do. Thrown you out, has she?"

"Something like that."

"About time, too. Big lad like you are. Nice to have somewhere to fall back on, though. I never had a schoolteacher to shack up with, when my dad banged the door behind me. You really landed on your feet, didn't you, lad?"

"Yeah, right, Barry," Rowan says, with only the least suspicion of a wary sigh, *yeah, sure, Barry, everything's rosy for me.* "I really landed on my feet. What's his name, this pedophile?"

"Oh, yeah. His name's Edward John Halliday, but he doesn't use it. Apparently he calls himself Root. That's all, just Root."

"Root. Okay. Any distinguishing marks?"

"As a matter of fact, yes. Cable-scar on his back and a tattoo like a tree-root to cover it ..."

"I meant his face, really, Barry. What does he look like? I'm not going to be seeing his back, am I?"

"We're printing up flyers now, with a photo. I haven't got the okay for that, but I'm doing it anyway. One way or another, I'll see him off my patch ..."

Treats happen, planned or otherwise. Juliet and David are late back from town, and Juliet's looking grim. Not such a treat for her, it seems; Rowan asks David what they did, and learns that they met their mother. An accident, in the street, just one of those things: but of course she wanted to know why they hadn't phoned in advance to warn her they were coming, and of course Juliet couldn't have said that they weren't, not coming to her, not planning to visit.

So of course they had visited, and David had had his treats; and Juliet had had to break the news for fear of David's doing so. And that hadn't been the plan at all, and so Juliet is bitter with the world this early evening, and Rowan can't pull himself out of his own introspection far enough to offer any comfort.

He hasn't thought to cook their tea either, which doesn't help. Juliet clatters pans while he stares into the darkness beyond the reflective window, not half so reflective as he is. It hasn't stopped raining yet.

Difficult days leave their difficulties behind them, when they go; it's a hard, edgy meal that they eat. Even David can sense an atmosphere this heavy, and falls silent under the weight of it.

Afterwards, he slumps in front of a mindless action movie, seemingly mindless himself and utterly inactive. Rowan makes coffee for two, takes one to Juliet, gets half a thin-lipped smile in response.

And takes a breath, takes a decision, makes a commitment.

Says, "Juliet, what I said last night when I got in, about me shagging a sixteen-year-old …?"

"Well? What about it?"

"Well, it was true."

They've always found it difficult to fight before. When they were teacher and pupil, when she was twice his age. He'd sulk or bluster and she'd patronize, both of them like cheap versions of what they were on the outside, what the world saw, nothing that either one could recognize in the other.

Tonight, though—no trouble at all. It's pyrotechnic, it's awesome. David just sits and does that Wimbledon thing with his head, even the TV forgotten as he swivels his round eyes between them, as they blaze and rage.

"You know I sleep with other girls, you told me to …"

"That was at college, I didn't mean here, with me …"

The words can't mean much to David, but they don't mean much at all; only the volume counts and the hissing interference in the voices, pure temper. The medium is the message. The words just give shape to their anger, a frame to display it in all its incandescence.

152

They move as they shout, they pace and gesture; when they fall silent, at last, they fall still also. Stand and breathe, no more than that, still glaring.

They breathe loudly, but David doesn't, air barely whispers in his throat.

Until Rowan moves again, sudden and decisive; until he stalks across the room towards the door, hooks his big leather jacket off the wall and shrugs it on.

Then David needs air and takes it, uses it. "Where are you going, Rowan?"

"Starwalk," he says, although the rain is still washing the windows. And, "You coming?"

And yes, oh yes, David is definitely coming. He's had too much of being left out, left behind. All his life, and far too much. So never mind Juliet, her flat forbiddal; David's up and out of there, grabbing his coat as he goes and leaving her yelling in his wake.

iv

They thought they owned the trees, the rain, the muddy mulch beneath their feet, the hidden stars themselves, by virtue of their long possession here; but these were not their woods the boys were walking in. The night and storm had ripped a change between the worlds and brought them somewhere other, where other powers ruled.

They did not know. They had a torch, which showed them paths that seemed familiar; there was no light else, which might have shown them otherwise. No moon, no stars, no glimpse of sky: only walls of dark and rain until they reached the woods, which held them closer.

"She'll be cross, that we've gone out."

"She'd have been cross anyway, whatever we'd done. It doesn't matter. Let's just walk a while, get good and wet, give her something real to worry about."

They walked more than a while, they walked a long long way. One of them, the one with the torch, perhaps he thought he knew where they were walking, and where home lay behind them. The other knew for sure how lost he was.

The one with the torch walked on in silence, in the rain, driven by his private demons; and realized late, too late, that he walked alone.

"David?"

He turned to shine the torch back along the path, saw nothing but trees that glistened wetly in the light.

"David!"

He ran back, calling, and heard nothing but his own noise, and the noise of falling rain. He came to where the path divided, where he might somehow have lost his friend and ran that other way and found nothing that moved, nothing that answered him.

He left the paths and plunged between the trees, slipping and falling in his urgency. Now, at last, he was beginning to see the strangeness, how the wood was altered. He sensed movement all around him, but when he sought it with his torch all he saw was thorn and bramble. Waving in the wind, he thought, bending under the weight of falling water—but the wind had died, and the rain was easing off.

There were voices, he heard them distinctly, hissing and scratching at the dark, sounds with meanings; but they could only be the sounds of rain, the abrasions of thorn and bramble in the wind. But the wind had died, and the rain was easing off …

By the time he did see his friend again, he had almost stopped searching for him, had stopped shouting altogether. He walked in wonder, torch hanging unheeded at his side, wasting its beam on the sodden beechmast. His feet followed a harsh summoning song, though there were no singers; his eyes followed a dance of light that couldn't be. The rain had stopped, the sky might have cleared, but he could catch no glimpse of it through the matted branches overhead; no moon or stars could find him in this dense wood, and yet he saw lights, green and glowing, green and flowing like water, flowing away from him and so he followed the flow and the call of the song.

And so he came to a place where there were no trees, a clearing, although the trees round about had closed their branches together above to roof it, to deny the sky still; and so he did see David, whom he had sought.

David, and others.

He saw creatures that were man-shaped, almost, but made of the wood, or of the detritus of the wood: creatures with bodies like cages of woven willow, with limbs of thorn and heads like leaf-crowns. Those he saw, and one other.

He saw what might once have been a man, only that its flesh was dried like leather, wrapped and knotted around a skeleton of green wood for bones and its face was terrible, dark pits for eyes with only a glimmer in their depths to see by. When it opened its mouth, he saw how it was choked with growing grass.

When it laid its claw hands on David—claw hands with white tips like roots thrusting out from its fingers' ends—he heard how David screamed.

And he screamed too, and turned, and ran away.

V

She can't go to bed. Not with David out there, David with Rowan and Rowan in such a mood, such a fury, and the weather a fury too and her own mind in chaos, all her certainties subsumed by shock.

She waits, that's all. At first she paces also, till her own fury dies under the great dead weight of betrayal; and the betrayal not fades but recedes, forced out by worry. She fetches towels from the bathroom for when the boys return, and waits.

When the rain stops, she waits a while in the open doorway, staring into the dark mass of the wood below, watching for movement. Her eyes deceive her; sometimes she thinks she can see a fireglow through the cover of the trees, but that must be nonsense, nothing could burn on such a night. Sometimes she thinks she sees

155

people on the lane, two young men returning, but she's always wrong.

She wants a cigarette, a whole packet of cigarettes, she wants to add her own small glow to the night and the cold stars overhead; but she quit smoking long ago. She goes back inside and puts the kettle on, and forgets it until it's nearly boiled dry, and can't be bothered to make the cup of tea she thought she wanted.

She waits; and in the end, as he must, Rowan comes back to her. Not as she expected him, though, sheepish and sorry and ready to talk, leading David by the hand.

He comes back wild, staring, staggering, filthy.

Wild, staring, staggering, filthy and alone.

"Rowan ...! Rowan, where's David? Where is he?"

Rowan doesn't answer her, or not with words. He cannot speak. He turns and gestures, a great and terrible gesture that says too much to bear; and then he weeps, racking sobs that tear his throat, her heart.

"AND MILES TO GO BEFORE I SLEEP," sighed the guiser, looking back at oh how far he'd come. If he looked forward, there was further yet before he reached his cave, his bed, his rest.

"Not so far," croaked the crow, a wheeling shadow against the stars above his head. "Look, I can see your fire from here, and your slaves who tend it."

"Not my slaves," protested the guiser, "my friends, who kindly keep my house for me while I am gone ..."

"As you wish. But there it is, see, a little way across the valley there. One puff of wind could carry me."

"I cannot fly, bird."

"Neither can I, in the night," cried the crow, laughing, swooping in moonlight. "You ought not to listen to the gods, if you're fool enough to believe what they tell you. But even afoot, it is not so far through the wood to find your fire."

Not so far, no—but he would not go the short way, through the wood. He had set himself this task, to patrol the borders of his land and be sure of his protection; and he would do that, he would beat his bounds again and again until his scent was pounded into the earth and the mere rumor of his footsteps coming was enough to scare away invaders.

It was a weary way to walk, but he would do it; even with this mocking bird for company, whose small bright eyes should not see so much even by daylight ...

"Why do you follow me, bird? By night and day?"

"This was a dull place, without you; it will be dull again when you are gone."

"I am going nowhere now. I have arrived."

"All the better. Then I will follow you until there is dust on my feathers and dust on my tongue. You interest me, guiser. I will not be your slave—no, I beg your pardon, your friend, to do you favors—but I will follow you, for no more than the interest of it."

The guiser would not welcome such an interest, but he lacked wings, and he lacked the faith to fly without them; or else he was too credulous, to believe the gods when they said that he could not. Whichever way that was, he could not fly, and the crow was safe from him.

All of that, the crow was certain of. For all the rest, what the guiser said and did, what he claimed and what he denied, the crow begged leave to doubt—though he begged it only of himself and not within hearing. He had seen the cat leave the wood, he had wondered what had happened to the bear; he had listened to the guiser and the naiad by the tarn, and had watched while the guiser bore away the jewel that had been the naiad's trust.

All of that, the crow had witnessed; and still all that he would swear to was that the guiser could not fly, and so he himself was safe.

"Bird," said the guiser, "how high can you fly, before you fall?"

"As high as the moon," said the crow, who had no more faith in the gods' truth than he did in the guiser's, but a great deal of faith in himself. "If I choose to."

"That must be very wonderful. What is it like on the moon?"

"I've never chosen to go so high. I like it here," the crow said, swooping about the guiser's head. "Where there are trees to roost in, carrion to eat, you to follow and watch."

"Would you go to the moon if I asked you to?"

"Probably not," said the crow. "Why would you ask it of me?"

"I have a treasure," said the guiser, "the most precious thing I know, and I want to see it safe. I think it would be safe there, where none but you could reach it. Will you take it for me?"

"What is this treasure?" asked the crow, who knew already what was the most precious thing the guiser possessed.

"I will show you."

◆◆◆

The guiser led the crow to his cave, and went inside; came out a minute later with a glowing jewel in his hands. The crow was amazed, to find so much truth in him.

"Will you take this for me," the guiser asked, "and set it safely on the moon?"

"Guiser, I will," said the crow, thinking that this lovely thing would belong to him, when once he had put it where none but he could reach.

The guiser climbed the high hill above the cave to come as near as he could to the shining moon. There he gave the jewel to the crow, who took it in his claws and beat his wings and rose swiftly into the air.

He climbed in circles, in a dizzy spiral, higher and higher. He climbed until his breath came in desperate gasps, until his wings thrashed madly, with his bulging eyes fixed on the disc of the moon, that never seemed any closer. And still the shimmering beauty of the jewel and the desire for it drove him on and up, round and around.

At last the air, it seemed, was grown too thin to support even his light weight. He flailed at it uselessly, and felt himself start on the long, long fall. With a cry of despair, of failure, he spread his wings wide to catch himself to glide back down to ground; but the heavy jewel dragged him down too fast. He heard the sharp sounds of his wing-bones snapping, and then he fell truly, tumbling, broken.

He dropped the jewel and cried again for its loss.

On the hill below, the guiser stretched out a hand to catch the jewel and smiled as it dropped smartingly into his palm.

He made no effort to catch the crow.

159

Unusual Suspects

"I don't get this," I said, hearing the sullen resentment in my own voice, sounding like a teenager even to myself. "You want to talk to me, okay—but why can't you talk to me out there? We can talk and search, can't we? What happened to David, it's my fault, I led him into it; I can't stand just sitting here, doing nothing. At least let me go and look for him. I know these woods better than any of your men, better than anyone …"

"Mmm," said the man sitting opposite. "That's one of the things I want to talk to you about."

Michael Aldiss his name was, Detective Superintendent Michael Aldiss, and he was not one of my biggest fans. Far from it. If I still had a fan-list at all, it had grown dramatically shorter in recent days; my own name wasn't on it, I didn't like myself at all right then, but his appreciation came lower by a distance, and he made no secret of it. This was the third time we'd sat like this, just the two of us, not even a constable taking notes: the third time in three difficult, dreadful days, and he wasn't out to make anything easier for me.

The first time, the first day following that night of storm and bewitchment, I'd still been shaking, exhausted, deep in shock. He'd listened to my story, gazed at me neutrally, then asked my permission to have a police doctor check me over.

Sure, I'd said dully, anything you like.

Blood tests and urine tests, a sample of my hair, a scrape inside my mouth for DNA; then a sedative, and a lift home. To my mother's home, not Juliet's, I couldn't go back there. I'd got my own bed to sleep in, the kids routed out of it; and I'd slept the rest of that day and the night that followed, on and off when I wasn't lying awake and shuddering, remembering, wondering …

The second day had been harder. I'd asked to join the search in the woods, and had been refused; had been interrogated by this pragmatic, earthbound policeman who didn't believe in mystic creatures or tales turned real, who didn't think that nightmares could come to life.

Now this was the third day and I had risen again, had asked again to join the volunteers who were scouring the valley for any sign of David. Juliet was out there, I knew, she'd have to be; and Andrew too, and many of my friends. I belonged among them, I ached to help and wasn't allowed to do so.

"There's nothing more I can tell you," I said helplessly, "you've heard it all already, all I saw …"

"Well," he said, "tell me again."

"What's the point? You don't believe me anyway." Who would? Even Juliet didn't believe me. My mother might, only that I hadn't had the chance to talk to her in any way that mattered. Too many kids around, too much Andrew in her life, and too much distress: David was her favorite kind of man, an adult with a child's mind, wide open to the mind-games that her stories were. She'd played too roughly with him sometimes, she'd seen him seriously afraid simply of her words; I didn't want to tell her how he'd been when I saw him last. Last of anyone, I thought, who'd ever see him now.

"So convince me," said DS Aldiss.

Well, I tried. Hopeless, but I did try. I explained to him one more time about the row with Juliet, about how I'd stormed out into the storm; how I'd taken David with me purely out of spite, because it would worry her, it would keep her awake. If I was going to be up all night, I wanted to be sure of her company in that.

God knows, I hadn't wanted David. Last thing I needed, another soul to be concerned about, someone trailing at my back and needing me, when I was in such a self-righteous, self-indulgent fury. Almost the last thing: apparently there was one thing at least that I needed more, some sense of vindictive satisfaction, the certainty that my lover wasn't sleeping any more than I was.

It wasn't big, it wasn't clever, but I'd done it; and I paid for it. Christ, did I pay …

If the superintendent wanted me to pay out one more time, fair enough. This was only small change by comparison; I deserved worse and far worse.

I told him how I'd blazed a trail ahead and trusted David to follow, how he'd let me down in that regard: how I'd turned at last to find him missing from my back, faithful dog gone astray.

How I'd searched and panicked, searched and screamed; and then finally how I'd stumbled into the silence and the dreamstuff where David should have been screaming and was not.

"There was this clearing," I said, fumbling for new words, different words, some other way to explain the inexplicable. "David was there, but he was held, trapped, captive. There were these— things, hanging onto his arms. He was fighting them, he was terrified, and he was strong like anything, David, bull in a china shop, and they looked light as balsa but he couldn't shake them off …"

"Things."

"I dunno, willow-men? Wicker-men, only nothing like the film. Like corn dollies, except they were life-size and not neat like that, real rough work. Greenstuff, leaves and thorns. And they were alive, and they held him, and he couldn't get free."

"And you didn't go to help him. Big lad like you, you left him to it."

"Not yet. That comes in a minute. There was this other one, too. Must have been a man one time, I reckon. Not any more. Roots growing out of its fingers and it had willow for bones, only it hadn't grown that way, looked like it had been cut open and its own bones taken out. Arms and legs, this was, all I could see. Shouldn't have been able to see that much, only there was this weird light all over, running like St. Vitus' Dance …"

"St. Elmo's Fire."

"Yeah, except this was all jerky. Jumped around, flickered a lot. St. Vitus' Dance. Grass in its mouth, it had, I saw that. Growing there. Looked like it hurt, something hurt, it hurt. All the time. It

163

had this way of moving, like there wasn't anything about it that didn't hurt when it did that, when it moved.

"And it reached out, touched David. Tore all his clothes off like they were tissue, tissue and rags. And then it put its hand on David's shoulder, and I saw those root-things dig into his flesh, and rip it open. From shoulder down to elbow, all the way, one neat tear with bone at the bottom. And then on down, two fingers, two channels down to his wrist and blood all over, blood everywhere ..."

And then, as the blood ran, David's voice ran with it, sobbing and howling; and I ran too. Sobbing and howling. That was when I left my friend, when I was sure, utterly certain that he needed rescue, that he was doomed and damned without it.

And that's what I told Superintendent Aldiss, that's how I gave myself away completely. But I'd done it already, more than once, it was no surprise to him. He sat and grunted, folded his hands across the desktop and said, "This row you had with Juliet, now. Tell me about that."

"I told you," I said, the ritual protest. Should have been unavailing, but,

"I know you did," he said, "and like you said before, I don't believe you."

"Christ. Ask Juliet, she'll tell you."

"Oh, I have. It's not the fact of it I don't believe, it's the facts behind it. You and Juliet, you've been together since you were a schoolkid and you've stayed together ever since, it's a Mrs. Robinson thing, she's been the great love of your life. She's the one you came back to, when things went bad for you at college—and you're trying to tell me you risked all of that for the sake of a quick shag with a schoolgirl? A girl you picked up by chance, one afternoon in a pub? Do me a favor, Rowan, you're not that stupid."

"I slept with other girls in Cambridge," I said. "Got the taste for it, if you like."

"No. I don't like that, not at all. You don't work that way. Your brain rules your groin, not the other way around. And I don't think your taste runs to little girls, anyway. Even at college. I've been talking to my colleagues; the word is that you always went for older women. Post-graduates. Yes?"

"Even so. It happened."

"Did it? I don't think so. I don't think you shagged that girl at all."

"You could ask her," I suggested.

"Mmm. I've done that, too. Nice and gently, with her father there."

"And?"

"What, did you think she'd back you up? She's sixteen, she's a rebel, she doesn't get on with her dad; and you, you'd be a real catch for her. Tall, dark and handsome, nineteen years old. That's big stuff, right? Of course she'd confirm your story. She pulled you in a pub, you took her away in front of all her friends—and then you slept with her. That'd be kudos, a major score for her. Was that what you were hoping? Sorry, Rowan. She says not. She says you waylaid her in the lane, no pub. She denies the pub. So do her friends, they all deny the pub. She accepted a lift back to her father's house, because she couldn't resist the bike; she gave you a snog for thanks, and that was it. Or it should have been. She says you wouldn't leave, though, you were a right pain in the arse. In the end she says she just left you in the house while she went for a ride on her pony, just praying that you'd take the hint and be gone by the time she got back. Not you, though, you were still there. Snooping around, killing time, I guess. She says she had to fetch the gardener in, to get rid of you. Oh, and he backs her up too, by the way. A hundred percent."

"Well, he would, wouldn't he? It's his job on the line. And her reputation, I suppose, with her father listening in. She's not that much of a rebel, she only wants to be ..."

"Well. Her word against yours—but she's got witnesses, and you haven't. It doesn't matter, either way. I still think you manipulated the whole scene. You set it up just for the sake of the row later, didn't you? Just so you could bang out of Juliet's and take David with you, it gave you the excuse you wanted ..."

"So what are you saying, that I killed my friend? I murdered him?"

165

"That's right, Rowan. That's what I'm saying."

"Why the fuck would I want to do that? He was my *friend*, I'd known him all my life, I loved him ..."

"Right. He'd become inconvenient, though, hadn't he? And there's a history here, I said I've been talking to my colleagues in Cambridge. You had another friend there, Simon Tarrant, and he was murdered too, just last month. Do you know, statistically, it's not very safe to have friends? If you don't want to be murdered? You're in most danger from your lover, but your friend comes a close second. With you, specifically, friends are top of the list. It's really not safe at all, to be a friend of Rowan Coffey. Is it?"

I gazed at him, took a slow, careful breath and said, "So I killed David because he was inconvenient. Getting in the way, I suppose, coming between me and Juliet. He'd done that all his life, but never mind, let's run with that for a minute. Why did I kill Simon?"

"Jealousy. You're used to being top dog, the smart boy, smartest of them all; but he was smarter. I don't think you liked coming second all of a sudden. I think you wanted the glittering prizes, and he was getting them. So you put him out of the way, into the river on a wet night when you could turn up soaked at a party and no one would ask questions. I can see how that would work: you'd arrange to meet him somewhere quiet, out of town. When he turned up you'd be there already, skinny-dipping. That way, when you produce the knife, you don't get blood on your clothes. That how it worked, was it, something like that ...? Nothing to say?"

No, I had nothing to say. I was too busy seeing the picture, pretty much the way he described it. Simon coming along the towpath in all his clothes, wet and worried; me pulling myself out of the water naked. Him turning his eyes aside for decency's sake, for a swimmer he was foolishly body-shy. And I'd have been counting on that, no doubt, to give me time to snatch the knife up and get close. And then him into the river and my using the towel I would surely have thought to take, rubbing myself roughly clean and approximately dry. The towel would go into the river too, surely; I'd pull my clothes on and head off to the party ...

"Then you came home for a rest, a year out, and found that things were changing here too, David was getting more difficult as he got older. You didn't like that, so you thought you'd do the same to him. It had worked before, so why not?"

"Okay. I took him for a walk in the woods, and I killed him. Hid his body, I suppose, came back all messy—and told Juliet about these monsters I'd seen, tearing him apart. You don't think maybe I'd have come up with something a bit more credible, if I'm so smart?"

"Oh, you're smart, Rowan. I haven't forgotten that. Let me tell you what the doctor says. He's done his tests, and he says you've been taking LSD. Recently, and regularly. Not that night, but that doesn't matter. He thinks you had a flashback. That can happen, he says, it's quite common: the drug nestles down in your system somewhere, then comes back and kicks you unexpectedly. Gives you hallucinations. You could see monsters, he says, no trouble at all. In the dark, in a storm, in a panic—perfect conditions for it, he says. It wouldn't be true, but you'd believe it. Does that sound reasonable to you?"

I shrugged slowly, cautiously. "I don't know how to respond to it. I'm sure your doctor's a very clever man; and yes, I take LSD sometimes. And yes, I've heard horror-stories about flashbacks, of course I have, who hasn't? I never had one, though. All I can tell you is what I saw. It didn't feel like any trip to me. You can interpret it how you like, but David's still missing, he's *gone*. Acid doesn't do that."

"Indeed it doesn't. My clever doctor thinks we're dealing with two different incidents here. He thinks David got lost in the dark and had an accident, fell into a sink-hole perhaps and we'll find him eventually; and he thinks you had a flashback brought on by your own anxiety and your mother's stories and the conditions of the night. He thinks they're independent events. I don't. I never did like coincidence, it makes me suspicious; and we're looking at two separate coincidences here, what with Simon Tarrant's death too. I think you're playing games with us, Rowan, I think you depended on that doctor's report. I think you budgeted for it. Maybe you had this planned, even, maybe that's why you took the acid a few days ago, to be prepared. So that you could feed us an incredible story, if you decided to go through with this. The same way you carefully had no alibi for the night of Simon's death. The harder an alibi is, the easier it is to break, if it's not true. That's why you're so vague about where you were that night, aren't I right?"

"No. I was just wandering, that's all ..."

"Just wandering in the rain, while your friend was killed. Like you were just wandering in your mind last night, while your other friend was killed. You knew we'd test you for drugs, and you'd come up positive. That doctor may be a clever man, Rowan, but you're cleverer—or you think you are."

"You don't know that David's dead. He could be out there, hurt, and I could help you find him, if you didn't keep wasting my time like this ..."

"Oh, I think we both know David's dead. There's only one thing I agree with the doctor about, and that's that we'll find him. Eventually. It's hard to hide a body. Simon turned up, in the river; and David will turn up in the wood. We've got men, we've got dogs, we've got volunteers; and I've got limitless patience. We'll find him, wherever you put him. Maybe not in the woods at all, maybe that's a red herring. There are people camping in the woods, not far from Juliet's place, did you know? We've talked to them, and they didn't see you that night. Didn't hear you either, though you say you were shouting your head off and running all over. Maybe you put him somewhere else, did you? In the tarn, say? I'm having that dredged in the morning. Or up on the fell somewhere, perhaps—down one of those old mine-workings, say? You'd know all about them. We'll search them all, if we need to. And we will find him. With or without your help."

"You won't let me help."

"Rowan," slowly, patiently, "we've got dogs out there that specialize in finding bodies, human bodies, that particular chemical cocktail that's composed of rotting people. Dead rabbits won't confuse them, nothing will. Don't ask me how they do it, I don't know; how they train them I don't want to know. But there are other dogs out there trying to find live scents, whatever's left after all this rain. David's scent they're searching for—and they're also searching for yours. Of course I won't allow you in the woods, you'd only muddy the trail. Were you counting on that? Perhaps you were, I can't see that clearly into your head. Your thought-patterns aren't normal. But the only help I want from you is that you should lead us directly to David's body, wherever you left it. If you'll do that, fine. If you won't, then keep right away, you understand me?"

"I can't take you there," I whispered. "I don't know where David's body is, I didn't leave it anywhere. I lost him. And then I found him, and then I lost him again." *Then I ran away*, but how do you say all that, with all that that implies? The language won't cover it. I tried a gesture that tried to encompass too much, and failed completely.

Drinks (5)

I could go, but not go where I wanted. He had his vicious suspicions, but no more; and he was an honest cop as cops go, unless he was paying out rope in the hope of a hanging. Maybe he was having me followed, I didn't know. Didn't much care. I had nothing to teach a shadow in secret, that I wouldn't declare face to face.

My mother's home was my home once again, except that it wasn't. I might have my bed back, but the cottage was still under alien occupation. When I had to go there, they'd have to take me in; but I didn't have to, yet. It was barely noon of a bleak dry day, and the Police Incident Unit—a Portakabin by any other name and smelling just as sweetly, stale tobacco and damp boots—was in a lay-by on the valley road, right at the heart of my devastated world. I could go anywhere, if anywhere would have me. Not the cottage, definitely not the boathouse. There was always the farm, I supposed, I could look for Malcolm or maybe Toby; chances were they wouldn't be around, though. They'd be out searching for David, and I was forbidden the woods. Not the campsite either, then. I took a moment to be glad that the police had found the campsite, though they were looking on that as evidence against me; at least Barry should have tracked down his pedophile, the man called Root. Wouldn't have run him out of the valley yet, most likely, he'd have other things on his mind just now, but at least he knew where to find the guy.

I stood at the heart of my world, and my world was closed against me. I took a breath, squared my shoulders against the wind and any watchers, and set off walking.

◆◆◆

It's a fair slog from the valley to the town. I was too chicken to go up to the boathouse even to reclaim the scrambler; I slogged it, measured out the miles with my feet. Didn't dawdle, and it still took an hour or a little more. I didn't look back; if I did have a shadow, I hope it appreciated the exercise.

I was chicken again when I got to town, took the long way around through the outskirts. My natural route was straight through the center, but that would bring me right by Juliet's mother's. Who of course was David's mother too, and I couldn't face her any more than I could her daughter. She was an old woman, she should be sitting behind closed curtains huddling with her grief, but I believed very strongly in the malignity of fate that day, and didn't dare to tempt it.

Bypass traffic on my right, rushing east and west; I made my own pedestrian bypass, rushing on my own account, hurrying to one place where I thought, I hoped I might be welcome.

When I reached the industrial estate I cut in towards the river, towards the last run of shops and little businesses along what used to be the highway before the bypass came. Rents were low now, to match the footfall; no tourist trade, no casual custom. Only specialists survived. I passed a violin-maker, a bookseller, a tailor; and reached a shopfront with boxes piled high in the window, behind a poster declaring "Interest-Free Finance Available." Above the door, a sign read *Clive's Computers*.

I ducked inside, squeezed between more stacked boxes and found Clive as ever behind his desk, scowling over sheaves of paper. For a man at what passed here as the cutting edge of information technology, he was embarrassingly primitive.

He glanced up, and his face shifted as it always did. Nothing extra, only that moment of hope followed by recognition: not a customer, just a friend.

"Rowan," he said. "Go on down. Don't talk to me, I'm frantic."

Clive was always frantic; I thought that was how he made the business work, by pouring nervous energy into every invoice, worrying his way to success. I nodded, slipped by him and down narrow steps into the cellar, hunching low to save cracking my head against the perilous ceiling. I'd bruised my scalp too often to forget.

172

Below, the bright humming fluorescent light above the long bench, where sick computers stood with their guts exposed; and sitting at the bench in his wheeled chair, looking round now to see who entered his domain was my friend Michael.

Old friend, best friend; good friend still, by the way he rolled his chair back from his work, stood up and came to greet me with a hug. No offhand or automatic gesture, that. When Michael hugged, he meant it.

"Rowan, mate. How are you?"

"Pretty crap," I said.

"Yeah, right. They haven't found anything, then?"

"Not a fucking thing. Cops think I did it."

"Oh, what? Shit, Ro …"

"Ach, I'm used to it. They thought I killed Simon, too. This one still does. He doesn't like coincidence, he says. Therefore I'm a serial killer. He'd arrest me, I think, if he had a body. Might do it anyway, see if I broke down in the cells …"

"Can he do that?"

"I don't know. I expect so. The police can do what they like, can't they? Remember the convoy. If what they did to that was legal, I guess they can stick me in a cell for a couple of nights on suspicion of murder."

Even I didn't like the way my voice was sounding, flat and dull, with no fight in it; by the look of him, Michael was seriously worried.

"Well, look, sit down, yeah? I've just got to get this finished, be twenty minutes or so …"

"As long as you like. I'll just watch, you know me."

This had been a regular gig since Michael found Clive's, four years earlier. Nothing could make him happier than twiddling with a screwdriver deep inside an electronic tangle; nothing, it seemed, could make Clive happier than having an eager-beaver kid with platinum-contact fingers running the repair side of his business. At first, he didn't even have to pay him; Michael did it for nothing, for the experience, for the fun. Then he left school, and Clive employed him; now they were partners, the only way Clive could be certain

173

of keeping him. *Clive's and Michael's Computers*, the sign should read.

Michael twiddled and I watched, and we'd been doing this also for years. He was happiest, but I was pretty happy: it was a switch-off thing for me, a chill, almost a meditation moment, a mantra to the eye simply to sit and watch while he played with his intricate Meccano.

As often as not twenty minutes would turn into an hour, as he got absorbed, as I did; but not that day. We both had too much else on our minds, in our lives. It was probably not so long, he was probably not even finished when he packed his roll of tools away and started clicking switches, turning off power, turning off lights. Certainly he hadn't put the case back on the computer-frame he'd been working inside, which was the usual sign that a job was done. Equally certainly he didn't test it, which he always did.

"Okay?"

"Okay."

I followed him up the stairs, flicking the last light off at my back as I reached the top. Michael was already bidding Clive goodbye.

"See you tomorrow, then. If anything new comes in, leave it up here, I've got no space downstairs ..."

Clive looked about him, at the maze of piled boxes that was his showroom. "No chance," he said amiably. "But I'm leaving myself in a minute. You'll probably be lucky."

Hard to credit, perhaps, but Tuesday was and is early closing, on my patch. Supermarkets ignore it and so do garages, DIY stores, a few rebels else; by and large, though, the shutters go up, the lights go out, the staff goes home. Been that way for generations, no one sees the need for change. They tend to close early on Saturdays too, and of course no one trades on a Sunday.

Michael didn't always stop when the lunchbell sounded of a Tuesday, but the option was always there, and I could usually persuade him to it. Today took no persuasion, and no discussion beyond a brief question from him as we left the shop.

"Where's my bike?"

"Up at the boathouse." *At Juliet's*, but I couldn't bear to say her

174

name, even, for fear of all that came with it, grief and guilt and loss. Loss redoubled, perhaps, if we couldn't find a way to come through this together. I couldn't go to her, that was all I knew.

We marched fifty yards along the street, to the Goat and Compasses. Née "God Encompasseth Us," according to popular rumor, but I always preferred the literal version. So did the landlord; the board above the door showed a caprid with a map and a pair of dividers, measuring out its route.

We knew our route, we'd measured it many times, pace by pace: in through the door, pause at the bar, head for the window-seat.

The Goat is a truly sad drink, the Drink that Failed. Abandoned by the town and the highway both, stranded a long walk from absolutely anywhere else, it has almost no custom left, bar Michael and me on occasional Tuesday afternoons. It can't even hang on to the teenage trade, though it tries harder than most, running Aussie soaps on the big screen and filling its fridges with alcopops. It has no beer worth drinking, nothing at all in a hand-pump, and why we ever go there is a mystery to me. It's not even so-awful-it's-great, it's just awful. Perhaps we need reminding how lucky we are to have the Agric; perhaps you have to sniff shit once in a while, to keep your everyday perfume smelling sweet.

Whatever. It's handy, it's immediate, it's there; and so, sometimes, are we.

Faced with a choice of bad drinks, we made the usual choice of Guinness served too cold and drawn too fast, given no chance to settle. Heresy, of course, but what can you do? Drink pressurized piss-poor lager, or premixed Malibu-and-blackcurrant? I don't think so ...

Once in the window, Michael propped his elbow on the ledge and turned his eye to the street outside, and I thought he was just avoiding too much contact as he said, "I've been thinking, Ro. What you saw that night, what you said—well, they reckon if you eat fly agaric too often, you get to see fairies. Elves, little people. They reckon that's where the myths all come from, shamans doing fly ..."

"I've only done it a couple of times," I said quietly. "You know, you were there." And we'd seen auras, we'd seen the visibility of air and music, but we'd seen no people but each other, and we were not little.

"Yeah, but it's hallucinations, that's the thing; and acid does the same, and you can flashback any time, and most flashbacks are bad trips from what I hear, so …"

"Michael," I sighed, "the police are way ahead of you. That's what their doctor reckons, at any rate, that I was out of my skull on resurgent lysergic. His boss disagrees with him, he thinks that's what I want 'em to think. He thinks that's why I took the stuff before, to have it there in my system for the excuse."

"It was my idea," Michael said.

"Tell them, don't tell me."

"Haven't you told them?"

"No, of course not. And don't you either, I was joking. What difference does it make? It's immaterial."

"Not to me. It's my fault, see? My idea—and if we hadn't done that starwalk, you wouldn't have flashbacked, and then you wouldn't have lost David …"

Actually, if we hadn't gone for Michael's starwalk that night and so upset David, I wouldn't have thought of taking him for another when I wanted to upset his sister, and he would never have been in danger of being lost. But that was a line of thought I didn't want Michael to follow. No sense feeding a foolish conscience. I just said, "Bollocks. I've got five years' acid stacked up somewhere, ready for its big comeback. What's one more dose, on top of that? Anyway, that assumes that the doctor's right."

"Isn't he?"

"Christ, Michael, I don't know. It's an explanation; that doesn't mean it's the truth. I don't believe in weird creatures haunting the wood—but my mum does." My mum used to, at least; I thought she was having doubts, now that I'd reported back on seeing them. Evidence spoiled her faith, she only liked a fight against the odds. "One of us has to be wrong. Could be me. All I know is what I saw; and I did see them, I really did …"

"Sure. But what you see isn't necessarily what's happening, you know that."

Of course, I knew that. Objectively, scientifically and experientially, I knew it. And I still chose to believe in what I saw: don't we all?

"Drink up, Ro. I can see Clive locking up."

"So?"

"So I'm taking you back in. Something I want to show you, in private."

That was unusual; we were pretty much private anyway, down in his basement. Clive was a man of bulk who found the stairs difficult, whose rare arrivals below were always preannounced by a deal of huffing and groaning. Michael wouldn't talk; he just shook his head to my questions, watched the street until he'd seen Clive drive away, then told me to drink up and follow. Another day, I thought, any other day he'd have been grinning to add a tease to the mystery. This wasn't a good time for grins, which took the gilt off his gingerbread a little, but whatever his secret was, he was still fizzing with it.

On the way out, he stopped at the bar to buy a four-pack of imitation Pils. We were in for a session, seemingly.

Back into the shop, turning on lights, turning off the alarm; he locked the door behind us, then led me downstairs. More switches, more lights and the power to his bench, one computer humming into life. This one was decently dressed in its case still, no innards exposed.

"Pull up a chair," he said, "crack open a couple of those cans, and watch this."

His fingers played with the keyboard, with the mouse; menus scrolled down the screen, and were followed by images.

Half a dozen images, photographs, one after another. He gave me a couple of seconds to look at each, before he called up the next. That was enough, too much; six of them was way too much. He'd shown me similar stuff before, but that was back when we were kids, eager to be grossed out by the adult world, and none of it had been as bad as this.

"Well?" he said.

"So you've got one sick customer. So what?"

"So the customer's name is Sir Julian Ricks, MP. The man who wants to turn our valley into a lake."

"Jesus Christ …"

The pictures weren't just porn, they were kiddie-porn, little naked girls having disgusting, dangerous things done to them by big naked men.

"He'd picked up a virus off the Net," Michael said. "People just don't listen, when we tell them they have to keep their protection updated. I cleaned up the virus, no trouble; it was just playing games on his monitor, it hadn't touched the files. I had to look at a few, though, just to check; and maybe I looked at a few more than I needed to. Well, you would, wouldn't you?"

Well, Michael would. Michael would read somebody's diary, if they'd left it lying around.

"I found this stuff hidden under a password," he went on. "Didn't take long to crack that, it was just a challenge; but now I don't know what to do …"

"Yes, you do," I said.

"Well, maybe—but I don't want to. I shouldn't have been nosing …"`

"But you were," I said, "and you did find it. You can't change that. I'm sorry, Michael, but you've got to call the cops on this one."

He said nothing, just fiddled with the mouse, closing down the files.

"Even if he was nobody," I said determinedly, "just a pervert, you'd have to tell. People who like that sort of shit, they don't just look at pictures. Christ, you've got a kid sister, Michael …"

"I know. I keep thinking about her."

"So do it, okay? This bastard's an MP, for God's sake, he makes the laws that send pedophiles down. He's a fucking hypocrite, you've got to blow the whistle." And then, when I still got no reaction, "Look, call Barry Carter. This isn't exactly his jurisdiction, but he's a mate, he'll make it easier for you …" And Barry had pedophiles on his mind already; I knew how he'd react.

"Stay with me?" Michael said.

"I can't. I'm *persona non grata* at the moment, it'll only muddy things up if I'm here. Besides, I know Ricks' daughter," *in the biblical sense*, "and that'd cloud the issue too. But I'll stay a while, there's no point phoning Barry just now anyway. He won't be there." He'd be out in the woods, where I was not allowed to go, doing what I was not allowed to do, looking for my friend.

I helped Michael as much as I could, mostly by not drinking much so that he got the benefit of three cans out of four. I talked him through it all again, and then again; and I did stay while he made the phone call, and only left after he'd got hold of Barry and persuaded him to come, persuaded him that it really was more important than supper and bed for an exhausted constable.

"Don't mention me, okay?" I said, on my way out. "I'm sorry, but this has to be your baby."

"Yeah, all right. I see that. I'll do it, Ro, I will. Too late to pull out now, anyway. That's what I wanted you for, to get me started. Thanks …"

I left him at the doorway, looking tense and pale and determined through the glass.

Ill-Met by Torchlight

Time was, when there was a decent bus service all along the valley road. That's how we survived our childhood, how we survived our teenage.

Not any more. Woe betide the new kids: no escape but Shanks' pony, pedal-power or their parents' cars. The best they could get from public transport was the coast-to-coast lo-liner that stopped at the Agric a couple of times each way, each day. You could get to town and back, so long as you could shape your life to fit. Basically, you had to spend all day there, or else all night.

I'd walked in, but I was lucky; I could bus back, the time just fell right. I almost begrudged the fare, I'd covered the ground so easily at lunchtime. But I'd been storming then, riding on emotion, feeling nothing under my feet. Right now I was emotional again and the road beckoned; I didn't trust it, though, not to bite after a mile or two, after the chance of a ride had passed me by. My legs must be tired, though I couldn't feel it, and the night was rising at my back.

I caught the bus.

Stepping off at the Agric was like stepping into a world I didn't recognize. I hated that. No thought of stopping for a pint or two; my valley had been invaded. The car park was full of vans with dishes on their roofs, full of TV journalists doing reports to camera. The search for David was big news; all the networks were there.

The road too was lined with people, volunteers waiting for the bus in the other direction to take them home. No searching in the dark. I ducked my head, trying for once in my life to hide my height as I positively scuttled out of sight. I couldn't have borne it if one of those cameras had spotted me. David's companion on that fateful walk: they'd have loved to get me cornered, to shove their mikes under my nose and ask me all the questions I couldn't answer.

Safe away—or at least some distance down the road—I straightened my back, stiffened my pride and wondered quite where I was heading now. The sky was darkening, this close to winter's heart, but it was early yet. I was running out of options, though, even here where I so much belonged, I was harried where I should find rest and shelter. I couldn't go to Juliet; my other friends were doubtful. I could go to the cottage, to be sure, spend a long evening with my mother and Andrew and his kids. I would do that, I would go there in the end, I had no choice about it—but I could at least shorten that long time, if I spent some time out here in the valley on my own.

And if I stepped into the wood, where the trees crowded down to the roadside on my left, then at least I'd meet no late volunteers straggling to the pub, no police off duty at last after a fruitless day of searching, no journalist still sniffing for a story.

Technically I was forbidden the wood, the whole wood and the fells that rose above it; but this part of the wood, this southern stretch was where they'd searched already. Hence no barriers to bar me, no tape stretched from tree to tree, no watching officers.

What they had not found already, they never would find now. No harm then in my tainted presence, my corrupting scent. The dogs must have sniffed me out before this, as much of me as there was to sniff after days of rain, and no good had it done them. That I could guarantee.

So I broke their order and my oath. I stepped illicitly from the road's shadow to the dark beneath the trees, and shivered as I did so. Softness underfoot, smells of damp and rot, the chill breath of the wind and nothing, nothing I could see: all this was memory unfurled, unfolding instantly to engulf me in the last place I would have chosen to be.

But I had no choices now, I'd been denied them. I stood still, there in the wood's margin, and closed my eyes against even the filtered passage of light as a car rushed past at my back. Opened them to the dark again and waited, until it was not so dark after all: until there were degrees of darkness, black overlaid on black, some hints of gray above and all about me.

No colors now, even after my eyes adapted, when I could see again. No green and flowing light tonight, no. Nothing moved at all.

Neither did I move, for a while. Frankly, I was scared. I'd known this wood, almost each individual tree within it, all my life; all my life I had known my mother's stories, which had always seemed to me to be personally and explicitly about this valley, this wood, these trees; for the first time in my life I was scared now, I thought the wood was cursed.

But you can only stand still for so long, when there's only yourself to watch you. When you're not performing for others, playing hero or coward or whatever it might happen to be tonight.

I walked into the wood, and not for the first time changed my life by doing it. My mother will tell you that places have atmosphere, the power to enchant, midsummer nights' dreamstuff, what you will. This was winter's margin, and I believe in maths over magic, every time; but perhaps trees are the higher mathematics after all. Perhaps they spend their centuries counting and dividing on their countless dividing limblets: every twig a digit, more ways than one. And perhaps the consequence, the result of all those sums is one misty moment when the world shifts and blurs, and what comes into focus after may not be quite the same world after all.

All I know for certain is that I was afraid that night, where I had never been afraid before; and that I had reason to be afraid, more than memory. There was no acid flashback tripping me, tripping me up, and I saw no pretty lights, no terrors; but I sensed a watchful, patient presence somewhere in the wood. I knew I was being hunted. I jumped at sudden noises; it took a strong and constant effort not to look behind me, not to stare and stare and make out figures that tracked my progress on either side of me.

Trying to pretend—to the night, to that presumptive witness, to myself—that I was going nowhere special, I wove an indirect route by narrow paths, through thorns and ferns and over babbling brooks until at last I came to somewhere that was very special indeed, at least to me.

Here an old oak overhung a glade, broad enough to seem bright-lit by starlight after the encroaching shadows of the wood. If there were magic in the valley, this was the heart and focus of it all, where secrets lay; there were paths that led here more straightly than I had come, but they didn't seem to be of human making. In the stillness, I could believe that I was the first man ever to stand in this place, though I knew too well—who better?—how false that was.

Stand I did, and in my sorrow and confusion, in that privacy I wept for what I had lost, what I might never find again.

And was still standing—though quietly now, wet-faced and weary, close to despair—when I saw a light among the trees. A light that moved, that jerked and stretched, that was a bright point or a pale bar and then a point again, seeking, searching ...

Voices too, hissed whisperings quite meaningless to me but voices nonetheless; there were words in what was said, although I could not hear them.

I might have run, I might have slid away to hide in undergrowth; I might have stood to face whatever came, bold and upfront and *here I am, if it's me you're looking for.*

I did none of those things. Other choices I had, one easy and safe; that the one I took.

The light came first into the clearing, proclaiming like a herald, peering like a spy. Behind the light the voices, and behind those they came themselves, in their bodies, indistinct shadows but I knew them anyway. Their voices made them clear.

"Somewhere round here," Toby said, shining his torch all about him, ruining my nightsight and their own. "I don't know where, exactly, I always lost him before he got this far; but it was this direction, definitely."

184

"You don't know where," said Juliet, sounding infinitely dull, not my sharp love at all, "and you don't know what it was, either?"

"No. I'm sorry, Juliet."

"Me neither," Malcolm added. "Just some big secret that he had, that he wouldn't share with us."

Toby stabbed the torch's beam left and right and down to the ground at his feet, every direction but up.

"Not such a great secret," I said softly, barely loud enough for them to hear, not to startle them too much. "Just a tree that I love."

And I swung down from the branches of that ancient oak, and dropped to earth in front of them; and they startled anyway, of course they did. Juliet gasped; I thought she bit her lip, I thought she must be tasting blood, only to stop herself screaming.

I could have wept again, I could have wished myself still silent in the tree above, not to have caused her that much pain and shock; but I did neither. I only stood there and tried to see her face, and could not because Toby was shining his torch right in my eyes now, blinding me completely.

"Toby, do you mind?" I said mildly, shielding my face.

"Oh—sorry, Ro ..."

He turned his light away, leaving me with glowing after-images in sickly colors that were, no, nothing like an acid trip, only a fierce frustration. I blinked and rubbed my eyes, which hardly helped, and had to stand gazing at my feet for a minute before at last my dazzled pupils had dilated enough to show me something of Juliet's expression.

Which was schooled, neutral, showing me nothing except her overwhelming exhaustion. What she saw of me, I couldn't venture to say.

We neither of us spoke. Nor did the other two.

In the end I had to; we'd have stood there all night else, broken statues in a glade, heedless of the world's turning. But I couldn't say anything that mattered. *Not with witnesses*, I told myself, trying to appease my conscience; *not with her as a witness* would have been closer to the truth. Some of the things I wanted to say to her, I couldn't have borne for her to hear.

"You should go home," I said. "You need to sleep."

"Yes." That wasn't her, it was Malcolm. "I've been telling her that, but she won't …"

"I'll go home," she said, and this time her voice was like a drawn string, dreadfully tight and close to snapping. "I'll go now," only she stood there and didn't move, just stared about her at the trees that closed off the clearing, unless it was the walls of the night that she saw.

"You guys want to take her?" I suggested, with just a hint of acid.

"Yes." Malcolm again. "Yes, sure. Come on, it's, uh, this way …"

Surprisingly, it was.

"Take the torch," Toby called after him, turning him, bringing him back.

"You not coming?"

"No. I'll stay with Ro."

I don't need you, Toby—but nor did Juliet with Malcolm to guide and guard her, reliable and sure; and I didn't need to be alone any longer, either. Perhaps Toby was right and I was wrong, perhaps I did now need not to be alone. I couldn't tell. All I knew was that I made no protest, that I stood with my friend at my side and watched as my friend and my lover left me. My ex-lover, perhaps, but still the woman I loved past reason.

"So what was it you were looking for, Tobe? Out here, in the dark, just the three of you?"

"Well, not you. Christ, you scared me shitless, coming down like that …"

"Not me, no," and never mind the gall of it, that Juliet was so actively not looking for me. "So what, then?"

"Something, anything. Somewhere you might have brought David one time, that he might have found his way to on his own. We knew you had a place out here, that you came to …"

"Somewhere secret, right. You said that. You said you followed me …"

"And lost you. I always thought you knew, I thought it was a game we played. I wasn't looking for a tree, though. I thought it'd be a cave, maybe, an old mine-opening, something like that. Some-

186

thing to hide up in, that you didn't want to share. Not a tree. There's millions of trees, what's so special about this one?"

"Couldn't tell you. This was the one I climbed one time, when I wanted a think; it's the one I always came back to, after. That's all. I never had a special hiding-place, why would I? Are we going home now, or what?"

"I guess, yeah. Come on. So what were you doing here tonight, then?"

"Having a think. Obviously." And then, with a small, small gesture of my hands, "Trying to make what I saw match up with what must really have happened. Maybe I did see something dreadful happen, to David; and the acid kicked back at me then, by chance or what you will, or maybe I grabbed at it like a defense, like some people grab at amnesia, you know? Maybe I'm blocking a true memory of what I saw. Sometimes it helps to go up high," with a backward jerk of my head towards that convenient oak.

"Not tonight, though?"

"No. Not tonight. Still can't get a grip on anything. Christ, my head's a mess, Tobe. And there's only one person I can really talk to about that stuff and I can't talk to her either, and I don't know what to do about that …"

"Give her time, Ro. That's all you can do."

"What, and let her harden up the way she is, the way we both are, torn apart? We need grafting, mending, not leaving alone. Before the scar tissue grows over the wound, or we'll never grow whole again."

"I dunno," and I could hear him frowning as Juliet would have frowned when she was our English teacher, at such a wrenched and overextended metaphor; but Toby was a gardener, I thought he'd understand. I thought probably it was the problem he was frowning over. "You can't expect—"

"I don't expect," I interrupted harshly. "I'm not that stupid. This was the first time we've seen each other in three days, and she couldn't even speak to me, didn't you notice? That's what I expect. She avoids me because there's too much hurt and doubt and grief that lies between us. But if we let this run, then it'll just become habit, we'll avoid each other because it's easier that way, we may go on hurting but neither of us bleeds. And then I expect I'll go back to college, she'll get another job or at least another house, and no more Rowan and Juliet. That's what anyone sensible would expect to come out of this. But I don't want to let it, and I don't know how to prevent it."

"I could talk to her …"

"No. Thanks, Toby, but I'd never expect that. I wouldn't ask it. Go-betweens just end up getting caught in the crossfire. Bleeding on both sides, like as not. You let us be. We'll sort it out, or else we won't. One thing at a time, and Juliet's lost David. You help her deal with that, if you can, and don't you even mention me."

And so through the wood—with no watchfulness now, on its side or my own, only walking side by side with my disturbed, concerned and doubtful friend—and so out onto the road where no traffic was running now, as though the police had sealed off the entire valley for the night. Not so, but people I thought must have sealed it in their heads. They might come to gawp in daylight; by night, they'd keep away.

Not me. It was valley nights I'd missed the most in Cambridge, it was the dark containing promise of the place I loved the best; even now I felt sheltered and protected, just to be here.

We came to the lane and climbed it side by side, quiet now, thinking our own thoughts. At the path to my mother's cottage, he said goodnight and left me; I stood and watched him go on up, a shadow in starlight headed for the distant gleam from the windows of his parents' bungalow.

A turn in the lane took him out of my sight. I turned then, towards the dark bulk of the cottage. One thin line of light showed between drawn curtains; with my eyes fixed on that, I could see nothing else. Nor did I hear anything until a single gasp of breath warned me, just a moment before a thin figure launched itself from the wooden fence on my left and clung monkey-like to my back.

I managed not to yell, nor to throw it off. Just.

A girl's shriek of laughter, from my right; I turned my head, and grinned into glittering eyes.

188

"Hullo, Icarus. Flying tonight?"

Antony grinned back; I gripped his legs and shrugged my shoulders, hitching him a little higher, shifting him into a position more comfortable for us both. His sister rose from where she'd been crouched below the bird-table.

"Shouldn't you two be in bed?" I suggested, playing the good grown-up.

"We can't," Emma said. "Alice and Andrew are talking, in that room. They told us to go away."

"They told us to go up to your room," Antony elaborated, inveterately more honest or else more pleased with himself, with the pair of them and their mini-adventure. "We played cards on the bed, but she kept winning. She always wins."

"Girls always do," I told him, confidingly. "That's one of the rules. So how did you end up out here?"

"Just under your window, there's a roof you can slide down …"

I knew it well: the original lean-to, that used to house the outside toilet before we got civilized. These days, my mother kept her gardening tools in it. Throughout my childhood and teenage, she had often wondered aloud and loudly just why it was that the tiles on that little slope of roof so often cracked or broke away from their moorings. She never did anything to close that route to me, though, nor gave any sign that she was thinking of it; I think we both felt that regardless of house rules or lack of them, there were times when it was simply a boy's duty to slip out of a night without his mother's knowing. Some things are only fun if they're hidden or illicit. Or illegal.

In gratitude, I'd learned simple roofing as I'd learned stone-walling also, monkey see and monkey do; since I was fourteen I'd kept the whole cottage watertight, and would do for so long as my mother lived in it. I had the skill, so I had the duty. Also I owed her more, far more than that. Also it added to my own comfort and convenience; also, I enjoyed it. Any one of those reasons would have been enough, and I had them all.

"Uh-huh. And you weren't scared, out here in the dark on your own, with no one knowing what you were up to? Nah, not you, of course you weren't scared …"

"Only a bit," Emma confessed. "That's why we didn't go far. We wouldn't go in the woods now, whatever you say …"

"I say you're very sensible, sweets. I wouldn't go in the woods now, either. Not if I was you. How were you planning to get back indoors without anyone seeing, had you thought that far? It's quite a climb, up onto that roof …"

"We were going to build a pile of logs, and stand on it."

"Very smart." Though it would have left the evidence standing behind them, which was not so smart; deniability is king, in any criminal enterprise.

Not that they needed it now. I was there; and two may be a partnership, but three is definitely a conspiracy. They didn't want to stay outside anyway, with me turned up. I was something new tonight, and hence better company even than each other. Also, I was conveniently tall and willing. I boosted them lightly back onto the roof of the lean-to, and stayed until I'd seen them through the window; then I wandered casually in at the door. If Mum and Andrew were talking secrets, they'd likely stop at my arrival. It was likely the secrets were about me, though not my own.

One thing for sure, they hadn't been canoodling; though my mother rather wanted me, I thought, to think they had. At any rate, she sprang up off the sofa as I made my entrance, leaving Andrew sitting; she said, "Rowan! Have you eaten? I wasn't sure when you'd be coming back, so we didn't wait. I saved you some, though …"

"Thanks, Mum."

She positively bustled into the kitchen, and she's not the bustling type. I followed more slowly, and cut myself a plank or two of her homemade bread while I watched her ladle out a bowlful of something rich and dark and aromatic, brewed no doubt of vegetables and healthful mud.

"What's up, Mum?"

"I worry about you," she said. Something to be thankful for, at least she was direct. She wouldn't hedge, I didn't have to dig.

"Yeah. I worry about me too, sometimes."

"Have you talked to Juliet?"

"No. I can't. How could I?"

"Did I ever tell you the tale of the rat and her litter? She was a

190

first-time mother, she had post-natal depression, one morning she ate one of her young. And then she didn't know how to tell her mate, which made her anxious and more depressed; and so she ate another. And so on. And he never noticed, until there were none remaining."

That was it. I never got the full-on storytelling, not for my own use; only the plot. She left me alone, to eat in the kitchen and work out the moral on my fingers. All my life she'd been doing that, I was pretty good at it by now. I could read what was plainly written between the lines, and I could read also what lay behind that message, which perhaps she would rather have kept hidden. My mother was concerned about me, of course she was, my comfort and happiness meant a lot to her; but her own comfort and happiness were important also, and they were much impeded by my presence here. There really wasn't room for me in her life now, not physically, not in the cottage. She wanted me gone, back with Juliet, in the valley but not in her hair. Juliet and I were a double star, a fixity, safe and untroubling; she wanted that surety back, and all the conveniences it brought with it.

And so did I, as with all my sureties that seemed so shifty suddenly; and oh God, I wished I could help my mother with her problem, I really wished I could.

PLACES OF SAFETY

i

They were six and eight, and too wise to play in the woods where monsters lurked; but theirs was only a little wisdom, and they thought it was enough, and they were wrong.

They knew the night could bring friends and laughter, gathered round a roaring fire or coming unexpectedly along a lane; they thought they could depend on that, they thought it would always be so.

Above all they thought that home was a place of safety, they thought it had to be. They thought that was what home meant.

Now, too late, they were learning otherwise. Now they were at home, and it was terrible. Now they lay together in the darkness, keeping each other cold, shuddering with pain and shock. Naked they were, their small bodies sticky with blood, their faces sticky with dried tears but they were long past crying now. Tightly gagged and cruelly bound, it was hard for them even to breathe; what little air they caught could do them little good, heavy with the stink of themselves in their terror and sharp with the smell of something else.

Nothing they could do but lie and wait, helpless and hopeless: lie in the absolute blackness that engulfed them, listen to the thunder of the rain and wait for a fierce, brutal light that was coming slowly, slowly.

ii

She doesn't often get visitors out at the boathouse, and certainly not unexpected ones; it's not a place you happen to be passing. If people are coming that far, ordinarily they call first.

Or they used to. Since the night when Rowan went out with David and came back alone—the last time Rowan came, perhaps the last time Rowan ever would come, but she doesn't want to, she can't let herself think about that—it's been different. The police have come and gone and come again since then, always unannounced; the press came unannounced and unwelcome and stayed for days, lurking in cars and vans around the tarn, have only recently given up and gone away in search of other stories; and now that everyone it seems has given up, now that the searching is over, still she isn't left alone. She doesn't know how to feel about that. Friends and colleagues keep dropping in of an evening, checking up on her, reassuring themselves. She thinks they might even have some kind of informal rota; certainly their visits never clash.

Tonight it's Maria's turn. School secretary for twenty years, a cheerful soul who's been mother confessor to staff and pupils both and could gossip for England normally, she's abnormally subdued in the face of Juliet's smothering despair. She's come late, perhaps hoping to be defeated by drawn curtains and darkness, but she's had no luck in that. Juliet doesn't sleep, these nights. It's raining buckets outside, the surface of the tarn is black and choppy in the light that falls from the wide window, but it's not the hammering of wind and water on tile and glass and wooden walls that's hammering both women into silence.

Maria sits uptight and edgy, with her hands wrapped around a cooling mug of coffee that she seems to have forgotten how to drink. Her gaze flicks across Juliet and goes away, flicks back and goes the other way. Fixes on the window where the rain streams down like an extra liquid layer of glass—and then fixes on something beyond the glass, something that stands tall and true and broken on the bank of the tarn.

"Juliet …"

"Yes?"

"Is that Rowan Coffey out there?"

Now, at last, there is movement against the stillness of that room. Juliet's on her feet, half against her own will, staring and staring. She doesn't say *Yes, that's Rowan Coffey*, but she doesn't need to. It wasn't really a question; Maria knows. Maria knows or knew them all, Rowan and David and every friend they shared.

"I'll leave you alone," she says, not meaning *alone* in any sense that Juliet knew it a minute ago. "If you want to go to him."

Juliet still doesn't know what she wants; but he's come to her, she knows that much. He's come almost to her, and faltered just a moment short. Whatever happens, wherever this leads, she can't leave him out there in the rain.

And so Maria leaves with no more farewell than that, taking silence as consent; she dashes to her car and drives away.

It's still a long time, a long and agonized time before Juliet goes to her door, goes out into the storm, goes to him—

She came to me.

I'm sorry, I can't pretend any longer, not about this. A storyteller should choose one voice and keep to it, I learned that from my mother; but I've been lying to you too long, and this at least demands the truth. I don't know what Maria did or said, or how Juliet really felt. That was all guesswork, I was making it up. Telling stories. Not playing games, I wouldn't do that, there was a purpose to it; but I wasn't there, in the room or in anyone's head bar my own. Obviously, that's been true all along. I've made up quite a lot of what I've told you. Call it guesswork, call it lies; you can make your own choices. That's your responsibility, your duty, as my auditor. It doesn't matter, anyway.

She came to me, and that is ultimately all that matters, all that this whole sad tale is about. Juliet came to me, and stood before me, and the rain washed down on us both and washed nothing away, as it could not. And for a while neither one of us could speak, but it was on me to do that first, it had to be; and so I forced the words out, one by one.

"Juliet, it's happened again. The kids—the kids have gone, and we can't find them. And I couldn't search any more, I couldn't bear it. I need ... No, I don't know what I need. No, that's not true either. I needed you. I left Mum and Andrew searching, but ..."

But I didn't know if I deserved her, or could have her; and so had come regardless, and had failed just a few meters short of her door.

She came to me and took me in, where I couldn't have gone without that express help: where I couldn't go, indeed, until she laid a hand on my arm to draw me forward. I couldn't move at all until she touched me. It was only a gesture, but I had to have it; and she, I think she had to make it.

And she did, and so we went inside. I stood there, soaking, dripping on her floor; she fetched me a towel. I took that from her and rubbed it vaguely through my hair and over my clothes; she made no move to help me.

"Tell me," she said, just that, no more help now.

That was right too, this was her need and my turn to meet it.

I told her my tale bluntly, almost crudely, no disguise. Harsh words, for a harsh night that was dreadful to us both.

"We went to bed early, all of us, we were all tired; but I couldn't sleep. I got up to make myself a drink, and when I went downstairs, the kids weren't there. They've been sleeping in the living room, but they'd just gone. The window was open, the rain was just starting. I thought they'd be out in the garden, sheltering under a tree or something, being wicked. Being kids. So I went out to fetch them in quietly, not to worry their dad; but I couldn't find them. I couldn't find them anywhere. I had to fetch Mum and Andrew in the end, and we all went out to search. We took torches and we yelled their names, but there wasn't any answer. I came through the woods to where those people from the Ride are camping, and I routed them out to help, but none of us could find any sign. In the end I just couldn't stand it—so I came back, I came here. I'm sorry ..."

She nodded, understanding just how very much I was sorry, that I had to come to her of all people, with such news as this.

"Are they still looking?"

"Yes. I guess. They must be ..."

Of course. What else could they do?

"Are you fit to go back?"

"If you come with me. Not alone."

For a moment she only stood and looked at me, and I felt the tremendous balance of that moment, how everything could pivot on a word; but she said no word, she only turned and fetched a jacket, two jackets from the lobby. One of them was mine.

She drove me back, and we ran and searched and flashed lights until we found others running, searching, flashing lights of their own. I found Scar, and found a question in my head, in my nervousness, on my tongue before I could think better of it:

"Scar," I said, "is Root around, is he out here looking, have you seen him?"

"No," she said. "I haven't seen Root all night."

For a moment I felt nothing but relief until I stopped to think about it. Then I ran again, searched again, looked for my mother and found her.

"Mum," I said, "I think you need to call the police. Right now, don't leave it till the morning."

The police as a body didn't come, but Barry Carter did. Eyeing me oddly, but I must have looked odd: soaked again and frantic, my eyes ever searching for a shifting shadow in the dark that might have been a wayward stray returning. I knew what I looked like, I stood among a group of us and we all looked just the same. Desperate, defeated, drenched.

Barry hadn't bothered with uniform, and I loved him for it, though his hasty jacket-and-jeans—already sodden from the ride here on his bike—might get him into trouble with his superiors when they turned up. "In a couple of hours," he said, answering someone's question, I hadn't heard whose and didn't care. Might have been my own. "No point turning everyone out in this light, in this weather. They're organizing now, they'll bring a fresh new shift up ..."

And the clouds would clear, no doubt, and the sun would rise to show the dazzle on their boots; and two little angels would come running in white from the trees' shadow, clean and bright and shining with their haloes chiming softly …

"Dogs aren't much use in the rain," Barry said, definitely talking to someone else this time, "and coppers are worse in the dark. Honest, love, it's better to wait. Won't make any difference, like as not."

He thinks they're dead already, I realized; but then, who among us would not? And on what grounds? I decided not to mention Root. I was surely not the only one who could make connections, but lucky those who could not.

I'd thought Barry would marshal us into searching in some more organized way, but no: he marshaled us all into the cottage instead, and set us about making tea and changing, getting dry. "No point losing anyone else now, or breaking a leg in the mud," he said, though I thought he meant *you've all mucked up the evidence enough already, broken the scent and lost the trail and churned up any footprints we'd have found; too late to be cautious, but let's not make it worse, eh?*

So that's where we were, where we all were, in the cottage with the curtains drawn back and all the lights burning, to make a beacon for lost souls against the darkness. I was by the window with Malcolm and Toby, who must have been fetched out while I was fetching Juliet, unless they'd fetched themselves; and we were all three of us gazing blankly out through our own ghosts, our reflections in the glass that looked about as solid as we felt, when we all three of us seemed to see it at the same time, something out there in the real, a beacon far brighter than the cottage could ever be.

It was Toby, sharp little Toby who put a name to it.

"Fire …" he whispered once, and then said it louder, shouted almost. "Fire! Up at the farm there, see it …?"

Oh, we saw it. Nobody believed it until they'd seen it too, pushing us out of the way for a better view, this was not a night for fire; but we all streamed out and found that the rain had ebbed to a drizzle, as if deliberately to give the fire better hold.

We ran up the lane in a pack, in another kind of panic; and no, it was not the farm that was burning, nor anything that belonged to the farm.

It was the Castle, Andrew's abandoned home, ferociously aflame where it had stood locked up and rusting so quietly on the verge all this time. The heat was incredible; no amount of rain could have put that fire out. The drizzle surely wasn't getting anywhere near it.

Neither were we. We huddled oddly, uncomfortably close, although there was all the width of the lane to take us; something so primeval raised an equally primeval response, herd instinct to the fore.

Barry took one, two paces closer, and the heat seemed to make a shimmer around his silhouette. He could only bear it for a second; then he turned, and I swear his face was glowing like dull coals for the brief moment I could see it, before he pushed blindly past and ran back down the lane.

Fire brigade, I thought, and, *clever Barry*. Slow me, rather; but it was hard to think fast, hard to think at all under the impact of those leaping flames. Twenty feet high they must be climbing, and carrying with them the ashes of everything that was or had been Andrew's. I could see the steel skeleton of the furniture van showing now, where the skin had entirely burned away. Following that thought with something like it, I turned my head to find him.

And found him stepped a little to the side, a little ahead of the rest of us, with my mother standing quiet in his fire-shadow. Lit red in profile, his face had a dreadful cast to it; I thought I could see his own skeleton also, or his soul's skeleton perhaps, where his skin had been flayed away.

The others watched the fire, everyone watched the fire bar my mother and me. Both of us, we watched Andrew watch the fire.

Took an age before the fire engine came. We'd been joined by Malcolm's dad and Toby's, but they were as helpless as the rest of us, just trapped as we all were in the vicious glare of destruction.

It was diesel fueling that fire, however much Andrew had left sitting in his tanks, that no one had thought to drain off. There were chemical extinguishers to hand now, both men had come up laden; but those were child's toys against this inferno, and in any case we had no hope of getting close enough to use them. I heard Barry say that several times, each time with more force against Mr. Gardale's natural protests.

At least the fire threatened nothing but what it contained already, there were no outbuildings close enough to catch. Sparks rose and flew on the wind, but the persistent drizzle and the wet ground were enough to douse them. Best just to let it burn, and wait for the professionals.

That we did, and at last the professionals came, grinding in low slow gear up the hill. We scattered to the sides to allow the engine past; a police car came up behind it and we let ourselves be chivvied to a greater, safer distance before we formed into our pack again, our little pack with its pair of strays, Andrew and my mother.

The police from the car moved among us, quietly taking names, asking the obvious questions. I don't know who told them first about the children; Barry, most likely. Andrew was saying nothing, only standing, staring at a light that slowly died.

Dawn came sullenly, a red glow in the sky to substitute for what was red no longer, the smoking foam-clad wreck of the Castle; and we were all still there, still watching.

At last I saw a man, two men in breathing-masks and heavy protective gear approach the ruin of the van. There was no floor now for them to walk on, nor walls nor roof to hide their progress; they ducked under twisted metal spars and gazed about them, made signs to their colleagues that I could read even from here, *can't see anything, nothing left to see …*

Andrew moved, then. He shrugged off my mother's restraining hand and walked forward, his shoulders hunching, like a man bearing a weight that should be too great to bear. He spoke to the policeman who intercepted him; that policeman spoke to one of the firemen, who climbed up into the engine.

They must have had radio contact with the men in the masks. I watched them stoop, to search among the buckled axles and the split and fallen tanks; I saw them find some kind of metal box, the size of a filing cabinet it looked.

I saw them force it open with their axes, and then I saw them straighten, turn, step away.

News spreads, sometimes faster than the words that carry it. Barry was already urging us back, further yet and all the way down to the cottage, even before the man in the fire engine had climbed down and gone to speak to Andrew.

"AND MILES TO GO BEFORE I SLEEP," I sighed, looking back at oh how far I'd come ...

Actually I was not so far from home now, from either home, though I'd walked a great circle to get here. That was traditional, surely: *what goes around comes around, blood will out, those who forget the past are condemned to repeat it.* I was footsore, but not sorry.

Things would be what they were, what they must be; that was their nature, and my own.

Things would be as they used to be, if I could make it so. That was my nature, if not their own. Change and decay in all about I see, and it offends me. I hate entropy.

It had been a long walk, to come back almost to the start again. I was tired, but content. I'd walked with friends, with stars, with tragedy in hand; I'd seen the Greenfolk and the truth of them, and their glimmer would lay glamour over all my life to come. I'd set off with burdens and I'd lost or left them all before I'd reached this far; veiled with sorrow, I could yet stretch half to the stars now and tingle with the ease and freedom of my body, all unhindered, unafraid—

Oh, I'm sorry. Again, I'm sorry. Did you think I meant any of that literally?

King Harvest ...

At least Andrew had not been asked to identify the bodies. That would have been impossible twice over: impossible to ask of him, impossible to do for anyone.

So Barry told me, at least. Later, days later, over a lunchtime pint at the Coach. More pints than one, to be honest: Barry was on sick-leave, leaving all the valley in the untender care of a locum who understood us not at all. Barry wasn't sick, but he had a lot of sorrows and he meant to drown them all, in company or alone. I counted myself a friend, by virtue of long acquaintance; it was my public duty to see him home safe afterwards, and my social duty to sit with him and drink with him until he needed seeing home, whatever the quality of the drink. How Barry counted me I wasn't certain, but he'd been giving me sidelong glances for years, no difference there. And no man is an island, to be eroded alone.

"You've seen films of Hiroshima after the bomb," he said. "The people, I mean. The kids. Like mummies, black skin over bones. This was worse. That steel box they were in—the oubliette he called it, he *built* it, Christ, it was meant to be a place they could hide up, somewhere that was *safe* for them—but it was like an oven, it just roasted them. And it was meant to. That evil bastard, I tell you, if I caught him he wouldn't live to go to trial. Never mind what they'd do to me, it'd be worth it ..."

That was why Barry was on leave, his masters didn't trust him. There was little enough chance of his finding Root, there'd been no sign of the man anywhere, but no one was taking chances. The papers were full of Root's picture, and there were the usual reports of sightings country-wide; who knew which—if any—were true?

205

"They were both tied up," Barry told me because he needed to, not because I needed to hear it. All the valley knew. "That's why they couldn't get out. He tied them up and burned them. After he'd played with them a while. Burned them alive, the pathologist reckons ..."

I sat with him while he talked, while he drank, while we both did. At last his common sense cut through the alcohol, unless it was just his sense of quite how far he had to walk to get home, to get to his bed and sleep these pints away so that he'd be fresh to start again.

I went with him all the way to his door, thinking mostly about my own bed and how welcome that would be, warm and enfolding; and still had a long trudge to get there, but trudged it willingly enough.

The Castle was gone now, they'd found a truck from somewhere that was big enough to take it, finally and far too late. Despite the clarion call of sleep, I stood for a while in the lane there, looking at the swathe of scorched earth it had left to remind me of that night and the day that had followed.

There had of course been more policemen, and more questions. Specifically there had been Superintendent Aldiss back again: our blighted valley his personal curse, it seemed, and for a while I was his demon once again, hauled off to that same Portakabin for another interrogation.

"Little *children* this time, Rowan? Tell me why the little children had to die."

I just sat there, mute of uttermost malice. I was exhausted, numbed, filthy, stinking of smoke; I had nothing to say to him.

It was one of his officers who pointed out that my movements were accounted for and witnessed for hours before the Castle had gone up in flames, that there were a dozen people who could testify that I was nowhere near it when it went.

"An alibi this time, is it, Rowan? Ringing the changes? Well, I told you, any alibi can be broken."

Christ, I wasn't offering him any fucking alibi. I wasn't offering him anything at all. I was sick at heart, and he only made me sicker.

206

Barry came in at last, to tell him that Root hadn't been seen by any of his fellow-travelers since yesterday evening and couldn't be located now. Root the known pedophile, Root who had announced his own arrival so loudly, Root who dragged a lifetime's record of abuse and child-murder at his back ...

"Well, find him," said Superintendent Aldiss; and then to me, "This doesn't let you off the hook, Rowan. Not for anything."

It did, though, and he knew that it did. Next day the papers were baying for Root; I was no substitute sacrifice that he could offer them, not without at least some grounds for suspicion beyond a series of desperate coincidences. Faced with the choice between a manhunt and a witchhunt, for once a policeman jumped the right way.

And so I was free and clear, although for sure the superintendent would rather have had me caged. I was never sure how much he believed in Root's guilt; I was certain he still believed in mine, for Simon's and David's deaths if not the kids'. When I said that to Barry he only grunted into his beer, confirmation enough. I had the sensation that I'd been generously allowed a little more rope, to see how high I'd hang myself; but the Castle had burned down, and that was one monstrosity they couldn't hang on me. Try though they might, though they had, though they would yet.

Which Root must have known, I told Barry that. He'd seen the hunt for David all around him, perhaps he'd even joined in; he'd know that I was under suspicion, everyone knew. A fresh murder in my past, a vanished lad under my feet—who were they going to call on, when two more kids went missing? Or were found dead ...?

My fault, I said dismally, it really is my fault. He might not have done it, probably wouldn't have, without that chance to use me as a scapegoat ...

But people who use scapegoats shouldn't run away themselves, it diverts attention and causes grief. The whole point about scape-goats is that no one hunts them, they're allowed to skip off with your sins on their back. Spoils the metaphor, to set dogs on their trail. Spoils the whole scenario if the goat goes one way and you go haring off the other, guilt like scorpions whipping at your ankles. You have to stand your ground, I think, or the magic doesn't work. God wouldn't take you seriously; and he must.

So here I stood like a bird in the wilderness, like a bow-shouldered and bewildered boy in the rain as it came on again; and it was the increasing weight of water flattening my hair and running down inside my collar that at last impelled me back down to the cottage. Otherwise I might have stood there by Andrew's cold hearth till night, aye, and all night too.

I went home instead and stood dripping politely on the flags just inside the door, while I considered the competing temptations of bath and bed. There was hot and wet, which sounded good against the cold and wet which I was now; or there was asleep, which sounded good against my current state, awake in a cruel world. The rain had taken the urgent edge off all that beer, though; I was swinging towards the bath, and maybe bed after.

But there were slow footsteps overhead, and then a figure on the stairs in front of me; and that was Andrew, and both bath and bed were instantly postponed.

Andrew was no longer what he had been, the middle-aged dropout living free and easy with his family on the road, in the Ride; neither was he what he had then become, a man making the very best of a bad situation, warming my mother's bed while he and his children also warmed her heart. Now he was a gray and shrunken shadow, dispossessed of all comfort, all hope of warmth. I'd hardly heard him speak, these latter days. Fair enough that he didn't speak to me, that was mutual; what could I possibly say to him? But as far as I was aware he wasn't speaking to my mother either, and that was serious.

He startled when he saw me, although he must have heard the door bang at my back. I spread my arms wide, as if to say that I was no threat to him, which he really should have known already; then I saw the bags in his hands, the old rucksack on his shoulders.

"Andrew, what's happening?"

"I'm moving on, Rowan." His voice was thin and hoarse, unrecognizable; more than disuse had worn it to a fraying shadow. "I'm sorry, I can't stay ..."

Of course he couldn't stay, I hadn't expected him to. Some events are so terrible, their impact overrides all other considerations; I knew that. I'd fled college, he was fleeing us.

My mother appeared behind him, presumably the hardest of the considerations he'd had to override. Certainly it was hard on her, that much was clear to be seen. She looked a mess, my darling mum: a mess and distressed, and I hated to see her so.

I stepped aside, wet as I was, to give him easy access to the door.

"Where are you going?"

"I don't know," meaning—transparently—*anywhere that's not here. It doesn't matter anyway, how could it? My children are dead. Everywhere I go, I take that with me. I can leave a great deal behind, but never that. Them, but not their deaths. Your mother, but not her witness to their deaths.* And then, immediately, as though the slightest tempering of the truth were intolerable, "No, that's not right," *not yet.* "I do know. I have to find my wife. I don't know where she is, but I'll find her." *And tell her how it was, and then not stay because neither one of us would be able to bear that.* He was giving out so many messages this evening I felt overborne, my system couldn't take it; I looked down, to where water was pooling around my feet and soaking into the rug.

Then my mother spoke to him and I turned away altogether, walked as far away as I could, wished there was a way to close the living-room door on them without being obvious. She's not a soft-spoken woman, my mother, I could hear every word and I really didn't want to.

She wasn't arguing his choice; if she'd done that at all she'd done it already, and lost. But my mother can see a natural, an inevitable ending as easily as I can, so I don't suppose she had tried to resist it. She was only trying to make her own position clear, to a man who couldn't see anything clearly except the one thing, his route out of here. She even opened the door for him, to show him that it wasn't barred either against his leaving or his returning.

Not that he ever would return. Some endings are for real.

He left, and I didn't even say goodbye to him, nor he to me.

Neither did I say anything to my mother, until she'd closed the door oh so softly behind him, and walked over to where I stood, and put her arms around me wet as I was, and lowered her head onto my shoulder in a gesture of utter defeat.

I hugged her in silence, for as long as I could bear it; and then I said, "Well. Just the two of us, then ..."

"Yes, love. It comes out the way it's written, I suppose—but God," she said, her voice thick with tears, "sometimes I hate the guy who writes it."

"No, you don't," I said, rocking her gently until she let those tears fall. "Not you. You're not able."

(Drinks All Round)

I sat in the Agric, deliberately there, so that almost it ended where almost it had begun. This was no gathering of the clans, though, it was only Michael and me and we were being highly unusual, almost forgetful of our drinks as we leaned side by side across a table.

Spread across that table beneath us was the local paper, the *Gazette*, just arrived mid-afternoon. No newsagent in the valley: Rose had a batch dropped by daily, and sold them to anyone who could be bothered to make the trip to her pub. She didn't do deliveries; paper rounds had never been an option for us valley lads when we needed money.

It was the headline story, repeated on page two with more detail and further sensational pictures. *Local MP Landowner on Child-Porn Charges* ran the headline; and that was it, that was the story, more or less. Sir Julian Ricks, wealthy exploiter of the rural poor, had been under investigation for some time, following reports of pornographic material being discovered on a computer he'd sent for repair. That material was believed to include photographs of children engaged in indecent acts with adults. Scandalously divorced Sir Julian, who lived with his vulnerable teenage daughter Patricia, had now been formally charged with numerous offenses under the Sexual Offenses Act of 1958, and quite right too, and with any luck the filthy pervert would go down for the rest of his natural …

Well, it didn't quite say all of that in so many words, but the implications were there. Sir Julian had never been popular with editor or owner; having come out so strongly on the wrong side in the reservoir debate—and having so clearly his own interests in

211

seeing it go ahead—he was equally unpopular in the district now, and so fair game for all the contumely and vituperation that hard-drinking, hard-typing and no doubt embittered journalists could generate …

Big photo of Sir Julian on the front page, looking stony-faced and shifty both at once; nature had been no more kind than the reporters, he had one of those faces that would always shriek his guilt regardless of the facts.

He of course was denying all charges; the headline article said so, once, briefly, in the final paragraph.

On page two there were photos of his house, his oh-so-vulnerable daughter Trix in army fatigues and rebel stance, and the frontage of *Clive's Computers*, where a vigilant and civic-minded young employee had made this disgusting discovery. There was also a photo of Michael, looking as vigilant and civic-minded as he could manage.

The writers were clearly being careful of both *sub judice* and libel, but there was a long article on the evils of Internet porn sites, and how children corrupted in youth could never recover; there was another on the shadier sides of Sir Julian's business and parliamentary career, which carried hints that in fact the current charges were by no means the end of the affair, that having his computer legitimately in their laps had led the police on into another investigation altogether.

Michael and I were musing on what that might mean when Barry came in, the Agric that afternoon just one more stop on his determined marathon crawl.

We shifted up to make room for him on the bench; he glanced at the paper and smiled, glad I think to see a different story making headlines, and more glad still to have something new to talk about. Besides, if there were revelations to be made, he owed it to Michael to make them to us.

"They've brought a smart girl up from London," he said, "and I'm told she's snooped through every file on that bloody machine. You wouldn't believe what she's turned up; that's really why they had him in at the station yesterday. It wasn't for the porn charges, it was first round on all this other stuff."

"What stuff's that, then?"

"I shouldn't tell you—but it'll be all over the papers tomorrow anyway. There's going to be a leak," and he smiled briefly, and I guess we all knew where the leak would be coming from. Barry was no friend of Sir Julian's, certainly not any more. "He's been taking bribes from the water company, to push for the reservoir to go through. We found notes in his diary, even a letter of thanks to the chairman; you wouldn't believe how stupid he's been, keeping records. Not that they needed to bribe him, though I suppose they wanted to have a hold over him and he just can't say no to tax-free cash. But he was going to rake it in anyway, if it went through. He's got all that land they'd be buying, and he's got a major share-holding in the company, though he'd hidden that behind a proxy name. That's illegal too, he's supposed to declare all his holdings. Any which way he turns, we've got the bastard this time. It's not just a case of sleazy politician's sticky finger, it's blatant corruption. He'll get jail for this, as well as the porn. Consecutive, I hope. Shame to waste it on concurrent sentences."

Michael whistled appreciatively; I said, "What's he saying about it all?"

"Denies the lot, of course. But they always do, they have to, when their world's caving in around them. Denial's the only thing holds them together."

"How can he deny his own records?"

"Says he never made them. Oh, he admits not declaring the shares, but that's minor. He says it's a point of principle, and he's never declared any of his interests. Which is true. It's supposed to be compulsory, but they don't enforce it.

"The rest, though, he says it's all forgery. He's trying to blame you, Michael, says you must have done it at the shop. Downloaded the porn and faked the records, the lot. You got any witnesses, by the way?"

"No—well, only Ro, and he wasn't there when I found it …" His voice tailed off uncertainly, as he remembered that I deliberately hadn't been there when Barry came round, I hadn't been any part of this story until this moment.

"Ro?" Barry was frowning. "What's your involvement?"

213

"Only that Michael showed me the porn, and asked me what I thought he should do about it. I told him to call you. That's all." Brief, accurate and to the point.

Not enough; Barry wanted to dig a little deeper. "You'd been to his house, though, hadn't you? Before he took the computer in, you'd been fooling with his daughter ..."

"A few days before, yes. But fuck, Barry, I don't know anything about computers. Ask Michael."

"It's true, Barry. For a clever dick, he's a real moron."

"I just like to do my own thinking, that's all. With pen and paper. It's a nice conspiracy-theory, Barry, but it won't wash. Even if I'd thought of setting him up that way, I couldn't do it. And it'd be really obvious if I had, I wouldn't have the first idea how to cover my tracks ..."

Barry grunted. "Even so, I'd better let them know, back at the station ..."

"Oh, for fuck's sake, Barry, do me a favor ... A big one, eh? You're supposed to be on holiday, that's why we're talking to you; and I can't take another fucking interrogation, I just can't. I haven't done anything, but the more mud you sling, some of it's going to stick ..."

"Maybe some of it needs to," he said shortly, as though this were something it was safe to suspect me of; then he pushed his emptied glass down the table towards me, *I'll have another in there*, as though this at least were something that could be forgiven or paid off, and cheaply too.

I sighed heavily, and wondered not for the first time if he'd remembered yet about the fireworks we used to make and set off in his garden, with their slow, slow-burning fuses; and didn't ask, of course. Just felt glad that Bonfire Night was behind us, gathered up his glass and Michael's, took all to the bar and paid up.

... Has Surely Come

The sky had cleared as it often did at sunset, and the wind had dropped; we were in for another heavy frost. The boathouse would be bitter tonight. Wooden walls couldn't keep out the weather.

Fortunately, there was a stone-built chimney. I was outside, fetching logs for the fire while Juliet put an extra-thick duvet on the bed: familiar duties both, something to cling to in a slippery, changeable world.

I stood with my arms full of weight and potential energy, gazing out at the dark mirror of the tarn where it shivered with icy star-light. I was shivering also, and everything I saw spoke of numbing, destructive chill; but my thoughts were all of warmth and shelter, of getting warm and staying so throughout the long winter ahead, until at last the spring should come. As it must, as it always did ...

At last I turned and went indoors, dropped my load of logs into the basket and added a couple to the already blazing fire, set a jug of wine and spices to mull gently on the hearth.

Then I went upstairs.

Sounds of rushing water, steam billowing from the open bath-room door; no surprise then to find Juliet stripping off in the bedroom.

"I'm going to have a bath," she said, needlessly.

"Sure ..."

I lifted her dressing-gown down from its hook on the door, and held it for her like a gentleman born; wrapped it around her naked body, tied the cord and then took advantage of the moment. Nothing challenging, I just embraced her lightly, a grip she could break with a gesture if she'd a mind to.

215

A beat of stillness and then she hugged me back, tighter than I'd dared to, than I'd dared to hope for.

She pushed me away too soon, but that was fair. That would change.

I gave her ten minutes, before I walked quietly into the bathroom.

She'd tied her hair into a tangled knot atop her head and was sitting up, soaping her long legs. I rolled my sleeves back, perched on the rim of the bath and took the soap from her wordlessly; dipped my hands into the scalding water, worked up a lather and began to wash her back.

She leaned back just a little into the pressure of my fingers, sighed softly and said, "It was you, wasn't it?"

My hands stilled against her skin. "What was me?"

"Sir Julian's computer. That's why you screwed his daughter, just to get at his computer. It was you put all that stuff on it. Wasn't it …?"

"Jules, I couldn't use a computer to save my life. You know that."

"I know how bright you are. And I know you spent all last year in Cambridge working with your friend, working on computers. Are you trying to tell me you didn't pick up everything he could teach you? Or Michael either, all those years down at the shop? Do me a favor. You did all that with the pornography, just so that the police would look further, and find out about his share dealings and his bribes and all the rest of it. To save *my* life, and your mother's, and this whole valley …"

"Juliet, I swear, I didn't know a thing about Sir Julian's share dealings. How could I? No one knew." She was quiet, relaxing under the rhythm of my fingers; I kissed the back of her neck, tasting soap and warm skin and Juliet, and I said, "Trust me."

This is my true confession, and I have lied throughout; but I told you that already. What more can I say?

Chaz Brenchley

Chaz Brenchley has been earning his living as a writer since he was eighteen. He was Northern Writer of the Year 2000, and lives in Newcastle upon Tyne with one cat and a famous teddy bear, and indulges in good whisky, good cooking, and playing snooker badly.

Bloody Brits Press

BLEAK WATER

Danuta Reah

"A powerful, haunting book."—Laura Lippman, winner of the Edgar and Anthony awards

Beyond the new city center developments, the old Sheffield canal is overgrown, run down, and deserted. Signs of regeneration creep along its towpaths, including a small innovative gallery housed in one of the warehouses. But between the renovations it's a dark and lonely place—the perfect site for an exhibition reworking Brueghel's *The Triumph of Death.*

For Eliza Eliot, the curator, the chance to show well-known artist Daniel Flynn's work at the gallery is a coup. But when a young woman's body is found in the canal, Flynn's nightmare images begin to spill out into the real world. Still affected by the murder of her friend's daughter four years earlier, Eliza is drawn deep into the violence that seems to surround the gallery. Is this the work of a psychopath, or is there a link between present horrors and the tragedy of four years ago?

ISBN 978-1-932859-21-8 $13.95

Bloody Brits Press

THE SPIDER'S HOUSE

Sarah Diamond

When Anna's husband is offered a job in the small Dorset village of Abbots Newton, she's as happy to move as he is. While she enjoys city life, her career as a novelist is going nowhere—and she hopes that the country might inspire her.

After the move, however, it's a different story. With few ideas for her new novel and little else to do, Anna's getting increasingly restless when she makes a shocking discovery—Rebecca Fisher, the notorious child murderess of the 1960s, was the previous inhabitant of their picturesque old cottage.

At first, Anna's just curious, and begins reading up on the case that appalled and fascinated the nation decades ago. Yet as she learns more, she becomes increasingly convinced that she's close to discovering something else— secrets that have been hidden away for over thirty years.

But someone else has other ideas. As an unseen enemy threatens her marriage, her safety, and ultimately her life, Anna realizes that by understanding Rebecca Fisher, she might just be able to save herself ...

ISBN 978-1-932859-27-0 $13.95

Bloody Brits Press

OUTSIDE THE WHITE LINES

Chris Simms

"Real fear, real chills, real suspense—one of this genre's all-time great debuts."—Lee Child

There's a killer on the roads. Masquerading as a breakdown rescuer, he strikes without warning, killing brutally and remorselessly. He roams the motorways, not even knowing himself when and where he will find his next victim.

Andy, a young recruit to the traffic police, is determined to hunt down the killer, whatever it takes. After the third victim is discovered, he believes he's spotted something crucial but his jaded partner won't believe him. Increasingly alienated from his colleagues, his career in jeopardy, Andy's obsession grows unchecked.

The Searcher is an outcast; lonely and misunderstood, he unwittingly draws Andy and the killer together through his own bizarre midnight behavior.

As the police struggle with carnage that grows more savage with each murder, Andy finally takes action. The three men are drawn inexorably together in a finale as chilling as it is dramatic.

ISBN 978-1-932859-25-6 $13.95